THINGS
TO CHAN...

The two black-clo... ...nly through the dark w... of the canal, their flippers propelling them just under the surface as they sped away from the houseboats.

Unreeling behind them was an umbilical cord of wirebound primacord designed for underwater use.

They broke the surface only when they were safely out of range of the houseboats, then swam silently to the side of the canal where they had previously set up their command post. By gouging out bricks from the side of the canal wall, they had created footholds, handholds and a niche for their hand-held box.

After hooking up the wire to the small blasting machine, they waited for their signal.

They didn't have to wait long.

The first shot was still echoing in the night when it was followed by a second. Then came a steady rain of sniper fire. That meant O'Toole was at work.

Pressing himself tightly against the side of the canal, ready to push off into the water, Alex Nanos whispered, "This is it, Claude. Give them our best."

"Loud and clear," Hayes acknowledged, then pressed the plunger, triggering a blast through the detonating cord at 21,000 feet per second.

JACK HILD

THE BARRABAS SWEEP

A GOLD EAGLE BOOK FROM
WORLDWIDE®

TORONTO • NEW YORK • LONDON • PARIS
AMSTERDAM • STOCKHOLM • HAMBURG
ATHENS • MILAN • TOKYO • SYDNEY

First edition July 1990

ISBN 0-373-60105-0

Special thanks and acknowledgment to
Rich Rainey for his contribution to this work.

Printed in U.S.A.

THE BARRABAS SWEEP

CHAPTER ONE

A war party of reporters surged toward the yellow wooden barricades, waving boom mikes and long-necked cameras at the flock of NATO officials behind the tall iron gates.

Bright afternoon sunlight struck the gates, cast spired shadows over the ministers, making them seem to be looking out from behind bars.

Right where many of them belong, thought Alan Locke, a tall lean American who sliced through the crowd of reporters until he stood beside the yellow wooden horse.

Locke's eyes were hidden behind dark tinted glasses. His face was sunburned from too much time spent exercising his eyes on the topless beaches at Ostend. Except for the reddened skin baked taut across his sharp cheekbones, he was in fighting shape.

But there would be no fighting today. Just observation.

The barricades formed a gauntlet on both sides of the driveway leading to a private mansion in the Brussels suburb of Anderlecht where the latest "secret" meeting had been held.

Instead of the usual full-blown meeting at NATO headquarters in Everre, a suburb at the eastern edge of Brussels, this was supposed to be a small informal gathering attended by a dozen or so officials and their bodyguards.

It was a choice location. Regal oaks flanked the manor, and in front of the main entrance a well-kept garden provided a carpet of bright red and yellow flowers, bordered by black fencing.

The three colors of the Belgian flag, Locke thought. A nice subliminal touch by the patriotic lord of the manor, Pierre Hubert.

A cadre of grimly smiling Belgian gendarmes was lined up inside the barricades, sensing that the news-hounds were about to get ugly, demanding answers to questions best left unasked.

Yet another secret NATO meeting was about to be overrun.

Secrets were hard currency in Brussels, and someone inside NATO had already passed them to the media crews who now besieged the iron gates.

"They're going to make a break for it," moaned a woman reporter slightly behind Locke. "And I can't see!" She was trying to wedge herself beside him, poking and prodding him with her mike and recorder. "Can't you let me get any closer?" she said to Locke.

He looked down at the slight redhead. She had a pixieish grin and dark cheekbones that spoke of too much makeup or too many gins.

"Any closer and we'll have to get married," he said.

"Hold that thought," she said. "But let me in first."

Locke politely elbowed an overweight Finnish reporter next to him, stepped closer as the man turned, and gave the woman a chance to move up.

Reporters were a crazy bunch, he thought. Nosy. Pushy. Relentless. In fact, at times they could be just like him, never taking no for an answer.

Inside the mansion grounds, the long line of Mercedeses and Lincolns that had coiled into a circled-wagon formation began to take on passengers. A few cars slowly headed for the gates. The gendarmes pushed back the throng as the reporters in the back went into a frenzy. Like electronic pikemen, the Belgian, Dutch, French, American and British correspondents waved their logo-emblazoned standards in the air, trying to record some stray words from the NATO Eurocrats.

Amid the scuffle of mikes and cameras Alan Locke moved along the barricade, edging toward the gates. He did it almost unnoticed, with a light shove here and an accidental push there, until he reached a spot where he could make out the faces of the people gathered inside.

The redheaded reporter clung to him as he moved, alternately cooing "Excuse me" and "Out of my way!"

Locke peered through the Javelin scope of his video camera for a close-up of the NATO insiders, mostly recording faces that were familiar to him from dossiers that had passed across his desk.

With his single-minded approach of shooting everything in sight, including gendarmes, NATO-crats, the stately gray mansion and even other reporters, Locke appeared to be just like every other newshound in the crowd. He even carried credentials linking him to several genuine news organizations. But his footage would never show up in the media.

He was conducting surveillance in broad daylight. His target was the lord of the manor himself. Pierre Hubert was a Belgian adviser to the North Atlantic council, a man who worked behind the scenes and had great influence on the administration and military activities of the NATO forces.

Hubert was a dapper businessman and ladies' man, turned adviser. Locke had been shadowing Hubert for weeks now, acting more on his hunches than on any hard intelligence. And doing it on his own free time.

There was something not quite right about Monsieur Hubert. Locke suspected Hubert of trafficking insider information about NATO movements, projects and contracts. Part of his feeling about the man stemmed from the company, especially the women, Hubert kept, many of whom were in bed with East Bloc spy networks.

Right now Hubert was in the company of a Dutch transportation expert and a Swiss finance man. They'd become a bit of a triad in recent weeks. They'd taken some interesting trips together. Too many.

Hubert turned toward the throng, his aristocratic expression capping a strong military bearing. Unlike most of the officials, who looked like swimmers who'd just spotted shark fins, Hubert smiled thinly. He regarded reporters as a necessary evil.

For a moment Hubert's eyes seemed to linger on Locke, then moved to bestow the same condescending gaze upon the rest of the herd.

As more of the conference members waved and got into their cars, a lumbering British reporter behind Locke swore. "The buggers are slithering away again, aren't they?"

The cars approached the exit and stopped, waiting for the iron gates to open. A babel of voices shouted out questions doomed to die unanswered. The gates swung soundlessly inward and the first vehicles poured out.

Back near the main entrance of the manor, Hubert was bidding farewell to the last departing guests. Then, to Locke's surprise and joy, Hubert climbed into a Mercedes with the Swiss finance man.

"Good, good," Locke said, focusing on the license plate.

"What's so good about it?" the redhead asked. "We're getting nothing."

He laughed. He was still in a good mood from being lucky enough to get the chance to follow his prey right out in the open.

When the car got in line, he moved back through the closely packed crowd of reporters. In the hot afternoon sun, the crowd smelled of old perfume, beer, sweat, tobacco and other odors. Locke was glad his man was going to make a break for it. It was time to get out.

He hurried to the side street where he'd parked his dark green Volvo, a color favored by plainclothes operatives the world over because it was the hardest to see at night. He unlocked the door, slid across the seat and, after unthreading the Javelin scope, carefully placed the camera gear in the back seat with the rest of his equipment. Change of clothes, change of identity. Camouflage kit. Reporter's notebook. And, packed in a square nylon camera case, a 9 mm automatic. Everything he needed.

Locke switched on the engine, then peered through the Javelin at the manor gates. A glinting ribbon of black steel and chrome streamed out of the driveway toward the main road.

Hubert's car was the last one from the gate. It rolled through the mass of reporters, then turned right onto chaussée de Mons, a main thoroughfare that cuts

through the south of Brussels and heads south toward Mons and the French border.

As a betting man, Locke figured that Hubert
wouldn't be crossing into France.

"Après vous, Monsieur Hubert," Locke said. He
pressed the gas pedal and turned the Volvo toward the
chaussée de Mons.

He had a patriot to catch.

A KEY RATTLED in the lock, and the bolt turned with
an echoing thunk. As Lili Kavroleira hurried down the
plushly carpeted stairs someone opened the door.

She froze on the landing. Though Lili lived like a
queen in the house on boulevard du Régent, she had
no control over who used the place.

A black-gloved man stepped into the front hall.

The lock of hair protruding from under his chauffeur's cap made him look too young, too slender, too
cheerful to give trouble to anyone, but she had seen
Kaspar Ulrich matter-of-factly dismantle men twice
his size.

"Oh, it's you," she said.

"Yes," Kaspar said, bowing his head in mock cer-
emony and tipping his visor with his index finger.
"None other than me." Like Lili, he spoke French
when in Brussels, although he had a slight German
accent.

The streetlights shone on his white Rolls-Royce
parked in front of the house. It fit in well with the
other luxury limos patrolling the neighborhood. The
boulevard du Régent traversed some of the most elegant properties in Brussels, an area long staked out by
ambassadors, entertainers and multinational executives.

Then there were women like Lili Kavroleira, who came with the territory.

She was better known as a Czech actress than for any of her movies. Except for a few obsessive critics, few people in the West had actually seen any of the expatriate's films. Just as she had been captured on screen, she had also been captured by an intelligence network. It rescued her from the clutches of the Eastern Bloc controllers running her—and threw her into the arms of Western Bloc controllers. They were a bit more subtle, but the effect was the same. Instead of having producers dictate her life, she was directed by men who inhabited secret penthouses in Paris, Brussels, Lisbon and Amsterdam.

Lili now gave command performances, carefully scripted by the network. She didn't know who was behind it all. She just knew that some of the people who controlled her and the network called it the Realm.

Kaspar closed the door and leaned against it, his arms folded across his chest.

"Where are we going?" she said.

"In the car," Kaspar replied, telling her things as he usually did on a need-to-know basis.

Lili smiled. "I see." She continued down the steps, capturing his gaze with her clinging black satin dress, the front straps crisscrossing in an X-shaped and nearly X-rated bandolier. She was, as more than one of her paramours had said, fully loaded.

Her soft brown layered hair was frosted with blond streaks. Wisps fell over her eyes like a veil. Other strands curled loosely down her bare neck.

"Where exactly in the car are we going?"

The tall driver looked at her, his eyes momentarily shaded with regret. "You're going to see Monsieur Hubert tonight."

"Oh," she said, unable to keep the curiosity from her voice. "Why is that?"

"Well, maybe he is lonely, and he is a good friend of ours."

She laughed. "Ours? He's better than many a man, for sure. Still, don't you mean yours?"

"Perhaps it would be better to say a friend of the Realm."

"And I'm the one who made him such a good friend."

"We all do what we can," he said. "What we must."

She shrugged. For years her life had not been her own. The telephone call earlier tonight had simply instructed her to look her best and to be ready for the driver who would come for her. She had been requested by a man of great importance.

She had suspected it was Hubert. After all, she had been instrumental in snaring him into the Realm. "Let's get this over with," she said, her dark voice giving the lie to her dollhouse image.

Kaspar nodded.

She turned her back and spread her arms as if she were about to take wing. Kaspar draped the satin wrap across her shoulders, then escorted her into the warm and dry night.

Settling into the rear seat of the Rolls, she glanced back at the stately mansion on boulevard du Régent. Walled off from the street by a small iron fence and floodlit lawn, it was more of a safehouse than a home, a prison without bars. But she felt secure there.

She also felt safe from others when Kaspar was with her. But he was much more than a driver for the Realm. For that reason she never quite felt safe from him.

They drove south, and soon were cruising down the Mons-Paris road, leaving behind the baroque mansions and the chrome-and-steel towers of Brussels, heading for the dark haunts of the rich.

And one haunted creature in particular: Monsieur Hubert.

ALAN LOCKE CROUCHED in the dark woods, his face smeared with camouflage paint, his body coated with the faintly metallic smells of insect repellent and mud.

The Javelin Model 221 night vision device gave him a clear view of all the comings and goings in the château.

He'd been perched in the Belgian woods for hours, concealed from the house by shrubbery, cool moist earth and a clutch of pines.

But the house had not been concealed from him.

He was familiar with Monsieur Hubert's second home. It was one of the best of the NATO castles in the region. Nestled between NATO's civilian headquarters in Brussels and its military operation facility at SHAPE—Supreme Headquarters Atlantic Powers Europe—was a heavily forested region with small villages and large castles.

Though not exactly officially NATO castles, many of the medieval properties were occupied by the military and political elite from several European countries, who flocked to Brussels and Mons to buttress the alliance. Several conglomerate chiefs and descendants of Belgian royalty also lived in the area, doing their regal best to safeguard the NATO alliance.

Then there were the foot soldiers like Alan Locke.

Though he had the skills and equipment of a reporter, Locke was a CIA officer stationed in Brussels. His cover identity was that of a United States Army sergeant who served as a courier between Brussels and Camp Casteau, as NATO's military headquarters near Mons was called. But his real task was keeping tabs on Americans who'd strayed.

Every traitor who came under his gaze came under his dominion.

He swept the high-walled château once again, seeing some activity behind the upper windows. Monsieur Hubert was looking out into the night again, as if he were expecting someone important. Who the hell could that be? Locke wondered. He'd already seen a baker's dozen of high-powered NATO bigwigs coming to the château.

Locke hadn't been the only one to follow Hubert's Mercedes south. Most of the representatives at the meeting that broke up in Brussels had made the journey. Pointedly missing from the secret session was the American representative.

It was almost as if some kind of shadow NATO was convening.

Headlights speared the night, slicing through a tree-lined section of road. Locke watched the beams of light flicker through the tall thin trees.

From his hidden vantage point behind a slight rise in the woods, Locke studied the approaching vehicle as it slowed in front of Monsieur Hubert's château.

It was odd that someone was arriving now, since the meeting showed signs of breaking up. Several guests had already left.

Just the hard-core membership was left, the inner circle. Or maybe just a poker game, Locke thought.

But who was this coming now? he wondered, focusing the night vision device on the door of the white Rolls.

The driver hurried around to open the passenger's door, revealing a woman of rare beauty. Locke recognized her instantly, not only from the dossiers he was privy to, but from the tabloids that never tired of parading her on their inside page. "Lili Kavroleira," he said.

Monsieur Hubert, in regal evening dress, appeared in the oval portal of his château, the glow inside backlighting him.

Lili stepped out of the Rolls and took his outstretched hand. He kissed it in a pantomime of class. Lili blessed him with a smile fashioned in fantasy land—even after he refused to release her hand. She seemed a prisoner to Hubert's archaic manners. Then, as if they were partners in a minuet, Hubert led her toward the entrance.

Hubert was definitely bent if he was consorting with Lili, Locke thought. Her name had surfaced several times previously when the Czechs used her to entrap diplomats, soldiers and a general or two in Vienna. Locke didn't know whom she was working for now, but he knew how she worked.

She wasn't here to discuss finances.

Monsieur Hubert either owned her or was owned by her. It was impossible to tell at this point. But Locke was certain that Hubert was up for grabs and so was everything he knew about NATO.

Although he was distracted by Lili's grand entrance, Locke suddenly ducked, out of instinct more than anything else. A moment later he knew what his instincts had acted upon. It was an errant whisper of underbrush from branches whipping into place as someone prowled nearby.

Suddenly, from his left came a man's voice. It was little more than a sigh. A moment later another man's voice joined in.

A patrol. Dammit! Locke thought. He hadn't seen them leave the château. His heart drummed wildly, feeling as if it were blasting a hole into the earth as his chest hugged the ground.

The men were about twenty yards away.

Locke forced himself to calm down. He was in good position, his camouflage blended in with the woods, and it was dark, he told himself. They hadn't seen him. It was just coincidence that the guards were out here in the woods. Wasn't it?

His hand snaked silently down to the 9 mm Heckler & Koch in the holster rig on his hip. He exhaled softly, the familiar grip of the H&K bringing him back down to earth as he prepared to use the weapon.

But before that happened the voices moved away.

Locke slowly raised the Javelin 221 and scanned the forest, instantly picking out the patrol that had almost taken him out.

He breathed a deep sigh of relief. He'd been lucky this time. It could have been disastrous, not even seeing the patrol. I'm not as good as I thought, he said to himself. But I'm still alive.

"WHERE THE HELL are you calling from, Locke?" Lieutenant Anderson said. "And do you know what the fuck time it is?"

The lieutenant definitely wasn't playing the diplomatic spook tonight. He was in his hard-as-nails supersoldier mode. Locke couldn't really blame him.

"It's the middle of the night, sir," Locke said. "I'm calling from the apartment at place Rogier and—"

"And you better have a good reason."

"I believe I do, sir," he said.

The lieutenant had to know something was up, because Locke was using the scrambler.

Beside Locke in the narrow hallway of the sparsely furnished bachelor apartment on place Rogier was a Model SCS-370 scrambler. The open fiberglass suitcase on the desk beside the telephone contained a scrambler that could randomly employ more than six million codes and tie eavesdroppers up in knots while secure conversations were held. On the other end of the line Lieutenant Anderson had a matching unit.

"What is it, Locke?"

"I think I found a traitor working for NATO," Locke said.

"Go on," Anderson urged.

Locke told him about the surveillance of Hubert, the secret meeting of a group of NATO representatives and the arrival of Lili Kavroleira at Hubert's Mons château.

"Is this on film?" Anderson interrupted.

"No," Locke said, "not all of it. Just the daylight meeting at Anderlecht. I didn't want to lug all that other equipment with me into the woods. As it was I was almost caught."

"You're lucky you weren't. You could have set us back years in our relations."

"The hell with relations," Locke said. "I'm telling you that Hubert is bent. And the woman is known to half a dozen services as a professional swallow and I was—"

"You were disobeying my orders," Anderson said.

Locke was quiet. After a long uncomfortable silence he said, "I don't get you. I thought you'd be happy to know—"

"Worried is the correct word, Locke," Anderson said. "Damn worried." He fired several more questions at Locke, unable to hide his anger. It was an anger that had nothing to do with being jarred from sleep.

"One thing bothers me, Locke," he said. "Why were you tailing a Belgian national when I personally assigned other targets to you?"

"I was doing it on my free time."

"You don't have free time, Locke. Your time is mine."

"Yes, sir, but I saw a chance to make a case. A big case. Granted, I stepped beyond the bounds of my assignment, but the events bore me out. Would you want me to sit on sensitive information like this until morning?"

"Of course not," Anderson said.

"My point, sir," Locke said.

"But this will be a tricky business. These are powerful people we're dealing with, and Belgium is not our country. We've got to be careful how we walk and talk over there. These people might have good reason to be meeting with one another—secret or not. It doesn't mean it's some kind of anti-NATO plot like you've dreamed up. And that Czech woman is beautiful. Who could blame a man for wanting her?"

"Sir—"

"Relax. I'm just playing devil's advocate."

A bit too well, Locke thought.

"Just letting you know the arguments you're up against. You've done fine, Locke. I want you to stick with it."

"You do?"

"Yes, son," Anderson said. "This is your chance to make a name for yourself, and I won't hold you back."

"Thank you, sir," Locke said. "You won't regret it."

"Let's hope not."

Locke saw promotions. He saw himself running a few field agents. Moving to another posting. Moving up.

"What should I do now, sir?"

"Follow Lili Kavroleira," Anderson said. "Everywhere. I want to know everything about her, including who she's working for and how she works. I want to know the size of her bed, her favorite position in that bed and who she shares it with. Got that?"

"Yes, sir," Locke said. "Should I arrange for the surveillance team—"

"No team yet," Anderson said, cutting him off. "This isn't official. So far it's just you and me playing your hunch. Keep it to yourself and play it real low-key."

"Sir, I don't have to remind you that one man alone can't conduct a constant surveillance—"

"If she starts acting suspicious, fade away and pick her up another time. In the meantime, as soon as I can arrange it I'll try and throw a couple of men your way. So if you see somebody tailing you, do me a favor, Sergeant."

"Yes, sir?"

"Don't take them out. They'll be our guys."

SOMETIMES SHE HURTLED through the streets of Brussels in the back of the white Rolls, captained through the clogged streets by the dark-haired chauffeur. Other times she drove herself in a small Peugeot that weaved through the constant traffic of the Belgian capital. Tonight Lili Kavroleira was on foot, idly walking through streets brightly lit by neon signs and archaic-looking lamps.

Alan Locke was also patrolling the streets on foot. Like a man caught up in a nursery rhyme of deadly intrigue, everywhere that Lili went, Sergeant Locke was sure to go.

But he was getting tired of following the fairy princess of Czech cinema. He was almost convinced that he had set himself the wrong task. In a manner of speaking, Lili Kavroleira appeared to be innocent.

For two days Sergeant Alan Locke had shadowed her every movement. Unknowingly, she'd taken him on a tour of nightclubs and restaurants. Despite her apparently lofty position, she was a habitué of some of the wilder clubs in the night-life district surrounding the Gare du Nord. The glitzier bars were close to the train station to snare the steady flow of incoming passengers to Brussels.

But Lili hadn't met any mysterious passengers. In fact, she hadn't met anyone suspicious at all.

At the moment she was walking down the rue des Bouchers. Her mane of hair flowed over the collar of her unbuttoned denim jacket and she was sealed into a pair of soft tight black jeans. As she walked she produced a ripple effect on the early crowd pouring in and out of the restaurants and bars on the strip. Men invariably turned their heads to watch her, while the women with them shrugged or tugged at their elbows. The subtle commotion she caused as she eased through the crowd made it easy for Locke to follow her at a distance.

Locke maintained a casual walk as he followed her along the street, picking up his pace only when she turned into Grand-Place, the cobblestoned square that served as the cultural, political and geographical center of Brussels.

Gold light splashed over Lili as she walked past Hôtel de Ville, the grandiose town hall. The town hall, the Maison du Roi, and all of the baroque and Gothic buildings in the square were colored an illusory gold. With the street lamps serving as floodlights and the light from the café windows striking the street-side customers, the square had a magical quality.

Warm breezes caressed the pedestrians as they strolled lazily past the cafés and stores specializing in offering many kinds of beers.

Alan Locke meandered along the square, keeping close to the walls and pretending more interest in the architecture than in anyone in the crowd.

The upper floors of the buildings in the Grand Place were darkened as if they were resting from centuries of labor, and a lofty collection of gargoyles watched over the square. Griffins, phoenixes and wolves were perched on the majestic facades, their stony eyes looking down in regal judgment upon all who passed beneath them.

Busts of the dukes of Brabant also looked down, their still eyes seeing how their descendants compared to the ancient glory of Brussels.

Locke looked back, looked up, looked away, trying to prevent himself from watching his prey like a hawk. The last thing he wanted was for that prey to discover that it was being hunted.

He strolled along, mimicking the actions of Lili Kavroleira. When she settled in at an outside table at a café at the corner of the square, Locke took a table at another outside café several buildings away. He ordered from the waiter who quickly honed in on him.

For the next few minutes Locke concentrated on enjoying his coffee and his pralines while idly scanning the café in the distance. Lili was still sitting there sipping her coffee. Not at all dangerously.

Good God, Locke thought. What have I stirred up?

Perhaps he'd made something out of nothing. And perhaps he'd been a bit melodramatic when he called a contact in the DIA last night.

It was strictly a backup measure. The contact was outside the chain of command and even beyond the need to know. But Melanie Cowan, an investigator with the Defense Intelligence Agency, had a certain quality he couldn't resist. He trusted her.

Melanie had been alarmed when he first called her. And right now she probably thought he was quite the jerk. But he had played hunches all his life, and it wasn't the first time he'd contacted her. Just as she had contacted him now and then to sound off.

As he sipped the dark coffee he recalled their conversation, trying to put himself in her place and think how he would have reacted. Especially to the cloak-and-dagger aspect.

After a couple of minutes, he had told her the reason he was calling. "Melanie, I'm following a woman."

"Nice work if you can get it," she said.

Then he had told her about his first hunches concerning Hubert, the unusual meetings of NATO reps, Hubert's rendezvous with the Czech woman and the lieutenant's initial lack of interest in what could be a major spy case.

"Maybe it's not a major case," she suggested. But she didn't act put out and went on to solicit a few more details.

"I guess the real reason I called was to let you know what was going on, in case something—"

"Nothing's going to happen, Locke!" she cut in. "You owe me a dinner and a night on the town and I'm going to collect it."

The echoes faded in his memory as he looked down the square through a relaxed and slow-moving crowd. There he could see Lili at her table by the street. She was enjoying herself, daintily sipping coffee and being seen by the multitudes.

Locke finished his coffee and pralines, the taste of chocolate lingering pleasantly.

When Lili pushed away from her table a short while later, he counted out some francs for the bill, left a tip and resumed his nonchalant spy walk as he followed her out of the square.

She walked uphill along the Marché-aux-Herbes and the rue de la Madeleine, apparently moving at random. She seemed to be just killing time as she strolled up and down narrow side streets and then scurried across some of the wide boulevards that traversed the capital.

Locke had to fall back as the crowds thinned. The farther away they were from the square, the more noticeable a man became.

Lili was about thirty yards ahead, approaching a corner crosswalk. She had the light but she paused for a few moments to decide which way to go. Locke stopped completely, letting other pedestrians pass. She crossed the street just as the light was changing.

By the time Locke reached the crosswalk Lili was already on the other side. A ribbon of traffic cut her from sight momentarily and he leaned off the edge of the curb.

Someone bumped into him from behind.

Like an off-balance diver, Locke teetered on the edge of the curb for a split second and almost regained his balance. He turned and saw a face that looked familiar. A black-haired man. But he couldn't put a name to the face.

The man pushed him again. Although it was just a slight, almost imperceptible shove, it propelled him into the street just as a torpedo-nosed gray station wagon screeched toward him.

Whump!

The bumper sledgehammered into the back of his legs, levering him back.

Whump!

The back of Locke's head smashed against the hood of the car, imprinting a skull-shaped dent in the shiny metal. He slid toward the windshield, then flew off to the side, pinwheeling in the air as the car sped away.

He landed in a mangled heap, his head reeling. He felt as if he were disintegrating, crumpling in the street.

Several people surged toward him. One man pulled him to the curb, while voices swirled around his battered body, some speaking French, some English. "Get him out of the road...." "Let him breathe...."

The man who had lifted him by the shoulders and dragged him off the street said, "Give him some room." He laid Locke on the sidewalk with his head resting near the curb while he fashioned a makeshift pillow out of his jacket.

There was pain at the back of Locke's neck. Someone was pressing it against the curb, choking him. The pain shot through his spinal column. Couldn't they understand what was happening?

Locke opened his eyes and saw a forest of legs spinning around. The long-limbed forest was capped with faces that stared at the bloody spectacle on the ground. Locke's eyes were drawn to the man who'd just spoken. It was the black-haired man again. A thick curly lock of hair fell down over his forehead.

He'd seen the man earlier in the square.

But now he recognized him. Usually he'd seen him in a chauffeur's uniform and cap, driving for Lili Kavroleira. But tonight he was in street clothes and wore no cap. Tonight Kaspar Ulrich wasn't on chauffeur duty.

And now Locke understood what was happening. In case the hit-and-run didn't do the trick, a backup team was here to finish him off.

Locke moaned. He tried to speak but the words broke before they came out of his quivering lips.

A shield of men separated him from the genuine spectators as they crouched around him. They were all under the direction of the black-haired Kaspar Ulrich.

Locke couldn't breathe. He started kicking.

"He's having a convulsion," someone said.

Locke searched the faces around him and saw nothing human-looking. He tried harder, and summoned up the angelic face of Melanie Cowan, hovering cloudlike in the neon-tinted night. At least she would know—

"Someone get a doctor," Ulrich shouted over his shoulder. "Quick." Then he turned back to the accident victim, and with a gentle touch Kaspar Ulrich broke Sergeant Alan Locke's neck against the curb.

CHAPTER TWO

The Gothic mansion facing the Bois de la Cambres, a wooded park along avenue Franklin Roosevelt, was in immaculate condition. Like many of the embassies and aristocratic estates on the well-heeled strip a few miles south of the center of Brussels, it was a place fit for presidents and kings.

And their henchmen.

The pillared and corniced mansion was an unofficial adjunct to the United States's presence in Brussels. It was known as "the Reserves" because that was the function of many of the personnel who were temporarily attached to American agencies throughout Belgium. The think tank was charged with studying the penetration of NATO via military and intelligence services, and potential economic subversion of the European Economic Community.

Although the American embassy was located on the boulevard du Régent, actually a lot of day-to-day work was conducted in this mansion by a collection of foreign service officers, military attachés and analysts who shuffled back and forth between the embassy, SHAPE headquarters near Mons and the Gothic edifice beside the Bois de la Cambre.

Despite the elaborate scroll work on the iron gate, it was a functional piece of metal. At night when just a skeleton staff remained in the house, the gate was closed, meshing perfectly with the spear-pointed fence.

During daylight working hours the gate was kept open. It was under observation at all times.

One afternoon, General "Hammerhead" Hamelin arrived unannounced, a dark cloud on an otherwise bright day. Word of his arrival spread quickly through the building.

The bull-shouldered, khaki-clad general sported a bristly black crew cut that made the flat top of his head resemble a landing strip.

Hamelin struck sparks the moment he stepped across the threshold through the arched wooden doorway.

Although some of the staff were in uniform, most were civilians. But the chilling effect of his arrival was the same on them all; one glimpse of Hamelin made junior officers sit straighter and put more steel in their eyes. Women suddenly looked more intent upon whatever they were doing. Few met his eyes because Hamelin had a reputation for chopping heads.

Whenever things went wrong, the general demanded a sacrifice. He was as zealous about finding scapegoats as he was about ferreting out Communists. The nickname, Hammerhead, had originated in Vietnam, when his habit of striking first and asking questions later had won a good number of the medals now decorating his chest.

His hawkish eyes were scanning the suddenly busy staff and their cluttered desks in search of something to enrage him when a woman in a light brown skirt and white blouse, hair pulled back in a bun, intercepted him. "General Hamelin," she said, "it's good to see you again."

"It's always good to see you," he said. He cocked his head and blatantly studied her from top to bottom. The urge to conquer was apparent in his eyes.

Ignoring the leer, the woman nodded. "This way, General. Miss Laine is expecting you." She led him into the inner recesses of the building, although he quickly caught up to her and was soon leading the way through one corridor after another.

Some of the rooms were spacious plush offices for conferences, with adjacent smaller boxlike rooms, like rabbit warrens, with rows of file cabinets and desks covered with computers and communications gear.

General Hamelin knew the building inside out because some of his personal staff were assigned offices on the basement floor, "where the dirty work was done."

The two finally reached the back of the mansion. A thickly carpeted hall with paintings staring from the walls led to a large office. A small porcelain figure stood on a pedestal table on each side of the door, giving this part of the building the air of a museum.

Inside the office sat the "curator" of the covert museum, Monica Laine, a veteran foreign service officer who had worked as an assistant to several American ambassadors in Europe while steadily rising in the invisible ranks of the CIA.

She was a ripe-figured, attractive and elegantly dressed woman in her early forties, with black hair touched by gray. Her short bangs gave her a girlish look, but she was no shrinking violet. She couldn't afford to be, especially when her job occasionally entailed calling men like General Hamelin onto the carpet.

Earlier that day she'd matter-of-factly and diplomatically suggested he get his ass over to her office if the chance presented itself.

After her assistant had rapped on the door, announced the general and closed the door behind him, Monica stood.

"What's so urgent that you wanted a face-to-face?" the general said.

"Good afternoon, General," she said, sitting down again behind her desk. "Thanks for coming so quickly."

Hamelin dropped into a wing chair facing her, gripped the soft upholstered arms and slid it closer to the desk. It was as if he was saying: *you asked for me, you got me, and it better be good to warrant dragging me over here.*

"It's about Sergeant Locke," Monica said.

The general nodded. "A bad business. Tragic."

She nodded and studied the general a few moments before she opened a green folder and scanned the contents. Photographs. Reports. Background papers. "Yes," she agreed. "Maybe more tragic than you know."

"What have you got there?" he said.

"It's a file on Sergeant Locke."

"I've seen everything there is on him—"

"No, General," she said. "I don't think you have. At least not this."

She passed him the file and he scanned through it, then shook his head. "I told you that I was familiar with all of this. Locke was a straight arrow, a man who was going to the top. Lieutenant Anderson had nothing but high praise for him—"

"The word *nothing* seems most appropriate as far as Anderson is concerned," she said. "I've paid a few visits to his office downstairs to discuss the Locke affair."

"So?"

"So your Lieutenant Anderson had precious little to say."

"About what?" the general asked. "There's precious little *to* say about the accident."

"Keep reading," Monica told him.

General Hamelin leafed through the folder. "Like I said, I've seen all this before—" Suddenly, he stopped. He held up a picture of Lili Kavroleira. It was a photocopy of a newspaper article with a lurid headline. "What the hell is this?"

"That's Lili Kavro—"

"I know that," Hamelin snapped. "What's it doing in this file?"

Monica smoothed her hands over her desk. "That's the woman Alan Locke was following when he had his 'accident.' As you know, she might not be on the top-ten movies list, but because of her former activities for the East Bloc, she's still on all our watch lists."

"Yes, but what's it doing here?" He closed the file and slapped it with the back of his hand.

Monica reached for another green folder. "Actually, that photograph comes from this." She fanned through the contents. "It's an unofficial file concerning Locke's activities shortly before his death."

She passed the folder to the general. Hamelin quickly skimmed through it, shaking his head once again as he neared the end. He picked out three sheets, a report on Locke's activities by Melanie Cowan.

"Who the hell is Melanie Cowan?" he demanded.

"She's with the DIA, General. It's all right there in the folder."

"Dammit!" he thundered. "I know she's with the DIA. It says so right here. But I mean who knows her? Who really knows her? I never heard of her before today. She could be an *agent provocateur* for all I know. Here she is making all kinds of wild accusations about one of my lieutenants—and apparently you believe her."

"I haven't said I believe it all," she said. "Not yet, anyway. But I'm looking into what she says, General. Unlike some people, I don't ignore evidence just because I'm too pigheaded to believe it."

Hardly aware of what he was doing, General Hamelin curled up the folder and rapped it softly against the desk. "These accusations make Lieutenant Anderson appear to be a liar."

Monica Laine shrugged. "Apparently Locke didn't trust Lieutenant Anderson one hundred per cent. So he contacted an old friend he could trust—and she says Locke was shadowing Lili in connection with some splinter group in NATO. And she says Lieutenant Anderson sanctioned the surveillance. I've been waiting for him to come forward, thinking that maybe he's conducting some operation off the books. Yet he hasn't given me one word, General. When I mentioned Lili Kavroleira, he just played dumb."

"Why are you telling *me* this?" Hamelin asked. "You want to fry his ass, fry it."

"He's your protégé, General. I figured I'd ask you if there was some operation you knew of, or if you knew a reason why I should drop this. I figured I'd throw the ball in your court."

"Is there an investigation going on into this matter?"

Monica shrugged. "Not yet. At least not officially. But when Officer Cowan learned of Locke's death—in light of this business with Lili Kavroleira, she began asking questions. Questions that have to be answered."

"You want answers," Hamelin said, "how about this? For a start, maybe Locke went outside channels and revealed sensitive information to this Cowan broad for reasons of his own. Maybe Locke was turned. Maybe Cowan was. Maybe they were working together on something crooked. And now maybe this Cowan is in hot water so she spreads some disinformation around. How's that for an answer?"

"It won't play in Peoria, General," she said. "Too many maybes." She sat back and rested her elbows on the arms of her chair, clasping her hands in front of her, looking like a priest who has just heard confession. "To me it seems pretty obvious that Locke was simply confiding in an old friend. Using her as a sounding board. Most people have a mentor somewhere. Perhaps even you, general."

"Attila the Hun, Hannibal, guys like that," he said, waving away her suggestion. "I can't believe Locke would turn to some sob sister. According to her, Locke's superior officer is sitting on information and is practically covering up an active spy ring."

"She says what she says," Monica responded. "And we can't just hear what we want to hear. Her report has to be looked into. Unless we get some answers, this is going to become a hell of a situation."

"It's all rubbish," Hamelin snarled. He stared at the rolled-up file in his hands. Then his eyes traveled toward the trash basket beside the desk, as if he were going to toss the file in it, but instead he leaned forward and rapped the folder on the desk. "I want to look into this myself," he said. "May I take this with me?"

"By my guest, General. There's more where that came from."

General Hamelin nodded. He gripped the edge of her desk and leaned forward. "Thanks for telling me this. Sorry about being such a bear about it. It's just that Lieutenant Anderson is one of my best people. But if I find out he's a wrong guy, he'll be rocking away his retirement behind bars."

Monica stood. "Very well, General. I just thought, considering our—our friendship—it was best to try and handle it this way first."

He tossed her a half salute and managed a brief smile. But as he moved toward the door, his eyes turned hard, reflecting anger.

THAT NIGHT a Mercedes sedan eased to a stop in front of the closed gate on avenue Franklin Roosevelt, its headlights throwing their beams beyond the iron fence. A uniformed driver stepped over to the gatepost and inserted a plastic ID card into the slot in a square metal plate. Then the plate swung open, revealing a small phone.

General Hamelin announced into the phone that he had come on an inspection tour. "And give no advance warning of my presence until I walk through that door. If I find out otherwise, you'll be guarding snowmen at the North Pole."

The gate whirred inward. Arrangements could have been made ahead of time so the Mercedes wouldn't have had to wait, but Hamelin wanted to surprise the skeleton staff.

The driver parked the Mercedes in the loop in front of the main entrance and Hamelin got out. As soon as he approached the threshold, a tall and alert sergeant at arms opened the door.

Hamelin nodded to him and waved a green folder. "This is sensitive business. If I need you, I'll call. And you'll come running."

"Yes, sir."

Hamelin walked along the corridor to a stairway and trotted down the carpeted steps to the basement. He walked past several small offices, then rapped on Lieutenant Anderson's door. At the same time he turned the knob. The door was unlocked.

Lieutenant Anderson looked up when he heard the click. His brawny shoulders were hunched as he pored over a map of Belgium and environs spread on his desk. Next to the map was a notebook in which he was jotting names, destinations, times. As part of his activities at the Reserves, Lieutenant Anderson handled transportation and security arrangements for a number of American officers coming to Brussels.

He pushed the notebook aside and wheeled the chair away from the desk. "Ah, General," he said, "what brings you here?"

"Business," Hamelin replied, closing the door.

Anderson smiled. "Fine. I'm just about done here. What's up?"

"This, I'm afraid." Hamelin waved the green folder so that the sheaf of papers inside riffled in the air. Then he dropped the file on the lieutenant's desk. While Anderson's eyes fell upon the folder, General

Hamelin drew the .45 Colt automatic from his holster and aimed the barrel.

"What the hell?"

"You've come under suspicion, Anderson," Hamelin said. "About Lili Kavroleira and Sergeant Locke."

A look of disbelief flashed across Anderson's face. Stunned, he searched Hamelin's eyes for some sign of the camaraderie he'd thought they had. After all, they'd covered a lot of ground together, a lot of stations, and survived a lot of covert battles. "But General, you know I told you—"

Hamelin shook his head, then raised his finger to his lips, as if enacting a charade. He gestured with his hand, encouraging Anderson to play along. "Lieutenant," he said, "I'm going to have to ask you to hand over your weapon."

Anderson laughed silently. He shook his head but matched Hamelin's smile, as if willing to play along with the general. "Whatever you say, General." Anderson stood, flipped the holster lid, then wrapped his hand around the pistol grip.

"Slow," the general ordered. "And make sure that barrel doesn't point at me."

"General, you know I wouldn't dare—"

"Just lift it slow and easy and hand it to me with the grip first. We'll talk this out later on."

Anderson nodded. Following orders he lifted the automatic slowly by the grip until it cleared the holster. He was about to turn it around when the general shouted, "No! Don't try it!"

Anderson snapped his head up, staring at the general, the game now far beyond his comprehension.

Hamelin pulled the trigger of the Colt. The first bullet hit Anderson square in the chest, ripping apart his breastbone as it sledgehammered him backward. He bounced against the wall, then slumped forward, his pistol dropping to the floor.

The roar of the blast was still echoing when Hamelin fired again.

The second shot tore into Anderson's heart, knocking him back against the wall. Then he crumpled forward on the desk, blood pouring onto the map. He died right in the heart of Belgium, his dark blood staining the soft green colors of the map.

Startled voices sounded in the hallway. Then a clatter of footsteps moved from door to door. Someone pushed several doors open before discovering the source of the shots.

The sergeant at arms burst into the room, saw Anderson's wrecked body and Hamelin, Colt .45 held down by his side. "What happened?"

"That man tried to kill me," Hamelin said. "I confronted him with some possibly damaging evidence—but instead of trying to explain it, he went for me."

One after another the members of the skeleton crew entered, saw Lieutenant Anderson's body, then the stoic but saddened face of General Hamelin. This was a side of him no one had seen before.

"I thought he was a friend of mine," the general said. "I wanted to hear his side of the story—but then he panicked and went for me...." He walked over to the desk and tapped the shoulder of the slain lieutenant. "I had no choice."

Then he stepped back, ready for the inevitable investigation. "I want this done by the book," he said to the staff in the room. "Our people will handle it, but I want no cover-up. After damage control, we'll get this out to the press. We've got to prove to the rest of the world that no one is invulnerable to this kind of treachery. Not even me."

With that, General Hammerhead Hamelin fell silent, his words still sinking into the stunned audience. He couldn't have done better if he'd rehearsed it.

General Hamelin Turns Tables on Turncoat

BRUSSELS (API)—General Randolph "Hammerhead" Hamelin survived an assassination attempt in Brussels last night by a subordinate officer allegedly involved in an espionage ring. Hamelin, known for his strike-first-and-fast approach to warfare, served with Air Mobile Cavalry Units in Vietnam where he often brought the action to the enemy. Now those same tactics have helped save the life of the much decorated general.

The incident occurred at an as yet undisclosed location in Brussels when General Hamelin confronted U.S. Army Lieutenant Gerald Anderson with evidence linking him to an embryonic spy ring. Instead of refuting the charges, the lieutenant drew his automatic pistol, General Hamelin claims, forcing him to defend himself. With instinct honed by years of combat, General Hamelin fired two shots, killing the man instantly.

"It was just like war," Hamelin said coolly from his office in Brussels. "It was him or me. Him or the United States. There was really no hesitation. I drew my weapon and fired."

The general continued, "I'm just sorry it came down to that situation. Now that he's dead there's a good chance we'll never know just how much damage he did, and what secrets he revealed."

Cold War Heats up in Belgium

BRUSSELS (API)—In a shocking assassination attempt reminiscent of the brutal cold-war killings of the fifties, a turncoat American officer tried last night to gun down General Randolph "Hammerhead" Hamelin at an American diplomatic post in Brussels.

General Hamelin was conducting an investigation into a NATO secrets-for-sale spy ring and had discovered that Lieutenant Anderson, attached to an Army intelligence unit in Belgium, was connected to the ring. When the renegade officer was confronted with evidence, he drew a weapon on the general. The general fired first, killing the would-be assassin.

"Unfortunately some of his secrets will die with him," a spokesman for the general said. "However, we do believe we contained the operation before it did irreparable damage. In any event, we are now closing down the operations that may have been compromised by Anderson."

Although the country behind the espionage was identified only as "a foreign power," NATO insiders believe that it was connected to East Bloc's intelligence. There have been rumors that a female Czechoslovakian agent was involved.

After Agence de presse internationale (API), a small newspaper syndicate based in Brussels, filed these two reports of the assassination attempt, the world media picked up on the event with their usual satellite speed. Soon articles on the smashed spy ring and the heroics of General Hamelin were being carried by all the Western media.

The good guys had won for a change, courtesy of General Hammerhead Hamelin himself.

CHAPTER THREE

The granite slabs sank deeper into the earth with each step Walker Jessup took along the winding footpath to the country house overlooking the Meuse River. A fresh rain had soaked the grass, too, and stirred up a scent of mist and mud.

Jessup carefully picked his way over the wet granite. At one time his weight might have cracked the slabs, but these days the former CIA operator known as the Fixer was down to a relatively trim three hundred pounds. And though he was meandering slowly, compared to his former speed he moved like the wind.

Judging from the armored steeds parked in the small gravel lot, Jessup was the last of the covert cowboys to arrive. Unlike the other two power hitters scheduled for the meeting, he was a "civilian" and had flown in from D.C. on a commercial jet like a mere mortal. He'd landed at the Zaventem airport, taken the train to the air terminal by Brussels's Central Station, then picked up a Company car that had been waiting for him.

He'd driven south to Namur, a village with a medieval fortress where the Meuse and Sambre rivers met, then continued a short distance to the tree-shrouded retreat.

This part of Belgium with its dark forests and isolated châteaus was home to legend and myth. It was a place where you'd expect to find knights in shining armor cutting through the woods with swords. But Jessup was satisfied with seeing a body-armored guard in his mid-forties, sitting on a rocker on the shaded stone porch of the building and cradling a submachine gun.

"Hello, Jessup," the man said.

"Well goddamn," Jessup said, trying not to wheeze as he walked up the stone steps. "Look what Darwin cooked up. Glad to see you're doing honest work again, Bennett."

The man laughed and stood up. The right half of his rough face had been nearly fried in a raid on a terrorist arms cache two years before. Now it looked as if it had been put back together by trial and error. Skin grafts had finally taken, but his cheekbone still looked pretty well baked.

Jessup leaned a beefy hand against the pillar, eager for the chance to catch his breath. "When'd you get out of the hospital?"

"About a year ago," Bennett said. "After a year of therapy they said I was as cured as I'll ever be."

"And now you're shepherding God and apple pie all around Belgium," Jessup said. "Good. We'll all live longer with you around." Jessup had been involved in an operation Bennett had been running in South America, and knew firsthand that he was as good as his reputation. The scarred operative was one of the best graduates of the CIA's animal farm in Virginia.

"It's a good job," Bennett said. "Until now it's been a piece of cake."

"Is that right? What's changed now?"

"What's changed is that you're here now, Jessup. That means your gang of SOBs is coming in full bore any time now. And that means we're all in for some deep shit.''

"That we are," Jessup said. He nodded and stepped inside the cool dark house.

A sputtering fire glowed in the hearth across the room, taking the chill from the damp morning air. Bathed in the soft light, two men were sitting on long rustic couches on opposite sides of a wicker table, upon which a steaming pot of coffee sat.

The man with the gray beard who looked like a professor was Teddy Nicholas, covert controller for the National Security Agency. Also known as Tsar Nicholas because of his encyclopedic knowledge of Russian affairs, Nicholas was second in power only to DRNSA, the director of the NSA. Because it was the largest and most secretive United States intelligence agency, NSA was known in the trade as Never Say Anything.

Tsar Nicholas was here at Jessup's request, which made the cockles of his heart and the leather of his wallet feel warm and cozy as the Fixer approached.

The other man was not smiling. While he, too, had the look of a college man, it was more of a military college. Former CIA chief of station and chief of base at several European posts, Mitchell Rhodes was currently the CIA's main covert controller in Belgium.

The CIA operative had wanted to bring in Jessup alone and not the NSA. But because Jessup had something he wanted, the CIA man had given in and brought the NSA in on the operation. Without the NSA man, he wouldn't have Jessup. And without Jessup he wouldn't have the small private army known as the SOB, the soldiers of Barrabas. Led by Colonel Nile Barrabas, the SOBs could give total deniability to the CIA, NSA or any secret branch of government. There was no risk of exposure with the SOBs. No talking to the press. No whispering to Congress. It was that simple. They did what needed to be done or died trying.

"Jessup," Rhodes said, standing when he saw the Fixer walking toward them. "You're just on time. Sort of."

"You know how it is with us poor civilians." Jessup shook hands with the CIA man.

Tsar Nicholas laughed as he hurried over to clasp Jessup's hands in a more genuine grip than Rhodes's. The two covert operators had forged a solid working relationship these past few years, thanks in large part to the mercenary team Jessup could field. "The day you become a civilian," he said, "the earth will shake."

"It already does when Jessup's around," Rhodes said. "But not as much as it used to. You're looking well, Jessup."

Jessup smiled. Normally he was immune to flattery—mainly because of his past physical shape. Back then he couldn't believe any compliment that came his way. Now, shades of the old Walker Jessup who made his name as a CIA paramilitary chieftain were returning. He could almost believe it. "Thank you, Mitchell," he said.

Rhodes nodded toward the couches and said, "Jessup, let's get on with it."

Jessup and Nicholas dropped onto the couch across from the CIA man. Jessup grabbed a brown mug and poured coffee into it, welcoming the chance to fuel his brain for the long session ahead. After taking a near-scalding sip, he sat back and folded his hands across his considerable girth. "All right, Mitch," he said. "What've you got?"

"We've got a breakaway faction from NATO in the form of a united Europe group called the Realm."

"Hell, Mitch," Nicholas said. "The CIA's been bankrolling a dozen united Europe movements for forty years. They were still doing it when I was brought in as interim director a few years back. What are you complaining about?"

Mitchell Rhodes laughed. "Looks like we got what we wished for. In spades. We were angling for a united Europe that could handle its own defenses—not some bizarre network of militant monarchists who've shown they're willing to kill anyone who gets in their way. Including us."

Rhodes glanced at Jessup, then said, "Jessup here has been briefed somewhat by one of my people in D.C. Since he pressed for your participation, Ted, I figured it was best to wait until you both got here before getting down to the basics."

Teddy Nicholas clapped his hands together like a man about to play poker and said, "I'm ready to listen."

"I was hoping for more than that," Rhodes said. "Judging from Jessup's insistence that you be in on this—"

"You'll get a commitment from us if it concerns us," Nicholas said. "If not, we'll walk."

"Fine," Rhodes said. As he spoke, he reached for a small calfskin valise by his feet. He opened it, then handed duplicate folders to Jessup and the man from the NSA. "Does the collapse of NATO concern you?" he asked. "If it does, I think you'll find this interesting reading."

While Jessup and Nicholas leafed through the folders, Rhodes briefed them on the string of "accidents" and killings that appeared to be tied in to the group called the Realm. He outlined the capabilities of the massive organization, which drew upon international corporations, intelligence agencies and a paramilitary force called the White Brigade.

"How much of this is rumor?" Nicholas asked. "I've heard about both the Realm and the White Brigade. But nothing substantial—"

"Look," Rhodes said. "It's true that they've thrown a smoke screen over their activities, but the intelligence gathered by my people indicates that they are strong enough—or at least consider themselves strong enough—to make their move against the NATO alliance. That means cutting us out whatever way they can."

The Fixer shrugged. "I've heard of the Realm, too," he said. "We all have. Hell, in our positions there's not a hell of a lot we don't hear of." He put down the folder. "But what makes you so sure this is all connected to the Realm? We've got one guy named Locke killed in an accident—"

"Yeah, death by traffic mishap," Rhodes said. "But there was a slight matter of a broken neck, which seemed a bit strange to the coroner assigned to the case. It appeared to have been broken *after* the accident." Rhodes looked from one man to the other. "Fortunately, or unfortunately, for us, the coroner was used to working on delicate cases involving our kind of people. So not much fuss was made when it turned out that one of our people had apparently been strangled to death by a car."

"I'm not arguing that," Jessup said. "It has all the markings of a hit. I'm saying that just because he was whacked doesn't necessarily mean it was on the orders of the Realm."

Tsar Nicholas glanced sideways at Jessup. "You don't know one way or the other, Walker," he said. "And neither do I. My guess is you're just playing devil's advocate here."

"From working with the Company so long," Jessup said, "I've found you live a lot longer if you question everything you hear. No matter who you hear it from."

"No argument," Rhodes said. "We're getting a lot of conflicting stories from our own people. It seems that the Realm has reached some of them. That's why I'm trying to keep this limited on my end and bring in some outsiders who can't be traced." He gazed pointedly at Jessup. "If you recall, that was one of the reasons why I wanted just you and your people."

Jessup shrugged, producing a ripple effect through his now somewhat larger than necessary jacket. "The SOBs will need someone to focus them on their targets if they're to do any good. Without the capacity of the NSA to eavesdrop anywhere in Europe, my people wouldn't be able to do much. Plus I figure we're going to need some of their technical dirty tricksters close at hand."

Though he usually operated from the Puzzle Palace, the dark glass tower in Fort Meade, Maryland that served as the brains of the NSA, Teddy Nicholas could, in effect, wield and direct the power of the NSA from anywhere in the world. Since Europe was only one province of the NSA's own eavesdropping realm, he could place a lot of twenty-first-century spookery at the SOBs' disposal. Though it would require a covert nod here and there, the decision was basically up to him.

"So you've got a package deal," Nicholas said. "*If* I decide to commit myself."

"If you don't, you'd better start practicing your court manners," Rhodes said. "Because, gentlemen, if we don't stop them, no one will."

Rhodes ran down the sequence of events. The hit on Locke after he'd tipped off his lieutenant about NATO officials meeting secretly and Hubert's meeting with Lili Kavroleira. The report from Locke's DIA confidant that cast a cloud of suspicion on Lieutenant Anderson's silence. And finally, the killing of Lieutenant Anderson by General Hamelin.

"Then," Rhodes continued, "add in a number of killings of small-timers in the Brussels spook trade, and you've got a neat little loop that no one can break."

"Unless you bring in the right people," Jessup suggested.

"Exactly," Rhodes said. He leaned forward, the fingers of his right hand forming an eagle's claw as he tapped three times on the wicker basket. "As far as I'm concerned, the right people are sitting in this room."

"We might be at that," Jessup said. "But let's set the parameters right now, and determine how much this operation is going to cost."

"Oh, that's right," Rhodes said, laughing. "I almost forgot for a moment, Jessup. You're in the mercenary business now."

"Trade, not business," Jessup said. "And if you play your cards right, Mitch, maybe we can do business."

They began talking seriously about what resources they had at their command and what they might actually have to use against the Realm. The three men in the secluded country home could set up international front companies, deploy satellites and throw covert armies into the fray. But covert armies wouldn't do the trick, at least not at this stage. But an advance guard of mercenaries, a small force aimed like a laser, might just be able to pierce the armor of the shadowy group known as the Realm.

As they talked, Tsar Nicholas leaned forward, now and then tugging at his trim beard, his eyes keen, thirsting for knowledge. He vacuumed up the arcane lore about the Realm just as eagerly as his agency vacuumed up intelligence from around the world.

Walker Jessup listened politely but interrupted whenever he felt that Rhodes was skimming over some small details—like the need to crack a safehouse in a fortress here or wipe out an army of elite commandos there.

The CIA man told them that several apparently isolated crimes had been linked to the Realm. NATO matériel diverted from European bases was most likely in the hands of the subversive kingdom as it prepared its own alternate bases. There had been, Rhodes said, several infiltration episodes in which key lists used to encode communications of the United States and its NATO allies had been stolen—not necessarily by the Soviets. Along with the key lists, a lot of sensitive equipment used to decipher encoded communications had disappeared. With that equipment in their possession, the operatives of the Realm could monitor the counteroffensive against them.

"Sounds like we're dealing with some pretty sophisticated people," Jessup said.

"We are," Rhodes replied. "In a way they're just like us. Our opposite numbers, in fact. We have reason to believe that the leadership is made up of former heads of intelligence agencies and a number of would-be kings."

"What kings?" Jessup said.

"The ones in exile," Rhodes replied.

"And where would they be?" Nicholas asked.

"Portugal, for starters," Rhodes said. "It was a haven for many a king who lost his crown in World War Two."

"I can see why they might back the Realm," Jessup said. "Other than planting petunias or counting gold coins, they've got little to do but breed more princes or dream of regaining their crown."

"For now we can consider Portugal as a staging area, a haven for the kings," Rhodes said. "But we believe the real power base is in France, where the hierarchy of the Realm pulls the strings of their fiefdoms in Belgium and the Netherlands. And, unfortunately, of some of our very top people."

Jessup sighed, a hurricane of details and problems sweeping through his mind. He also saw the potential headaches—headaches soothed somewhat by the huge fees coming his way.

"Where do we start?" Jessup said.

Rhodes picked up some photocopies of a newspaper story featuring General Hamelin. "Right here," he said, handing a copy to each man. "This could be our main link."

Jessup studied the hard face glaring back at him as if from a Wanted poster, then scanned some of the text. "According to this, Hamelin's the hero of NATO."

"Don't believe everything you read in the newspapers," Rhodes said.

"Unless I write it myself, I don't," Jessup said.

Rhodes nodded. "If all goes well, we'll be making some headlines of our own. That is, if both of you are in?"

"Ask and you shall receive," Tsar Nicholas said. "For now, anyway. I'll give it a look—and a listen. If nothing turns up, I'll drop out. Until then you can count on my people helping any way that's needed."

Rhodes nodded. With Tsar Nicholas sanctioning the operation, however unofficially, he now had access to another commodity. "Well, Jessup? Can we get him?"

"We need him, don't we?"

"Yes."

"Then he'll do it," Jessup said. I hope, he thought. Although Jessup served as the cutout between the government and the Soldiers of Barrabas, he didn't command the SOBs. Only Nile Barrabas did. Barrabas was the one who decided if he'd work on any given case or not.

If too many hands were shuffling the deck, if there were too many agencies to deal with, Barrabas often refused a mission. He'd been burned too many times. And if the mission was on the questionable side, he'd break off negotiations immediately. It was often said of the SOBs, their skills were for hire but they couldn't be bought.

If Barrabas was going to risk life and limb, it had to be for something he believed in. That was why Jessup brokered operations for the SOBs only when the job was something he knew Barrabas would want to take on.

"When can he get here?" Rhodes asked.

"As soon as we agree on terms," Jessup said.

Nicholas laughed. "The usual ransom?"

"Five hundred grand a man—and woman," Jessup said.

"These people live well," Rhodes said.

"Yes," Jessup said. "But sometimes they die horribly."

With the main points of the meeting covered, Jessup paced the room to restore the circulation in his legs. He went over a few more details, arranged the next rendezvous, then shook hands with both men before leaving.

Outside, the house was still wrapped in mist. Droplets from the morning rain trekked from branch to branch before dripping into the tall grass. The foliage was lush, vibrant and serene. Hardly the kind of place to plan to topple an embryonic kingdom.

Which made it just the right place.

Trees waved in the wind as Jessup passed, like a forest sharing a secret, old oaks spinning myths. As he made his way down the winding path toward his car, he felt almost as if he were walking into a dream.

His part, the easy part, was almost done.

Now came the hard part. Now it was up to the SOBs to walk into the nightmare.

CHAPTER FOUR

Nile Barrabas sat in a tavern in the middle of the Adirondack woods listening to bluegrass on the jukebox.

He finished a mug of Albany Amber dark beer while he savored the steel whine of a song about a woman crying a river of tears and a man who swam away in them.

Cool mountain air breezed through the open door. Outside, the jagged line of pine and oak trees merged in the dusk into one huge spindly shadow creeping closer to the tavern's picture window.

Barrabas had become a semiregular there not just because he was thirsty. He'd been reacquainting himself with a woman named Denise, who tended bar and fended off men with equal skill, often deflecting advances with a well-timed wink or a well-aimed slap.

Previously, every time they started to get to know each other, Barrabas had vanished. Denise never knew what to make of him. He never talked about his trade. All he told her was that he had to go away for a while.

But sooner or later he always returned to the tavern by the Ausable River.

He usually chose a spot at the bar where he could enjoy the scenery, both outside and behind the bar.

Today he was wearing a faded blue work shirt with the sleeves rolled up. His hair was the color of smoke, a shock of white that had come from battle rather than from age. It was the color of the ghost he should have been by now.

If anything, white hair made him all the more attractive to women. It gave him a distinguished look— although he wasn't at liberty nor inclined to discuss how he'd distinguished himself.

The former Special Forces colonel felt at home whether at an embassy affair or an Adirondack roadhouse. But more often than not he preferred the stripped-down comfort of a place like this.

Besides, from firsthand experience Barrabas knew that embassies weren't all that impressive. He'd left the embassy in Saigon by jumping from the rooftop to swing on the struts of a helicopter. Last man out, one of the first men in.

Though he'd left the service as a colonel, he was still a military man. Paramilitary actually. Since he'd become a civilian, his rank and his value had risen considerably in the eyes of those he chose to work for. He led his own private army now.

"What'll it be?" Denise asked.

Barrabas looked up at the barmaid, her brown hair pulled back in a long ponytail. As she leaned over the bar, the cleavage displayed by her sequined and partially unbuttoned black cowgirl shirt lassoed him in.

"What do you suggest?" he asked.

She pursed her lips into a smile and said, "I'll leave that up to you." Then she moved down the bar, glancing back. "Let me know when you make up your mind."

The question involved a lot more than just a drink.

Barrabas watched her coast down the bar, not facing him but definitely aware that he was watching her. Watching her was his favorite pastime lately.

He rested his elbows on the smooth oak bar hewed from the woods about 150 years ago to serve the crew of a logging camp. By the 1850s the inn was prosperous, transformed into a retreat for Manhattan millionaires who rode their private railcars up north. After those glory years, the inn sank into obscurity. But now it was gathering a good name again as a year-round place for tourists to hunt, fish and ski, and now and then glimpse the Ausable Chasm itself. It was also popular with the locals, and Nile Barrabas was almost, but not quite, a local.

During the periodic respites between covert wars, Barrabas often came to the hilltop hunting lodge he'd converted into a sprawling home overlooking Ausable Chasm. The scenery was spectacular. The jigsaw canyon had been carved from the glaciers a few aeons ago. The river and the forest still looked pretty much as they had back then.

The place was just one of several in several states that he owned. And though he liked to relax occasionally in a place where people weren't shooting at him, Nile Barrabas couldn't really consider it a home. Home was where the heart was and his heart was in combat. To his eyes, war never ended. It simply changed its name and its face. War was his calling and he wasn't about to turn his back on it.

Barrabas was just about to signal Denise when the wall phone by the mirror rang. Denise poured three fingers of whiskey in front of a customer, spun around and got the phone before it could ring again.

She frowned, then glanced in Nile's direction. A moment later she was standing in front of him. "Phone for you." She raised her eyes. "He sounds real mysterious. He also sounds like a real bastard."

"I think I know who it is."

He walked around the bar to the phone. "Hello?"

He was right. The curt voice on the line belonged to Walker Jessup, the man who served as a buffer between the Soldiers of Barrabas and the intelligence community.

The Fixer spoke briefly about a new mission, giving Barrabas veiled hints of what it entailed—enough hints to seriously interest him.

"If I take it, what should I bring?" Barrabas asked, knowing they might have to bring in their own weapons and identities unless the mission was endorsed by some pillars of the "community."

"A coat of armor and a battering ram for starters," Jessup said.

"I'm all out of shining armor at the moment."

"Then I'll settle for just you and your gang of five."

Good, Barrabas thought. That meant the weapons and logistics would be handled by the local powers that be.

"The fee?"

"The usual," Jessup said. "Enough to get a new coat of armor and make a down payment on a castle or two."

"When?" Barrabas said.

He noticed Denise sidling down the bar. Though seemingly absorbed in her glossy red fingernails, she had grown obviously tense at the word *when*.

"Three days," Jessup answered.

Three days, Barrabas thought. Three days to round up the SOBs: Liam O'Toole, an ex-Army captain and current barroom bard; Claude Hayes and Alex Nanos, a SEAL and a sailor; William Starfoot II, an Osage Indian and Marine Corps guerrilla warfare specialist; and to handle the inevitable casualties when the SOBs used their skills, a combat doc and woman warrior, Leona Hatton.

It could be done. The SOBs were probably as stir-crazy as he was by now. But he'd have to move fast and start making the calls tonight.

Jessup gave Barrabas the name of a Brussels hotel, then said, "Your answer?"

"I'll be there," Barrabas said, and hung up the phone.

Denise spun around, her ponytail lashing the air like a whip. She set her hands on her hips and stared at him with blazing green eyes. "Maybe you will," she said, blocking his path. "Maybe you won't."

The way she bunched her fists at her hips and stood at attention was more inviting than intimidating.

Barrabas smiled. He'd been in a lot of bars, but he couldn't remember a woman trying to pick a fight with him in a bar before. "I see," he said. He reached out, gripped her shoulders lightly and spun her around.

Denise looked over her shoulder, then nodded toward the door.

"Outside, soldier," she said. She waited until he passed, latched the swinging half door that led to the bar, then stepped outside.

Barrabas followed her to the side of the inn. She leaned against the log wall and folded her arms in front of her, then raised her knee and anchored her foot against the wood.

"Soldier, huh?" Barrabas said. "You seem to know a lot about me."

"I know what I see in your eyes," she said. "And I grew up around enough soldiers to recognize one when I see one. I also see someone who's going to take off again, just when..."

"Just when things are looking good between us?" Barrabas suggested.

"Yeah, or starting to."

"I've got to make arrangements," Barrabas said. "Get in touch with some people before I go."

"So you're taking off?"

"Yeah."

"For how long?"

"As long as it takes."

"Well, then, soldier," she said, stepping forward, "I think I just may have to stop by your barracks tonight. To help you with those arrangements—and to make sure you take off in style."

She pushed herself from the wood into Barrabas's arms. He held her by her shoulders and kissed her hard, lifting her on her toes.

Then he released her, the electricity singing in his blood as she went back inside to steal a few more hearts.

CHAPTER FIVE

The wind swept down Manhattan's East Side, kicking up newspapers, bright-colored wrappers and the skirts of the career girls streaming from office buildings at rush hour, a sight that put a grin on the face of Liam O'Toole.

The red-bearded Irishman couldn't hide his interest in the hurricane of high heels and nylons.

The woman on his arm, Gloria Gehlen, a small-press publisher of poetry who usually teetered on the brink of bankruptcy, squeezed his arm with all her might. To the former Army captain and current SOB it felt as if a butterfly had landed on his biceps.

"Always the lecher, O'Toole," she said.

"You've got it wrong there, darling," he said. "I'm just an observer of the human condition."

"More like a voyeur," she said.

O'Toole stopped in the middle of the street, a broad-shouldered barrier for the waves of pedestrians who detoured around him. "I can't close my eyes to the world, Gloria," he said. He looked down at her and ran his fingers through her long silky hair, then kissed her lightly rouged cheek. "Not when there's so much beauty to be seen."

"Maybe you should write greeting card verse instead of real poetry, O'Toole."

"No," he said. "But don't blame me if God's in cahoots with the muse today. We take our inspiration where we find it." He found it once again in the parade of windblown skirts as he guided her through the crowds.

The afternoon sun was mostly hidden by swiftly moving storm clouds. They continued up Lexington Avenue past Broadway, strolling by a string of expensive restaurants and nightclubs that sported fresh chrome-and-glass facelifts. Sandwiched between two of the East Side's finest watering holes was another kind of club. It was a walk-down bar that served as a reminder to the other places of what could happen if you weren't careful.

The glorious dive was named Club Exo. It was in dire need of a window washer, a street sweeper and an exterminator or two, but it had something else going for it. It was *their* place, the place where O'Toole and Gloria met.

Liam O'Toole liked living in New York when he wasn't touring the battlefields with Nile Barrabas, who was perhaps the only man he would trust to captain him these days. The city was the closest thing he knew to a combat zone, so he felt right at home there. Besides, New York was where the poets were. And it was also the place where a poet-loving publisher named Gloria Gehlen lived.

Since she'd discovered him at Club Exo—or "uncovered" him, as one critic had written—she and O'Toole had become an item. Despite his penchant for flirting and his wandering eyes, when he was in town he was a one-woman man. At least, as he often told her, only one woman at a time.

Gloria had had romances with other poets. It was only natural that her passion extended from their poetry to the poets themselves. But those poets had been of a different stripe entirely. Many of them had masked their inability to deal with the world with self-conscious, obscure poetry. O'Toole was different. He was the first poet she knew who really dealt with the world first, then described it. That was what made his work so potent, if not quite polished.

They skipped down the dusty cement steps and walked into the club. Here and there the darkness was broken by the glint of light on brown beer bottles and wineglasses. The usual crowd was gathered for the afternoon poetry reading.

Many faces looked up when the two minor celebrities entered. Berets, biker caps, biker boots, spiked hair, black mesh stockings, high heels, worn-out sneakers, mascara, black lipsticked smiles, pale nightlife faces and sunglasses were all in abundance.

O'Toole wasn't scheduled for a reading today, but as he walked through the club he was addressed with what amounted to praise or one-word critiques of his recent performances. Some people clapped. Others yelled out.

"Hail Caesar!"

"Hail Hitler!"

"Fascist!"

There were comments from admirers of his poetry, many of them women who liked the fire-breathing Irishman more for his performance than for his poems.

The bartender, Stu, hollered out, "Hail the Savior," as O'Toole passed. Not only did O'Toole draw a good crowd of poets and critics when he took his turns on stage, but he also knocked back a fair share of "postcards from County Antrim," as he called his shots of Bushmill whiskey.

O'Toole calmly accepted the epithets hurled his way as if they were warm greetings from the bizarre clientele of the club. The poet and his lady sat at a table off to one side of the club, away from the bar and near the stage.

"The place has gone upscale on us," O'Toole said.

Gloria brushed away some of the ambience of Club Exo, a piece of dust that had settled on her black V-neck top. "What do you mean?"

He glanced over at what had been a stripper's promenade and now served as a stage for poets and musicians. "They painted the walk."

Gloria smiled. A coat of flat paint had been splashed upon the old stage, drenching it with beatnik black. "Right down to the last splinter," she said.

"The paint's probably all that's holding it up," O'Toole said.

"Everyone's a critic," the bartender said as he approached their table, holding his chest as if O'Toole's comment had cut him to the quick. "I put in a lot of time reconditioning that baby."

"At least five minutes," Gloria suggested.

"You're not kidding," he said. He leaned over the table and took their order, like a father confessor about to hear the sins. His black shirt, black suspenders and neatly trimmed hair added to the effect.

"I'll take the usual, Stu," O'Toole told him.

"One vat of whiskey coming up." Stu turned to Gloria.

"I'll take the house wine," she said. "Easy on the formaldehyde."

"It's not that bad," he protested.

"Words can't describe it, Stu," she said. "And in a place full of poets, that's bad."

He nodded, then left.

Originally he'd scheduled most of his poetry readings for nighttime, but since many of his best customers were poets chasing but rarely catching the employment muse, he discovered he could get a fair crowd earlier in the day.

Work at the Club Exo was usually a one-man operation. Even on nights of music instead of poetry, when a girl at the door took admission fees, Stu liked to handle the crowds himself for the tips.

Even the musical performers of Club Exo were a bit offbeat. The club featured folk talkers who would recite poetry, then seemingly at random strum a guitar or plink the untuned keys of a stand-up piano at the edge of the stage.

O'Toole loved the club in all of its moods. It was as if an archaeologist had uncovered an underground cave full of beatnik princesses and black jacketed hipsters and revived them.

When their drinks arrived, O'Toole and Gloria settled back, watching the black-haired woman who took the stage and began to read her poetry.

O'Toole only half listened. The pressure was off him for a while. His latest chapbook, *Warmongrel* published by Gloria's small press, had assured a great reaction among the poets who worshiped at Club Exo's altar. In most cases it was an allergic reaction; many of the poets and critics were hooked on left-of-center, far-left and far-out poetry, and considered O'Toole to be slightly to the right of Attila.

Warmongrel was a ballad about a soldier of fortune who stayed too long in the trade, well past the time when his reflexes, instincts and humanity began to fail. He ended up as a burned-out enforcer for a terrorist outfit, and died in a shoot-out in a South American bar.

Several copies of the staple-bound chapbook were in evidence at Club Exo, some of them covered with beer rings, others well thumbed. The marbled cardboard cover was bloodred with *Warmongrel* embossed in black Gothic type. It was dedicated simply to "those who rose and those who fell."

The narrative was based on fact. O'Toole was the man who killed the soldier of fortune. He'd had no choice, but even so, the man he termed the Warmongrel had done a lot of good in his time. He just hadn't known when to get out. Always hanging on past his time. Even now it seemed as if he were still hanging around. But maybe now the ballad was printed, he would go and haunt someone else for a while.

O'Toole gathered the material for his poetry from his life. There were his days in Ireland. In Vietnam. In Africa. In Europe. Most of his sight-seeing was done while serving as an SOB. After leaving the Army as a captain, the red-bearded Irishman had captained a few mercenary crews of his own before he was recruited by Nile Barrabas, who'd been assembling a small group of similarly talented soldiers.

Liam O'Toole was certain of his military prowess. But when it came to poetry, he wasn't quite sure—despite his limited success.

"One of your admirers has her eye on you," Gloria said.

"And where is she?" O'Toole asked.

She nodded toward the bar, where a stunning blonde with short spiked hair and a clinging tiger top was leafing through his chapbook, occasionally glancing at him.

"Her again," O'Toole said. He'd noticed the blonde several times before. Usually she was at the front of the audience while he was reading. And usually she was hurling insults. "She hates my stuff."

"At least she bought a copy," Gloria said.

The chapbook had come out in a small edition, just five hundred copies, but it had attracted considerable notice among the poetry clique and in some of the small but vicious literary magazines that circulated in the clubs like car-wash fliers. Some of the genteel reviewers went for the jugular in their critiques of *Warmongrel*.

O'Toole had gleefully clipped out every one of the reviews. "*Warmongrel* is a paean to pain." "Nothing but out-and-out warnography." "A journal of a madman apparently written by one." "The title is perhaps the best thing about the book."

Such reviews didn't bother him. He had a thick hide. His own doubts mattered to him, not theirs, especially since these members of the cult of poets were so inbred, pretending their unsung, unpublished odes were the only ones that really mattered. As far as O'Toole was concerned, they wore blinders as they sat on the edge of their flat earth and crucified everyone they reviewed.

There had been a few favorable comments on his ballad, however. One of them, which he kept firmly in mind, came from a well-regarded reviewer who wrote, "This man is going to make a splash—a bloody red splash, but he will be noticed. *Warmongrel* is an assault weapon from someone who knows how to wield words."

Such an appraisal soothed any possible wounds from the rest of the pack of reviewers.

"She's coming your way," Gloria said.

A moment later the blonde sauntered over to their table, carrying her copy of his chapbook.

"Good afternoon," O'Toole said.

For a moment she looked as if she was going to argue the point, but she finally said hello. Then she handed over the book and asked him to inscribe it.

"You're sure about that, darling?" O'Toole asked. "The last time we talked, you called me a bloodthirsty storm trooper."

"I was feeling mellow that day."

O'Toole laughed. "But you still want an autograph?"

She nodded. "Hey, I love to hate your stuff."

"A pleasure, dear," he said, taking the book in one hand and her proffered pen in the other.

After she left, O'Toole and Gloria downed a few more glasses, while they and the faded interior of Club Exo took on a warm glow—a glow that was interrupted by the bartender a half hour later.

"A call for you," he said to O'Toole.

Gloria sighed and lifted her glass high to finish the last of her wine.

O'Toole nodded. There were only a few numbers where he could be reached during the day: Gloria's, Club Exo's and that of a gym where he went whenever he had to work off an overindulgence in alcohol.

And there was usually only one person who would call.

"What did he say?"

"He just asked for Irish," the bartender said.

"The whiskey or the soldier?" Gloria asked.

"Sorry, darling," O'Toole said. He pushed back his chair and headed for the phone. He returned a couple of minutes later.

"Well?" Gloria said. "Off to gather some more material?"

"Afraid so," O'Toole replied.

But in a way he was relieved at Barrabas's call. There was a chance that if he'd stayed around much longer, he would have been looking back at Gloria with marrying eyes.

"Why are you looking at me like that?" she asked.

He tapped the side of his face. "That's so I can carry you around up here."

"Most men would just carry a picture."

"I'm not most men."

"That you're not, O'Toole," she agreed, pushing away from the table. "Thank God and goddamn it all at once. Let's go back to my place, so I can remember you."

CHAPTER SIX

The teak-trimmed sportfishing yacht bobbed in the blue waters off Boca Raton, Florida.

Alex Nanos, lulled by the rhythm of the waves, had drifted off to sleep. He was sitting in the helm seat on the fly bridge, his stocky tanned legs draped over the control console. And though the Greek seaman always claimed that he could pilot any ship in his sleep, there was no chance it would happen today. The yacht was firmly anchored just a swim and a hop from shore.

The midafternoon sun baked down upon the bright enamel and chrome of the yacht, casting colored reflections in the sea. Though the heat was brutal, the Greek was almost immune to the rays. Nearly every inch of his powerful body was bronzed from the sun. Though his muscles had the definition of a weight lifter's, he was always careful to keep them fluid, preferring speed to bulk.

His weathered face often looked somber, but the twinkle in his eyes always gave away the imp who lived inside. That same twinkle served as beacon to the fair maidens of the sea who swam in schools to the Gold Coast of Florida year after year.

There was a straw-haired blonde sprawled on the companion seat behind him. Her name at the moment was unknown, lost in the Mai Tai clouds formed from the drink in her hand and the laughter on her lips.

One of her slender arms was draped over the side of the bench, the other was crooked above her space-age shades. Her tanned legs glistened with suntan oil, and surprisingly her bikini top was fastened for a change.

She was one of the multitudes who had made the journey from Boca Raton's beaches to the SOB's seagoing hotel, one of the legion of leggy blondes who followed the Greek pied piper of the sea, Claude Hayes thought.

The tall black man with the closely trimmed mustache shrugged and climbed back down the ladder to the cockpit. He'd been about to ask Nanos to go on a run into town, but he hated to disturb him and his friend during their siesta. After the most recent onboard bacchanalia, they deserved their rest.

Let the sucker sleep, he thought, dropping down into the fighting chair in the cockpit.

He reached over and tapped one of the expensive deep sea rigs in the rod holder. It might as well have been an antenna for all the use it got. Though Nanos's yacht was designed for fishing and cruising, for the past few weeks it had hardly lifted anchor, and its catch of the day was usually of the striped or string bikini variety.

Claude had had more than his share but had always thrown them back. Nanos, on the other hand, was a bit of a satyr, a trait he shared with many of the old-money millionaires who harbored in Boca Raton. Unlike them, Nanos never held on to money long enough to count it. Instead of nouveau riche, he was temporarily rich. The money all went to boats and broads and booze.

Inevitably, like the tides that rode in and out, his money would go the same way. Soon enough he'd be as well off as the nearest beachcomber. Until then, he'd be ringing the belles night and day.

Hayes handled his finances a lot differently. After having beheld the walking scarecrows that haunted the famine-plagued deserts of Africa, he couldn't see himself squandering the handsome fees he received from the mercenary trade. He quietly transferred some of his funds to a select few relief organizations that actually helped the people instead of siphoning off most of the cash for their stateside bureaucrats. Hayes also distributed some of his income in his hometown of Detroit.

By no means was he a saint. But he felt that if money came his way, he had to do some good with it. Of course, he made sure there was always enough in his account to keep his own house in order and, now and then, to fund one of his trips with Nanos.

Hayes believed there was a certain balance that had to be maintained in life. But whenever he was with Nanos it was like walking on a tightrope.

Despite their different approaches, both men had a lot in common. They were at home in the sea. That was one reason they often palled around between SOB operations. While Nanos had picked up seagoing skills in the Coast Guard, Hayes had got his from the Navy's Underwater Demolition Team.

Hayes had also served a couple of hitches as a SEAL, part of the Navy's elite Sea Air and Land special warfare teams. It was there that he had acquired the skills that kept him alive during his guerrilla tours in Africa before Barrabas recruited him for the SOBs.

He'd survived the fast-moving life as a mercenary. It was the off time, the slow time that was killing him.

"Dammit!" he said.

Suddenly he swung the cockpit chair to his left, braced both hands on the arms, then pushed himself off. He let the momentum carry him up and over the side of the boat. He arched his back, then straightened in midair as his spear hands knifed into the water.

The cold slap of the water woke him, removing the doldrums that had seized him these past few days.

He broke the surface, then treaded water while he looked back at the yacht where the sleeping captain sat, dead to the world. Hayes shook his head, went back under, then with long sweeping strokes swam back to the yacht. He climbed the ladder and shook off the trails of ocean water.

The sun went to work drying his skin almost immediately. He grabbed a towel to wipe his face and slung the towel over his shoulders.

"Alex?" he called up to the fly bridge.

There was a murmur from the blonde, some indecipherable but nonetheless sweet sound. But there was absolutely nothing from the Greek.

"Alex? Are you still alive?"

Silence. Hayes shook his head and went into the galley to brew up a strong pot of coffee. Soon the thick aroma was wafting up to the fly bridge.

A few minutes later there was a thump as Nanos jumped down to the cockpit. He crouched from the impact, then sprang up to his full height.

Hayes was sipping a fresh cup of coffee when the Greek stepped inside the cabin.

"Morning," Nanos said.

"Good afternoon," Hayes replied.

Nanos glanced at the watch that he often boasted could tell time, temperature and political climate nearly anywhere in the world. "Well, according to this it's morning somewhere, so let's leave it at that."

"Where's the girl?" Hayes asked.

"She's up there wondering what she ever did to deserve me," Nanos boasted, heading for the coffee to pour himself a cup.

Hayes dropped down into the U-shaped settee flanking the table. "We've got to talk, Alex."

Nanos slid across the table from him and knocked back a slug of strong coffee. "So talk."

"It's about the life we're leading here, man."

"Heaven, isn't it?" Nanos said, rapping out a two-handed drum solo on the table.

Hayes shook his head. "Man, don't you ever get tired of fast blondes and cheap thrills?"

"Are you kidding? What else is there in life?" He leaned forward. "Besides, how come you don't give me these lectures about my foolish ways until after you've joined in for a while?"

Hayes sighed and shook his head. "Man, you're losing track of what counts...."

"Oh, I don't know." Nanos glanced up at the ceiling. "I know I can always count on her for a blast."

"You're hopeless," Hayes said. "You've got to start—"

Nanos cut him off. "Hey, get thee to a nunnery, Claude," he said. "Or convent, or whatever it's called. They'll listen to you there."

"It's called a rectory," Hayes said.

"Ah ha, so you *are* studying for the priesthood."

"Alex, we're getting out of shape here."

"The shapes around here suit me just fine," he said.

Hayes shrugged. He knew he was getting nowhere. It was impossible for the Greek to have too much of a good thing.

Although the Florida boat trip had seemed like paradise in the beginning, now Hayes wouldn't have minded if a big hand came down from the sky and distributed a few fig leaves.

The hand from the sky came about ten minutes later when the buzzer rigged to the radiophone sounded two harsh bursts.

"Oh, no!" Nanos said.

"Oh, yeah," said Hayes.

Both mercenaries were extremely careful about revealing their whereabouts, except to those who might have to get in touch with them in a hurry.

Nanos picked up the small receiver. The operator of the yacht club's VHF station told him he had a call coming in from a Mr. Whitehat and gave him the channel.

"Who is it?" Hayes said.

"Some guy named Whitehat," Nanos said.

Hayes laughed. *White hat* was a term Barrabas used to refer to intelligence operatives on their side, or to describe himself when he was working with official agency people. It meant they were about to go on a mission, and since it involved the SOBs it had to be an intelligence operation with a strong military aspect.

Hayes eavesdropped on the conversation.

"No, we're not doing anything important," Nanos spoke into the receiver. "Interesting but not important."

He paused, listening to Barrabas. There was a look in his eyes that had been missing for some time now,

Hayes noticed. It was the look of a man about to trade in a beach towel for a parachute.

"Yeah," Nanos said. "Hayes will be there, too. Hell, he's been ready for a week now. If you hadn't called, he would've started a war of his own."

Nanos stayed on the line a few moments more, then replaced the receiver.

"What's up?" Hayes said.

"We're going into a war zone."

"Where?"

"Belgium."

Hayes looked sideways at him. "Belgium?"

Nanos shrugged. "Must be a secret war," he said.

CHAPTER SEVEN

William Starfoot II shucked off the tuxedo jacket as if it were a second skin. Holding it by the collar he snapped it like a whip, then let if fly across the room. It settled ghostlike upon the bed.

The Osage Indian never felt comfortable in that kind of duds, even though, according to the women at the party, they looked good on him. Too civilized, he thought.

From the ballroom downstairs he could hear the live band. Despite the late hour they were still giving it their best. Waltzing Matildas all around the room, he mused. True, his eyes had feasted on some of the belles of the ball in their silk dresses. But in their gazes he'd seen little more than the desire to capture a real live Indian. Or perhaps some of that Indian's wealth.

He pulled loose the thong that had bridled his collar-length hair, then kicked off his shoes and exchanged the rest of his monkey suit for a pair of sweats. He sat back against the deacon's bench in the corner of the room and exhaled.

The room was decorated in early American money. Everything was top drawer and depersonalized, selected by an interior decorator to create a turn-of-the-century atmosphere. Though this room on the second floor of the west wing was considered his and was reserved for his use, he seldom spent time there.

In his father's house—his mansion actually—William Starfoot II, scion of a wealthy Oklahoma oil family, felt separated from his Osage heritage.

In its place was an ersatz heritage, purchased by the oil that had made many of the old Osages wealthy beyond their dreams.

They were the wrong kind of dreams for him.

The Osage blood that raced in his veins carried other dreams. Warrior dreams. At times that made him feel that his father had exchanged his blood for oil, for wealth. But he never felt anger toward him. They were different people. The generations had strayed now and then, but there was always someone in the family who relished the old way. The way of the warrior.

That was William Starfoot II, or as the SOBs knew him, Billy Two.

As a youth he'd sought out Osage shamans and chieftains. He'd become a hunter and tracker and martial arts expert, multiplying those skills when he served with the Force Reconnaissance Marines.

Those skills never deserted him. In fact, they were called upon quite frequently by the one man he would follow in war these days—Nile Barrabas.

It seldom took Billy Two long to get back in condition. He was always in training. And he was always at war—often with himself.

It stemmed from an SOB operation behind Russian lines in which Billy Two had been caught and tortured beyond endurance. He had survived, but for a while his head had turned into a living laboratory, splicing and churning out thoughts that only a madman could fathom. The SOBs had been able to rescue his body but it had taken a lot longer for his mind to come back.

A normal man would have perished from the experience, but as Alex Nanos was fond of pointing out, no one had ever accused Billy Two of being normal. Billy Two accepted the good-natured ribbing. Especially since Nanos was always there when he needed someone, often hanging with him for those months when he was prone to psychotic fits and the head doctors considered him dangerous to himself and others.

Nanos matter-of-factly took it all in. "Hey, no sweat," the Greek had said. "Bounce off the wall if you got to. Bay at the moon. Talk to God if you want to, and while you're at it tell him I plan on reforming in about ten years or so. Don't worry about a thing, Billy. Hell, except for me, nobody's perfect."

Somehow that attitude worked for Billy Two. It was what he needed, along with the support of the other SOBs—including Leona Hatton, the black-haired siren, assassin and combat doc, who made sure he was mentally and physically prepared before coming back on assignments with the SOBs.

Billy Two had definitely hooked up with the right crew. They were his family. Others would have walked away from him, considering him a basket case when he began seeing things, hearing voices and gradually becoming convinced that he was in contact with an entity revealed to him as Hawk Spirit.

That was what had finally healed him.

Not a doctor of the body. Nor a doctor of the mind. It was a doctor of the soul. As he tried to explain to the others, Hawk Spirit was something like a familiar, a guardian angel, a god who'd been inside him all along and only now had emerged.

In the beginning they'd all kidded him about it. "As long as he's housebroken, bring him along," Nanos had said.

But on subsequent missions, the SOBs were grateful. With Hawk Spirit around, whatever it was, it was as if Billy Two had developed some kind of sixth sense.

A sense that was now very much in operation.

Something was happening. Something soon. He could feel it in the air. It seemed so tangible he could almost touch it.

Billy Two dug through the desk drawer, found some note paper, then wrote in a leisurely scrawl: *Thanks for keeping the door open, but I can't seem to get into the spirit of things here. I have to go.*

Billy Two left the note in the middle of the bed.

His father would understand. Even though he was constantly trying to draw his son into high society, he knew more than anyone that Billy Two was at odds with the world he lived in and had to go off and live in his own.

Billy Two opened the window, letting the dry desert air into the room. He slid out backward, supporting himself on the sill until his six-foot frame was stretched to its full length.

Then he pushed off and dropped to the ground with a soft, almost soundless touch.

At the side of the house the Caddies, Lincolns and Mercedeses were parked. Billy Two threw his leg over the seat of his 1955 Vincent Black Knight and wheeled it silently down the driveway to the road. He eased on his night-black helmet, tested the balance of the bike, then jumped. His instep came down hard and quick on the start lever.

The motor roared. He twisted the grip toward him and shot down the road.

The wind buffeted his bare arms, stinging slices of cold air slashing at his shirt.

It was flight.

He felt as if he were soaring. Hawk Spirit was near.

The Osage barreled down the road for a few miles, then turned off into a small dirt lane that led to his secluded ranch.

After a short uphill ride, he parked the bike near the stone front porch, then stepped inside the curved portal. The house was airy and simply furnished. Except for some handwoven rugs and a few modern accessories, he kept it sparse.

Just like the land outside.

It felt hot and dry tonight. Now that he wasn't barreling down the road, sweat was trickling off him. He poured a glass of water, took a small sip, then stripped off his shirt. He splashed the rest of the water over his head, and let it drip onto his chest and back.

He didn't turn on any lights. The moonlight was strong enough tonight.

It was late but he knew he couldn't sleep. Something was up. Something was missing—his peace of mind. He felt jittery, as he had in the early days of his recovery.

A mind ache, he called it.

Billy Two stepped out the back of the house and walked about two hundred yards on a zigzag path through the low grass to a small sandy hill he regarded as his observatory—where he went to look at things that could not be seen.

He dropped to the earth and sat, folding his legs. With his palms resting on his thighs, he looked up. The light of the moon washed over his face.

Then a shadow flew over his face. Something hovered above him.

Hawk Spirit.

The shadow flew across the inside of his mind. He could feel the beat of the wings, he could see through the eyes of the hawk above, looking down at the full blood Osage on the sand....

He looked hard and long, listening to the wings beat until the world around him disappeared. And he saw the world through the eyes of a hawk. He saw the world that belonged to a creature with wings.

He saw the SOBs who were shadows now, the ones who had not come back from their missions. Their spirits were up there, too, still taking shape. They were new to the world of shadows that Hawk Spirit soared through. But for a while the Osage could see them, hear them, remember them as their shadows stirred in the moonlight.

They fled with the dawn.

But Billy Two stayed there, chasing thought after thought, taming them into manageable concepts that were as still and light as his silent breath.

Then the sand stirred behind him.

A few moments later two shadows lined the ground in front. One stocky, one lean.

"Don't get your feathers in an uproar, Billy," Nanos said. "It's only us."

Billy Two looked over his shoulder, his eyes like those of a man awakening from a time long past. "I was expecting you," he said.

"Don't tell me," Nanos said. "A little bird told you."

The Osage laughed. "No," he said. "It was time. I knew something was up."

"Ever since you heard the car door slam, you did." Claude Hayes nodded toward the rental car just barely visible beside Billy Two's house.

The Osage shrugged, stretched his arms and legs and stood. He shook hands with Nanos, then Claude. "Good to see you both."

"Yeah," Nanos said, looking at the tall, weather-burned Osage, and beyond. "It's nice to see the two of you, too."

They laughed. For a moment it was as if no time had passed since they were last together.

Then they walked back toward the house and the war that awaited.

CHAPTER EIGHT

The dark-haired woman turned the green figurine slowly in the light that blazed through the shop window. While she was inspecting its beauty, the dealer was inspecting hers, watching the full-figured brunette's profile.

She was aware of the glance and unbothered by it. Years of experiencing similar looks had made her immune. Besides, the collector was not unattractive. A bit too feral, perhaps, expecting his dark good looks to conquer all. He was about forty and immaculately dressed as if this ocean-side shop were a world-renowned exhibition and he were a guide to its treasure.

"Ah, yes, the ancients did such fine work," the dealer said, sidling up to her.

"So did the guy who made this," she said.

The dealer raised an eyebrow. "I see you are a fine judge of art."

"And character." She leveled her gaze upon him and inspected him as if he, too, were a figurine of questionable heritage.

She replaced the figurine on an uncrowded shelf. There it stood guard over all the other treasures. Its price had already decreased because she knew its heritage.

It was still a fine piece of craftsmanship, however. The small malachite base a few inches in circumference supported a jade woman with a spear. Exquisite and expensive, the glittering green nude Amazon on the marbled green ore base had been made perhaps two hundred years ago. Old but not ancient.

"Everything here, you will see, is flawless. The island has certain standards to maintain."

Indeed it had, she thought. And that was one of the reasons Leona Hatton now resided a large part of the year on Lanzarote, one of Spain's Canary Islands off the Atlantic coast of Morocco.

Though she still kept one foot on Majorca where her family had lived for years, more and more she was finding that the island paradise of Lanzarote fitted her idea of home. The ever-present scent of the ocean drifted over its sandy beaches while the warm sirocco winds brushed through fig groves, castles and hotels.

The underground cave systems had proved fascinating, drawing her back for several visits to the grottoes. Naturally, since this was paradise, there were some cafés and nightclubs near the caves where the sightseers could quench their thirst.

The volcanos and castles gave Lanzarote a primitive if somewhat pricey atmosphere. But since the island was still relatively undeveloped, there was room to move. That was what she liked about it most.

At the moment she was in the town of Teguise, the former capital of Lanzarote guarded by nearby Guanapay Castle. While the sun and the beaches drew others, the small shop in Teguise drew her. Although she wasn't an avid collector of art objects, she had many fine pieces in her island home. Too many, all of them acquired recently. But she needed to do something, to go out and kill the fortune of time that was on her hands.

The shop was worth a look.

It had good word of mouth. The collector who'd opened it had brought with him oddities from the world over, including the Canary Islands. He had also brought with him his own considerable ego, carrying it in every step of his furtive gait as he followed her through the shop.

The dealer believed that his newest customer and potential conquest might elude him if he stayed in the background and kept his charm hidden. "Are you alone?" he asked.

"Not often," she said.

He smiled. "I meant that...I was only thinking that perhaps I could show you around the island."

"I live here," she said. "I know it well."

"Ahh, indeed, the spirit of the island has drawn you, too. We heed the same call." He paused. Then, as if a sudden inspiration just struck him, he said, "Well, if you live here, perhaps I could call for you at your villa and we could—we could continue our relationship from there."

She smiled and shook her head. "And you with a broken back."

"But it's not broken."

"Keep it up and it will be."

He laughed, thinking it was all part of a game she was playing with him—a ritual he was glad to join. But then he saw the promise behind her gaze. It wasn't a bluff.

When he realized that this woman actually could do what she said, he felt as if he had been slapped in the face. It was not what he would have expected from a woman with her riveting looks. Her hair was shaped in a short Cleopatra cut that accentuated her sharp cheekbones. The pastel summer dress clung to her, but somehow she looked cool despite the afternoon heat.

She was everything he wanted in a woman. But the eyes told him that she was too much woman for him.

She drifted back toward the figurine, once again picked it up.

"It is a most beautiful piece," the dealer said.

"Yes. Just what I was looking for."

He smiled.

"But now that I've found it, the thrill is gone. It's all in the chase, you know."

She put it down for a final time and left.

Lee Hatton walked through a maze of dry streets before heading down Costa Teguise to the modern Las Salinas Sheraton where she had booked a seaside room. She'd planned on spending the weekend in Teguise rather than at her villa on the south side of the island near Playa Blanca. She was attracted by the Verdes Cave system, the underground web of rocklike mazes. She needed something to take her out of the ordinary. For the past few weeks she'd been restless, felt expectant. Another need was arising. A need not anticipated in someone of her apparent background. It was a need for action.

She'd been on edge lately, and the cure could not be found in some shop on Lanzarote, nor in the arms of one of her many suitors.

The cure lay in a different kind of action. Because of her stunning looks, Leona Hatton did not fit anyone's idea of a soldier. Which made her an ideal recruit for the SOBs. She'd come on board during the first SOB operation in Africa. They'd needed a doctor for their wounded—and also someone to keep them from getting wounded. A soldier.

Leona had trained as a doctor and had served a lot of time in hospitals in the Third World. But she had also spent an equal amount of time in embassies, often working undercover. She was equipped to heal or harm.

The dark-haired doc's medical and martial arts proved a deadly combination.

Raised in a military family, Lee had had every opportunity to learn the craft of covert warfare. Her father had been a high-ranking officer with the OSS, the predecessor of the CIA. The covert blood raced in her veins.

It raced even faster now when she stepped into the lobby of the Sheraton and a young British woman behind the desk called out her name. "Miss Hatton?"

She stopped, forcing back the smile. There were few who knew where she was. Her house staff at Playa Blanca had been given her address for the forwarding of messages—but only for messages from a privileged few.

"Yes?" she said, approaching the desk.

"A message came for you. It seemed rather odd, so I asked the caller to repeat it a couple of times. I wrote it down word for word."

The woman passed over a note written on hotel stationery. Lee turned it around carefully and read: *Expedition with Nile about to begin. Proceed to Brussels at same.*

"I'm afraid it doesn't make much sense," the woman went on. "If your trip is along the Nile, I figured you'd fly straight to Cairo from here. But when I asked for the correct wording he said *with* Nile, not *along* the Nile. He said you'd understand. And he didn't give his name."

Oh, but he did, Lee thought. "It makes sense," she assured the clerk. "In its own way."

The note was obviously from Barrabas. It simply meant she was to make her way to Brussels. "Brussels at same" meant she was to book a room at the Brussels Sheraton. And there she would be contacted.

The SOBs needed her—just as she had needed them.

"I'm afraid I'll be checking out soon," she said. "Could you contact the airport at Arrecife and book me on the first flight out?"

"Of course," the woman said. "Sorry you couldn't stay longer."

"I'll survive," she said. *I hope.*

CHAPTER NINE

The house on the border was just five miles south of Breda, a medieval Dutch town surrounded by woods in north Brabant province. It was about fifty miles north of Brussels.

And at two in the morning it was about forty steps away from hell.

That was the distance that separated the man in the forest-green hood, Bernhard Vallance, from the sturdy old farmhouse. Beside him, a half dozen White Brigade commandos waited for the Belgian's signal to move.

Bernhard Vallance was a slender but sinewy man whose monklike appearance had led many an opponent to underestimate him. It was always a lethal mistake. Like a bowstring about to be drawn, the potential for action was always there in him, hidden beneath the surface.

With his fringe of thinning blond hair, soft blue eyes and refined aquiline face, he looked like a recluse, a monk who worked by candlelight in dusty towers. When he wore one of his fine tailored suits he could pass for a banker or lawyer.

A perfect image for a field commander of the White Brigade.

Now, however, his outer image matched the inner. He wore dark green camouflage garb. His web belt held spare magazines for the Heckler & Koch MP-5

SD3, the sound-suppressed submachine gun cradled in his arms.

He scanned the farmhouse through a monocular thermal imager, checking once more the position of each of the sentries. They were spaced so that if a sniper got one of them, his outcry and the sound of his fall would alert the others.

So they thought.

Tonight the White Brigade was going to rendezvous with the sentries up close and personal.

"Let's take them out," Vallance said softly.

Sordett, his right-hand man, nodded, then gestured to the man on his right. One by one the signal went down the line and they moved forward.

Like a poisonous fog, the dark shapes of the White Brigade commandos rolled over the heather. Their movement through the Dutch countryside was indistinguishable from the night. Except for a slight rustle here and a soft footfall there, the only sounds they made could have been natural, like a breeze skirting through the grass or a nocturnal creature scrambling through the underbrush.

The sounds they made did not disturb the four sentries posted inside the fenced-in farm ground. The sentries guarded only the front of the farm because the back, with its natural barrier of nearly impenetrable woods, was considered safe.

A second team of White Brigade commandos was even now moving through the "impenetrable" barrier. They had made two dry runs previously, advancing undetected through the dense forest. It was timed down to the second how long it took them to traverse the woods from the narrow road connecting the few isolated farmhouses to the E10 route that crossed from Holland into Belgium.

The backup team would approach the farmhouse from the forest, and handle any escapees, joining in the fight if necessary, while Vallance's team would clean out the hornet's nest inside.

But first Vallance's team had to eliminate the sentries.

Recruited from the underworld, the sentries were hard men and most of them had killed. Although they were dangerous, they labored under the belief that the night was theirs. That they were the ones the world had to beware.

The White Brigade commandos, however, had been recruited from some of the best paramilitary and covert agencies in Europe. Most of them led two lives. Along with carrying out sanctioned operations for their official covert agencies, they conducted operations for the Realm, their true masters.

One way or another, they were always at war. It would be no contest tonight.

Under cover of clouds and foliage, the White Brigade commandos infiltrated the fenced-off farmland, moving up to the periphery of the sentries' vision. They knew exactly how many sentries were on duty and where they were posted.

In fact, they knew everything about the security system because they had set it up for their cocaine and arms-trading "friends" in the farmhouse. They stepped easily over the trip-wire alarms. They slid through gaps between fence posts, dropped from overhanging branches within the perimeter. The deadly commando rain was about to fall.

Bernhard Vallance and Maurice Sordett headed for the sentry assigned to them like deadly arrows about to hit a target. Their man was hidden halfway up the dirt driveway that was bracketed on both sides by wooden fences.

Crouching, they cut through the underbrush, narrowing the distance with small but sure steps. Gripping their weapons, they scythed the air in front of them with their free hands. The sound suppressors threaded on the Heckler & Koch MP-5 SD3s gave the dull-colored submachine guns the feel of walking sticks.

The weapons were pointed at a bearded sentry who stood behind a fencepost, flush against an eight-foot wooden shed. Concealed by the shed from the road that passed in front of the farm, the sentry carried a double-barreled shotgun that could turn any intruders into ghosts.

The sentry watched the driveway and more distant road. Now and then he looked at the gray clouds passing above. Then he returned to his usual position and fell back into a trancelike state. His eyes dropped over the expanse of night-shrouded farmland, seeing nothing unusual.

When he was several yards from the sentry, Vallance crouched even lower, infinitesimally sinking into the grass as he inched forward. He reached out in front of him, touching the earth and anchoring himself as he eased into a prone position. He softly planted the H&K on the ground and uncoiled the garrote.

Sordett moved quietly past him in the grass.

Vallance waited a few moments, then rose from the ground six feet behind the sentry. Don't turn around, he willed the man. Not yet. Not until we want you to.

He stretched out the garrote between his hands like a clothesline about to hang out a man to dry. Then he stepped forward.

Now.

Sordett went into action at the same time, intentionally stirring the grass and drawing the sentry's attention.

Now.

As the sentry focused on that rustle of grass, Vallance hurtled forward and dropped the wire loop over the man's head.

Now!

Vallance pulled the loop taut, practically lifting the man off his feet. The sentry arched his back and tap-danced futilely, trying to wedge his feet into the slats of the fence to keep himself from being slaughtered.

Vallance pulled him away from the fence with the razor-sharp lasso. A hiss of blood and breath rushed from the sawed gap in the flesh as the wire cut into the man's throat.

Sordett had sprung up at the same time and instantly ripped the shotgun away from the sentry before he could trigger a blast.

Vallance finished off the sentry, crossing his hands as the wire cored through muscle and veins clear down to the bone. The man's death throes made him think of a gutted fish.

Die, for God's sake, hurry up and die!

When the man stopped kicking, Vallance dropped him to the ground. Red tendrils flowed from the fresh collar line of blood and dripped onto the grass.

Done.

Vallance backed away a few steps and fought off his revulsion. The man had had to be silenced. There had been no choice. Vallance had given himself that task for one purpose, to harden his resolve and make it easier to complete the job.

But it hadn't worked that way.

He wasn't yet immune to the awful majesty of playing God. This was new territory he was travelling into, a murderous realm. The sentry's death injected an element of horror that would linger in his mind.

He looked down at the fallen man and shook his head. The sentry had been only a hired gun, a thug dragooned into service from the waterside haunts of Rotterdam. The man inside the house, Jan Ostermann, was Vallance's friend—in a manner of speaking. While working undercover, Vallance had befriended Ostermann, helping him set up the underground organization. He had even helped the Dutchman set up security for the farmhouse, telling him the best places to deploy sentries so he could sleep safely at night.

Sordett studied the field commander for a moment, as if he could see through Vallance's hood and observe the lines of doubt on his face.

"Come on," Sordett said. "He's no more threat."

He never was, Vallance thought.

Sordett lifted the slain sentry and propped him against the fencepost, so that if someone from the house looked out, they would see him still on guard.

Vallance and Sordett regrouped with the other commandos, who had also left the blood of their targets sprinkled on the ground. Vallance led them to a spot about thirty yards from the house. The commandos spread out in a loose arrow formation pointed at the front porch.

The windows were dark—and so, most likely, were the minds of the inhabitants. Darkened with sleep and drugs. The cocaine crew inside the house had received another batch of stolen weapons yesterday from their military contacts.

They'd probably dipped into some of the cocaine currency to barter for the weapons. They'd probably partied long into the night, assured of protection by the men outside. Their deal wasn't supposed to go down until tomorrow night. They probably felt they had nothing to worry about.

The White Brigade commandos stood in the tall grass, ready.

"We should hit them now," Sordett urged.

At the words of the second in command, the other night-clad commandos looked pointedly at Vallance, members of a wolf pack waiting for the top wolf to strike first.

"No," Vallance said, after glancing at his watch. "The other team needs two more minutes to get into position."

"Let's go with it," Sordett urged. "It's gone so well, don't break the momentum. The men are ready...."

Vallance knifed the air with his right hand to cut him silent. The gesture was short and quick, that of a priest about to give benediction or perform last rites.

Sordett settled into silence.

Vallance understood the man's eagerness. The first part of the assault had already gone well, the first line of defense totally silenced. And it was tempting to continue the strike alone. But another minute or two could make all the difference. The backup team would be in place to take care of any escapees from the house.

There was little chance the cocaine crew would break out. But it was anticipating the small chances, Vallance knew, that had kept him alive through his career with the Belgian antiterrorist unit. Escadron spécial d'intervention. The secretive ESI group, usually referred to by its code name of Diana, drew from the best military, intelligence and police units in Belgium.

If anything, Vallance had to maintain even more stringent standards for the White Brigade detachment than he did with the ESI. The ESI went on sanctioned operations. The White Brigade went on operations that were supposed to be untraceable. Silent. No sign of them until they were gone.

That was why Vallance made his men wait.

In the silence of the night, the men scanned the farmhouse for any sign of life behind the darkened windows, as well as the dirt driveway where a late-model Porsche, a Volkswagen and a Jeep were parked near the front of the house.

There were no tractors. Evidently, the only cash crop the crew in the house were interested in came from clandestine laboratories in Marseilles, Berlin and Amsterdam.

A few more cars and an older van were parked beside the house. Painted in dated psychedelic designs, the van lent an aura of a commune to the house, rather than the underground cell it really was. Several bicycles were leaning against the wraparound front porch.

A small stream meandered through the property, gently zigzagging through a gauntlet of trees. One could almost have fished from the porch.

It was an idyllic location for the cocaine crew, who'd prospered these past two years. But every idyll has to end sooner or later.

Vallance gave the command to move forward, then hefted the Heckler & Koch submachine gun as he sprinted softly for the front porch. The muffled footsteps whispered through the grass, then the men stepped softly up the wide stairs.

The commandos spread out on the porch, some sidling up to the windows, others waiting behind Vallance and Sordett.

Sordett tried the door. If it had been locked, it would have taken only a moment for Sordett to open it. But it was unlocked. The only security the cocaine crew had believed in were the four guns outside that were now silenced.

The White Brigade commando opened the door, then entered, the barrel of the suppressed Heckler & Koch leading the way. The other commandos followed. It was only slightly darker inside and took just a few moments for their eyes to adjust.

Most of Vallance's men knew the house inside and out. He'd brought them here in ones and twos for previous meets with the underworld crew. They'd handed over bundles of currency in exchange for stolen weapons the Dutch gang collected from military bases.

Ostermann, the leader of the crew, believed that Vallance was an underworld armorer involved in the international terrorist scene. In a way he was right, Vallance thought as he and the men spread out through the farmhouse.

The first room was empty, but two of Ostermann's crew were in a longer room to the right. A man in stovepipe jeans and a flannel shirt was sprawled on a small couch, his long legs dangling over the wooden arm. He'd tucked a holstered automatic inside one of his tall leather boots.

A second man was stretched out on a heap of blankets on the floor, his lanky frame running along the gray stone border in front of a wide and dark hearth. An assortment of empty wine and beer bottles were lined up on a low coffee table beside ashtrays full of stubbed-out cigarette butts and crushed roaches.

Vallance gestured with his right hand.

One of the hooded commandos dropped into a padded rocking chair and made himself at home, a silent companion watching over the two gunmen with a silencer.

Two more White Brigade commandos moved toward the back of the farmhouse, positioning themselves by the bedrooms on the lower floor.

Vallance headed for the stairwell, testing each step for creaking before moving up. Behind him came Sordett and the others. They wound their way up to the first landing, then crept up several more steps and paused at the top.

Strains of jazz music drifted down the hallway, slowly fading, followed by the muted voice of a Dutch radio announcer. After a few seconds a discordant drum and bass duet kicked off another song.

The music gave Vallance an eerie sensation as he crept down the hallway, as if he were following the commands of an invisible conductor. In a way that was exactly what was happening. His actions tonight and just about every night these past several years had been orchestrated by Auguste Bayard, the former grand master of French intelligence, who now sat upon the invisible throne of the Realm.

Bayard had personally given Vallance the orders for tonight—after Vallance had refused to carry them out on just the say-so of General Hamelin, his usual commander. Hamelin had turned red when Vallance demanded that the command be verified by Bayard himself.

But the general could turn red, white and blue for all Vallance cared. In light of the general's recent foul-ups, on a mission like this Vallance wanted his instructions to come from the top.

They had. And here he was dancing to the dark music of murder. Not assassination. Not war. Murder.

The sound of the radio seeped under the doorway of the second room on the right. He followed it and stood quietly outside.

Sordett took the room opposite him. The two other commandos took their posts outside the remaining rooms.

Vallance could hear breathing from behind the door of his selected target. This was the largest bedroom, the one with three wide windows looking out upon the front of the farm. Ostermann was fond of doing business in his bedroom, surrounded by women, weapons and cocaine. All of the toys of his profession. At times his quarters had all the charm of a whorehouse.

Soon they would be a charnel house.

Vallance opened the door to his protégé's room and stepped inside. Two shapes were huddled under a quilt, lost in the warmth of deep sleep.

Vallance stepped closer to the double bed.

Ostermann's breathing changed its pattern. As he stirred under the blankets and turned his every move was tracked by the silenced snout of the Heckler & Koch. The Dutchman's massive arm rolled away to reveal a blond woman, who had been his most frequent companion of late. Aside from being his lover, she was an invaluable cocaine courier and had good contacts in the underworld and in the military.

Her name was Giselle and just four nights ago Vallance had sat across from her in an Amsterdam bar, toasting her health.

Hello again, Giselle.

Any moment now it would happen. The White Brigade commandos had all had time to get to their targets undetected.

Ostermann muttered something while he tossed about, as if his subconscious was aware that a bad dream had come to life and was hovering by the bed.

Phyyt. Phyyt. Phytt.

Sound-suppressed rounds punctured the sleep of the room across from Ostermann's. There were a couple of surprised outcries. Last murmurs. And then stillness.

Phyyt. Phytt.

Thumps. Moans.

Phyyt. Phytt.

Someone fell onto the floor downstairs.

From one of the rooms on the second floor a man cried out, his death throes drowned by a gurgling sound.

Bernhard Vallance stood still with his finger on the trigger. But he didn't fire. Not yet. It didn't seem right somehow. He knew he couldn't stop it from happening. The shots had been as good as fired from the moment he told Bayard he would carry out the operation. But still, it wasn't right yet.

Vallance was more than a thief in the night, a coward hiding behind the mask. He grabbed the lip of his hood with his left hand and flung it onto the floor.

Osterman's lips moved. He was muttering louder now, the words tumbling out in the deranged language of the sleeping. They didn't make sense but they served their purpose anyway, waking him up slowly as sounds from the other room invaded his consciousness.

The silenced bursts and the sounds of bullets thumping into flesh and blood had finally turned up the alarms inside Ostermann's brain.

He rose from the bed, snapping into a sitting position. At the same time he cast off the thick quilt. It fluttered to the floor. The blonde lay on her side, curling up instinctively to replace the lost warmth of the blanket.

The sight of the silenced Heckler & Koch opened Ostermann's eyes wide. Naked, the bear of a man looked indignant at being taken so easily. Taken while his men were supposed to be guarding his house.

For a moment there was relief on his face when he realized that the man standing at the bottom of his bed was his good friend, the man he'd been dealing with for so long. But when he continued to hear the silenced rounds thwacking into the bodies of his crew, he realized that a hit was going down.

"You!" he shouted. "But we're friends. Why are you here—tonight—it's tomorrow night we meet."

Giselle stirred, telling him to be quiet.

"*I* am here because we are friends," Vallance said. "It has to be face-to-face."

"No! No!" Ostermann shook his head. "I don't understand."

"And you never will," Vallance said. "For that I'm sorry."

Vallance couldn't have lived with himself if he'd done it the easy way. If ever he wanted to know who he had really become, all he had to do was summon this memory of Ostermann staring at him wide-eyed.

He pulled the trigger.

The 3-round burst piled into the Dutchman's head, wiping out the shock, the hurt, the anger in a split-second fusillade. And then he was tumbling backward, the top of his head split open by the 9 mm burst.

His death cry awoke the woman at last. She jumped from the bed, saw her lover's slain body, saw Vallance standing there with the submachine gun. "Oh, no," she said. "Oh, no, not me—not me..."

The naked woman dived for the floor. Her hand clawed under the bed, then reached back up toward the bedside table and yanked open the drawer. Her slender fingers darted for the revolver within—

Bernhard Vallance was moving on instinct now. In a split second he was upon her, grabbing her wrist and pulling it away from the weapon.

He had to kill her.

He couldn't kill her.

He had to kill her.

She started screaming. Dammit, he thought, he was screwing up a hit. Making a shambles out of it, like an amateur. He tugged on her wrist, then flung her away. She pinwheeled across the room, lost her balance and went headfirst into the window.

Beautiful, he thought. She had been beautiful.

The glass shards exploding around her were flecked with red. Instead of tumbling through the window and out into the night, she was impaled there. Kicking and screaming.

He triggered a burst.

Another.

Another.

The silenced rounds did their work and Giselle collapsed on the sill, no longer beautiful, no longer screaming.

He backed out of the room. Then, as on so many other operations, he regrouped with his men, thumping down the stairs, checking all the members of the Dutch gang to make sure they were dead.

He was on automatic pilot now. Just as if it were a legitimate operation.

The woman upstairs had never quite realized what she was a part of, that the cocaine she and Ostermann dealt in was like a white powder fuse that would one day be set off by a cold man like Bernhard Vallance.

It was a simple operation in its way. For years the Realm had been siphoning off huge quantities of weapons from NATO bases across Europe. Now that the tremendous loss of inventory was being investigated, the White Brigade needed someone to pin the thefts on. Someone like Vallance's good friend Jan Ostermann.

The backup team of White Brigade commandos filed into the house, working quickly with the others to pull aside the frayed carpets and pry up the loose floorboards over the vault where the cocaine crew kept the stolen weapons they'd received.

Automatic rifles. Submachine guns. Magazines. Grenades. Communications equipment.

There was enough matériel here to supply an underworld arms bazaar. Some of it was still in crates stamped with their point of origin.

Vallance's men took most of the weaponry but left a few automatic rifles so the authorities could trace them. Along with the weapons, the commandos took bricks of cocaine and heroin. These would be used to start another underworld ring that would remain active until it had to be discarded like Ostermann's crew.

In a few hours a phone call would lead Dutch security services to the farmhouse. The caller would tell the security men that the massacre stemmed from a gang war between a stolen-weapons ring and a gang of cocaine traffickers.

Though the ring had brought in only a small fraction of weapons, the Realm would make sure that it and a few others took the blame for the real massive thefts orchestrated by Bayard and his covert generals.

"All right," Vallance said when his men had carted out all they were going to carry tonight. "Let's get the hell out of here."

As he moved back out into the shadows of the night, Bernhard Vallance knew he was no longer the man he'd thought he was. He lived in two worlds now and could never be at home in either.

From now on, he was a creature of the Realm.

CHAPTER TEN

"A castle tour," Nanos said, as he watched images of a French château flicker across the wide video screen suspended from the ceiling of the rustic safehouse. "All right! And I thought this was going to be hard work."

"Wait till you see the tour guide before you start doing handstands," Barrabas suggested. "Then you'll see just how much of a holiday camp this is going to be."

"Nanos needs another holiday like I need a picnic in Pretoria," Claude Hayes said.

The SOBs were sitting around a long trestle table in the dining room. Splinters of light poured through the narrow cathedral windows upon the table, but not enough to interfere with the assembled footage provided by Jessup.

After they'd arrived in Brussels in ones and twos and gathered at the Sheraton, the Fixer had sent a couple of cars to drive them south to the safehouse.

Though the CIA had given them the run of the place—or perhaps because they had—Walker Jessup had brought in some of Tsar Nicholas's NSA techs to sweep for bugs. At the moment two carloads of NSA security men were patrolling the area to see just who might be interested in the mercenaries who'd arrived from America.

"Here comes the tour guide now," Barrabas said as a slender figure appeared on screen, walking along the inside of the battlement.

At first the man's face was cloaked in shadow, indistinguishable from the gloom. Then the high-resolution image showed him up close. His was a narrow aristocratic face, the lines of age around his eyes taking nothing away from his hawklike gaze. He was still a hard man.

"That is Auguste Bayard," Barrabas said. "At his main base of operations in the French Ardennes."

The name brought the SOBs to attention. Count Bayard was something of a legend in the covert world. And like many legends there was a sinister aura to his name. He was a brutal man. Though he was responsible for some incredible successes of the French covert services, his name was also linked with a number of atrocities.

"When he was the head of DST—Direction de la surveillance du territoire," Barrabas said, "Bayard was one of the most powerful men in France. And he wants to be that again. From what our friends in the intelligence community have been able to determine, Bayard is most likely the man behind the Realm."

Barrabas outlined the scope and the agenda of the United Realm of Europe organization, highlighting the series of murders, thefts and subversive actions tied to the group. He tracked the covert threads that connected the Realm to intelligence, paramilitary and corporate empires across Europe.

"By Saint Antrim himself!" O'Toole said. "That includes just about every damned spook outfit in the business. While you're at it, you might as well throw in the Illuminati and the International Bankers."

Barrabas laughed. "Look, I know it sounds like a wild conspiracy theory—but the men behind this aren't wild. They're very deliberate, efficient and ruthless men. And they may even have the ability to carry out their goal."

"And we're supposed to stop them?" Lee Hatton said. "The six of us?"

"The six of us plus a few allies we can enlist as we need them," Barrabas said. "But yes, that's our target." He pointed at the smiling face of Auguste Bayard, whose patrician countenance seemed to be looking down upon the SOBs as if he knew everything about them, to be watching them and listening to them even at this moment. "Bayard is our long-range target," Barrabas emphasized.

"Why don't we just hit him now and be done with it?" Billy Two asked. "That castle of his doesn't look too well protected."

"Yeah," Nanos agreed. "We could chart a flight path for Billy Two and Hawk Spirit to drop in on them."

"Two reasons," Barrabas explained. "First, the castle may look like it's not defended well. But then again, you could say the same for right here. This retreat looks like a summer camp." He gestured at the screen and at the video deck and bank of security monitors below it that watched over every approach to their retreat. Then there were other items like bulletproof glass, hidden steel shutters, weapons caches in nearly every room. "At a moment's notice we can turn this retreat into a redoubt," Barrabas continued. "So imagine what Bayard can turn a fortress into. Jessup is looking into that right now, in the event we do have to hit it."

On the screen behind him, as if the film were in sync with his briefing, the château was shown from every angle. It looked as if it were part of the craggy promontory it had been built on, settling down over the centuries until it had become one with the rock.

"The château has been in Bayard's family for hundreds of years," Barrabas said. "And the wealth that made it possible to build it in the first place has been growing ever since. That's the second reason we can't touch him until we have absolute proof that he's behind the Realm. If we take him out before then, we'll be on the hit list of every spook service in the West."

"Not my idea of a holiday," Nanos said. "But I can see their point of view. If the French thought he needed killing they'd do it themselves, rather than have us waltz in and do it."

"But more important," Barrabas said, "if we take him out now, without hard proof he deserves to go, we'll be no different than the people we're supposed to be fighting."

There was no argument from the SOBs. They were mercenaries, not murderers. But Barrabas could tell from the looks on their faces that they thought it was just so much red tape they had to cut through before eliminating a man they all believed was guilty. But it was part of the job.

The video screen went to white for a moment, then more spliced footage came on, showing the chiseled features of a silver-haired man in his sixties. He looked more like a military man than the count.

"Although Auguste Bayard is our long-range target, this is the man who might help us close in on him." He pointed at the hard-jawed face on the screen. "All the time Bayard was running the DST, the main thorn in his side was Pierre Duval, his opposite number in SDECE, better known as the Service de Documentation Extérieure et de Contre-Espionage. When Duval ran the foreign intelligence branch he tried to drive Bayard out, claiming he was a mole, a psychotic, a thief and a murderer."

"Which he probably was," Lee Hatton said.

"'Probably' is the key word," Barrabas said. "It's also the billion-dollar question: was Bayard corrupt or not? Before Duval could get the answer, Bayard managed to frame him and get him purged from the SDECE. Naturally Duval is still gunning for Bayard. If we get on his good side, we may be able to help each other out."

O'Toole jabbed the air with his cigar. "That's a big if. Duval doesn't strike me as the type to welcome any outsiders with open arms."

Barrabas nodded. "Duval's a dangerous man. He's currently running a think tank and a private security agency in Paris that gives him considerable power."

"He's like us," O'Toole said. "He's still in the game, but he's not listed as a player."

"Right," Barrabas said. "And he plays by the same rules. Unless we win his trust, he may try to take us out of the picture the hard way."

"How do we approach him?" the Irishman asked.

"Jessup's already set up a meet for me with him."

"Thoughtful of him."

"It's one of the risks we have to take to get to the top," Barrabas said. "We have to try every avenue...which brings us to our immediate target."

He shut off the videotape. Then he riffled through a stack of newspapers, photocopied magazine articles and green folders on the table and passed them out to each SOB. "Enter the hero," he said. "This is where the trail starts. Read these press accounts, then take a look at the summaries in the dossiers and see if we can read between the lines."

He left the room for about ten minutes while they sifted through the material about General Hamelin's heroic breakup of a spy ring, then he came back and stood in front of the table.

"Any questions about our hero?" he said.

"Yeah, I've got a question," Lee Hatton said. "How the hell did he get away with it?"

Barrabas nodded. "That's exactly what I've been asking ever since I read those accounts." He paced around the table and stood behind Lee's chair. After gesturing for the dark-haired woman to stand up, he slowly pulled the chair out for her.

Even though she was wearing a soft clinging top that hugged her curves and a pair of snug stone-washed jeans, Lee was accustomed to being treated like one of the guys. A look of surprise flashed across her face. "What brings out the gentleman in you?" she queried.

"I have a favor to ask," Barrabas said.

"What's that?"

"I want you to try and kill me."

She shrugged. "You're the boss."

Barrabas walked away from the table to a wooden deacon's desk against the wall. "Say this is the desk that Lieutenant Anderson was sitting at when General Hamelin confronted him." He smacked his hand on the wood. "And say I'm Anderson." He slipped into the chair behind the desk.

Lee Hatton circled around behind him. "And I'm General Hamelin."

"A bit easier on the eye," Barrabas said. "But you'll do for now."

The SOBs pushed away from the table and grouped as an audience around the two mercenary players.

"Okay," Barrabas said. "Let's act it out now." The SOB chieftain turned away from her, dropping his arms at the desk. "Now you come in the door."

Lee Hatton stepped behind him.

"I turn around and stand up," Barrabas said. He rose and looked down at Hatton. "And you charge me with being a spy."

She stood there, hands by her side, looking stern.

"And then I draw a gun on you." Barrabas shot his right hand down to his side in a motion he'd perfected over the years, then pointed his hand at her as if it were holding an automatic.

"What happens now?" Lee Hatton said.

"Now you draw your weapon and kill me," he said.

She reached for her side.

Barrabas shot forward and knifed his hand into her rib cage. He bellowed at the same time, his roar echoing like a gunshot.

And Lee collapsed backward as if she really were shot—before she had a chance to draw her weapon.

Barrabas tugged her to her feet. She brushed off her jeans.

"So?" Barrabas said. "What just happened?"

"You killed Lee and she came back from the dead," Nanos said.

"Right," Barrabas said. "I killed her just like Lieutenant Anderson really would have killed General Hamelin."

"Hamelin was a hard man to kill," O'Toole said, playing devil's advocate.

"So was Anderson," Barrabas said. "The lieutenant was in the trade. He knew what he was about. No matter how good Hamelin was—or is—he's not going to beat a guy like Anderson who's already drawn his gun."

"So maybe General Hamelin decided to just walk in there and kill a traitor," O'Toole said, persisting in the argument. "We might have done the same thing."

"Perhaps," Barrabas said. "But if Anderson was the only link to a NATO espionage ring, you don't just go in there and blow him away. The general could have arranged it differently. He could have had security men take Anderson away quietly. No, he wanted it to go down like this."

"So where does that leave us?" O'Toole asked.

"Right behind the trigger. It's our turn to go against the general. Right about now he's thinking he's got everything closed out. All the loose ends wrapped up. It's our job to make the general think there are a few loose cannons on the battlefield."

Barrabas led them to the back room of the safehouse, which had floor-to-ceiling bookshelves lining both sides. He pressed a vertical centerpiece and then pulled out two wings of false-backed bookshelves, revealing an armory of sanitized Heckler & Koch weaponry: automatic rifles, submachine guns and side arms.

"Things are going to get a bit rough," he said, gesturing toward the weapons. "Take what you need to survive. From here on in we're on a war footing."

THE BLACK-HELMETED BIKER crossed lanes at the last moment and headed straight for General Hamelin's black Mercedes cruising up the road from SHAPE headquarters at Casteau.

Sergeant Monahan swore and spun the wheel to the right to avoid colliding with the biker.

"No!" General Hamelin shouted. "Hit the bastard!"

But the driver followed his instincts and stomped on the brakes.

Revved up like an angry hornet, the biker deftly wheeled away at the last moment and rode harmlessly past, calmly studying the occupants of the screeching Mercedes through his black visor.

The Mercedes skidded wildly out of control. It careened down the road on two wheels and tilted precariously toward the trees that lined the roadway. But instead of rolling over onto its roof, it levered down onto all four wheels again.

The driver edged the car onto the narrow shoulder.

General Hamelin leaned forward, digging his nails into the back of the driver's seat. "Crucify that son of a bitch!"

"I think that's what he's waiting for," Monahan said, looking in his side-view mirror. "He wants us to try something."

Stopped about forty yards down the road, the biker was nonchalantly straddling the motorcycle and looking the general's way. Long black hair coiled from under the helmet, splayed out on his broad shoulders.

Hamelin spun around and looked out the back window. "I'll get him myself."

"Step out of the car and we're both dead," the driver said. "We should move on."

"I want his ass."

"This could be a hit, General," Monahan warned.

Hamelin bulled his way out of the back door and shouted at the man who'd narrowly avoided a head-on collision.

The biker revved the engine, drowning out the red-faced general's words with a raucous whine.

"Back in the car, General," Monahan said, climbing out of the driver's side, his hand by his holster as he stared at the biker.

The biker also lowered his hand to his side, without drawing a weapon.

Hamelin stared at the figure in black, whose very presence was taunting him. "I don't think that son of a bitch knows who he's dealing with—"

"Actually, General," Sergeant Monahan said, "I think he does. Get in the car."

Hamelin nodded and climbed back inside.

The driver eased the car off the shoulder and drove slowly off, heading north toward the Belgian capital.

The mood inside the car was tense, as if a bomb had just gone off. Monahan caught the general's florid face in the rearview mirror, he realized the bomb was still ticking.

WHEN THE MERCEDES WAS out of sight, the biker removed his helmet. His weathered Osage face broke into a wide grin as Billy Two lifted the transceiver from his leather jacket and said, "I think I got his attention."

A moment later, Barrabas answered. "Good. We'll take it from here."

FIFTEEN MINUTES LATER, as the Mercedes continued on to Brussels, General Hamelin had almost forgotten the run-in with the biker. If the incident lingered in his mind, it was merely as a shadow that wouldn't quite go away.

Suddenly a green station wagon shot out from a crossroads and cut in front of the Mercedes. The Mercedes braked, almost ramming the slow-moving vehicle. Monahan beeped his horn but the station wagon kept moving.

A second car pulled out behind them.

"This is a hit!" Hamelin said.

Pressing on the accelerator, the driver backed up, torn between evading the threat or charging forward. "Let me call for assistance."

"No," Hamelin said. "Not yet. They're not showing any weapons."

Even as the general spoke, the driver of the station wagon saluted him. After tipping the brim of his cap, he spun the steering wheel and hurtled off toward Mons.

"These people play any more games with me and I'll take them off the board," Hamelin said.

TWO MILES DOWN THE ROAD, the green station wagon pulled over. Nile Barrabas and Liam O'Toole emerged from it, both wearing blank prescription glasses and caps with leather brims shading their faces. Looking like a pair of nondescript tourists or businessmen, they abandoned the car that they had hot-wired and liberated from a restaurant parking lot.

Within a minute Alex Nanos and Lee Hatton pulled up in a black van, sliding open the side door.

"Any word from Claude?" Barrabas asked, as he and O'Toole dropped into seats in the van.

"He's finishing up," the Greek said. "Leaving the general's house right about now. He said he left the present for him."

Barrabas smiled. "Good. I imagine it won't be long before the general starts to raise holy hell."

THE MERCEDES CRUNCHED to a stop beside a green jeep on the gravel drive outside the general's sprawling ranch-style cabin home.

Midway between SHAPE headquarters and Brussels, the cabin was in the perfect location for him. Convenient to both places where he did most of his official business, it was a secluded retreat where he could host clandestine visitors for his unofficial business.

The place had been expensive, even on a general's salary. Fortunately, Hamelin wasn't limited to a general's salary. The coffers of the Realm had made the cabin possible—just as his duties in the Realm made it necessary.

Hamelin hurried up on the fieldstone porch, his keys jangling in his hands. But as soon as he slid the key into the slot the door opened.

"What the hell—"

The lock had been stripped.

He pushed the door fully open and stepped inside. There, hanging from one of the exposed beams, coiled around it like a snake, was a microphone. It wasn't plugged in, and obviously whoever had planted it hadn't tried to conceal it.

"Those bastards!" he said. "They're trying to play games with me!"

Sergeant Monahan walked through the house, checking for signs of anyone's presence while Hamelin stared at the microphone. The message was clear. He was under observation. Being listened to. And he was being shadowed by men who could take him out at any moment.

They weren't his own people, he was pretty sure of that. He'd ensured that the official investigation ran into a stone wall—the gravestone of Lieutenant Anderson.

This was definitely a warning from someone.

But from whom? The Realm? One of those back-biting court jesters? Or one of the action teams? He'd been pushing pretty hard lately....

Hamelin's driver returned. "There's no sign of anyone," he said.

Hamelin nodded. "The only sign they'll leave is one they want us to see. Like this."

The driver nodded. "We've got to report those incidents on the road and this break-in, sir. It's pretty clear that someone is out to get you."

Hamelin shook his head. "If they wanted to get me, they had plenty of opportunity. No, this is something different. Someone's got a funny way of making their point."

"Sir, just to be safe, I think—"

Hamelin waved away his concern. "Don't breathe a word to anyone," he said. "Go back to your quarters and forget all about this. I'll handle it my way."

Sergeant Monahan nodded and turned for the door.

"Hold it right there," Hamelin said. "If that look on your face means you're going to do the right thing and spread this around—I want you to reconsider. You've driven me around long enough to know I mean what I say. Cross me and you'll spend the rest of your days driving a diaper truck for the officers' wives.''

"Yes, sir," the driver said, managing a phony smile.

The general forced himself to calm down and then, speaking more rationally, said, "This could be a warning from some of our European allies—about some toes I stepped on. It doesn't necessarily mean I've been selected for a terrorist hit." He put his hand on the sergeant's shoulder. "This kind of thing happens now and then. So, like I say, forget it, will you?"

"Consider it forgotten, sir."

"Well done, sergeant." Hamelin clasped the man's shoulder and ushered him outside.

When the sergeant had driven off in the jeep, Hamelin returned to the dead microphone that hung from the beam.

Just the sight of it was a slap in the face. Someone was following him. Some had broken in here. Someone was taunting him.

Hamelin muttered and yanked hard. The microphone wire uncoiled. He wrapped it around his palm, then spun the microphone around and around over his head, before letting it fly across the room. It banged into the wall and smashed into small pieces.

General Hamelin clenched his left hand into a fist. He squeezed harder and harder, using the tension to ground him, to balance him until he could find an appropriate target.

He knew the events today were calculated to drive him wild this way. But even so, he couldn't avoid it.

General Hamelin was going to war.

CHAPTER ELEVEN

Barrabas scanned the crowd streaming by the outdoor café on petite rue des Bouchers to see if anyone was watching his rendezvous.

But the people cruising the cobblestone street did not seem to be paying attention. He saw nothing out of the ordinary, just the usual parade of Belgian beauties in their brightly colored summer dresses, whisking through the narrow medieval streets of the L'Ilot Sacré neighborhood on their way to the square in Grand-Place.

Tourists and natives were lured into the many restaurants by their tempting aromas. It seemed an average day along Brussels's restaurant row.

Barrabas didn't expect anyone to take much notice of Walker Jessup sitting across from him at the small round table on the terrace, patriotically living out his cover as a lover of Belgian cuisine.

The Fixer was making short work of *moules et frites*, washing down the seaweed-and-leek steamed mussels and Belgian fries with a bottle of beer.

But at least he had only one serving, Barrabas thought. The Fixer of old would have decorated the small round table with three meals.

Barrabas sipped from his glass of brew. Although he acted like a man with nothing on his mind, he needed an intel fix from Jessup, who'd been working behind the scenes as liaison with the Agency and the Belgians. To coordinate the SOBs' strikes, the Fixer had to find the right man in the Belgian ESI. Someone they could trust and someone who was high up enough to watch their backs in case they had to bring him into it.

And someone who could help the SOBs without bringing much notice to himself.

In short, they needed someone who wasn't part and parcel of the Realm.

Finally Jessup finished his meal and pushed the plate aside.

"Now that we've saved you from famine," Barrabas said, "maybe we can talk."

Jessup wiped his lips and nodded. "I'll try and manage."

"Fine." Barrabas finished his mug of beer and slid it aside. "How's it working out on your side?"

"This is a dangerous game you're playing," Jessup said.

"*The most* dangerous game," Barrabas said. "But it's the only one we have."

"You need a special license to go hunting for game like General Hamelin," the Fixer said.

"Do we have it?"

Jessup shrugged. "If he's guilty, yes. If he's guilty and you nail him, the CIA will give you a gold crown and swear loyalty and gratefulness forever. Which amounts to about three weeks, in their book."

"What's the other side of the coin?"

"What else? They'll crown you with thorns." The bulky man leaned forward, clasping his hands together on the table. "If the general's not guilty and we take out one of the Agency's beloved war-horses, the best we can hope for is we get pinged."

To be pinged, Barrabas knew was a spookspeak for what happened to someone who was declared persona non grata. The usual practice of a host country was to classify a foreign service officer involved in espionage or subversion as PNG and dismiss him from the country. Thus he was PNG'd, or pinged, as the action came to be known. If the agent refused to play by the rules and returned to the host country, he was fair game. There were no second chances.

In this case Jessup meant that he and the SOBs would be pinged from their own country. They would be treated as outlaws by the country they were working for. It wouldn't be the first time covert teams had been cut loose and hung out to dry.

"I can live with that if I have to," Barrabas said. "What's the worst-case scenario?"

"Worst-case scenario is that instead of getting pinged, we get whacked," Jessup said. "End of game. Do not pass Go. The only thing we collect is tombstones."

"We'll take that risk," Barrabas said. "They're not paying us to waltz with Hamelin."

"No argument," Jessup said. "You call the shots— I provide the guns." The Fixer smiled innocently, as if he was just commenting on the Belgian beer he was quaffing. The white-haired controller hardly looked like someone who had just agreed that the SOBs could take out a United States general.

Nile Barrabas sat across from the Fixer looking relaxed, the navy-blue windbreaker concealing the 9 mm Browning Hi-Power nestled in an underarm holster.

Barrabas looked like a silent partner to the Fixer, a troubleshooter who went out into the field to handle the business of war. Despite the casual and confident poise of the coarse-haired soldier of fortune, a look that had prompted inviting stares from women passing by, up close it was possible to see that he was here for more than just sirens in satin sheets. His eyes had the look of a man who was ready at any moment for war.

"Has Hamelin attempted to bring in the security people since we started setting fires under his foot?" Barrabas asked.

"No," Jessup said. "At least not any of our official security people."

"Is that guaranteed?" he asked.

"The Tsar has a small army of technicians monitoring everything General Hamelin says, does or thinks. Anything happens, they'd know about it."

Barrabas nodded. With Tsar Nicholas, the NSA's covert controller here to push the buttons, a lot of buttons were going to be pushed. The National Security Agency was in a remarkable position, since its satellites and ground monitoring stations could practically eavesdrop on any electronic communications in the world.

NSA field teams could plant monitoring devices that were as nearly undetectable as the teams themselves. The NSA spooks in the Special Projects division were hardly ever spoken of in the intelligence community.

"They gave him the full treatment?" Barrabas said.

"If the general wants to watch a home movie of himself, all he has to do is aim his satellite antennae straight over his house," Jessup said. "Of course, without the right decoding equipment it'll come in scrambled. But you could say he's one closely watched man."

Jessup's voice lowered as their waiter drifted toward their table, nodding at them to see if there was anything they needed.

Barrabas ordered two coffees.

"And a side of beef," Jessup suggested under his breath, for a moment the inner man surfacing once again.

When the waiter left, Barrabas asked, "Have the Tsar's people turned up anything?"

"A lot," Jessup said. "None of it conclusive. Hamelin's smooth. Everything he's done can be interpreted two ways. He had a number of contacts with Monsieur Hubert, who seems to have the same expensive tastes as the general. But he can always explain those contacts as part of his unofficial work for NATO. Still, the general made several interesting calls right after your crew started harassing him."

"Can you tell me about them?"

"Better than that," Jessup said. "You can read the transcripts yourself." He pushed away his plate and took out a rolled-up magazine from his jacket pocket. He smoothed it out on the table. "Look through the gossip section," he said. "You'll find everything there is to know about him."

Barrabas took the magazine. "Thanks. I'll look it over. But two things before I go."

"Shoot."

"First, I want the NSA to stop spying on Hamelin. I don't want any record of us when we go after him. No home movies."

"Done," Jessup said.

"Another thing," Barrabas said.

"Shoot."

"What's the name of our ESI contact and where does he stand in all of this?"

"Henri Goliard?" Jessup asked, smiling broadly. "He's standing right behind you."

Barrabas slowly turned around. The waiter looked down at him.

Goliard was in his forties, unobtrusive, wiry. His dark brown hair was cut close, blending in with his well-trimmed beard. Barrabas had paid him little notice. "Monsieur Barrabas," he said. "Can I get you anything else?"

"What do you recommend?"

"A guillotine would do just fine," Goliard said. "For our friends in the Realm."

Barrabas smiled. The Fixer had found the right man.

GENERAL HAMELIN TOOK the late-night call to his Belgian country haven south of Brussels in stride, picking up the phone on the third ring.

In a way he'd been expecting it. Whoever was going to the trouble of shadowing him and harassing him wasn't doing so just for the hell of it. There had to be an approach sooner or later.

"Yes?" he said.

"Good evening, General," a man said. "I was hoping you'd be in tonight. But then again, you've been holed up in your place for days now."

"Who is this?"

"We've met before."

"Where?" Hamelin demanded.

"On the road. Briefly. Here and there."

"I know who you are," Hamelin said. "What I don't know is what you want."

There was a pause before the caller continued. "The question is, General Hamelin, what do *you* want? Silence? Or do you want the real story of Hamelin the hero to come out?"

"Is this some kind of blackmail attempt?"

"Of course it is," the man said. "The best kind. We've got you dead to rights."

"What do you want?"

"I think we should meet face-to-face, to hammer this thing out."

"Where?"

"We'll come and get you," the caller suggested.

"Not on your life."

"It's your life that hangs in the balance, General. But I can understand your fear—"

"Dammit, you listen to me—"

"No, General, you listen. You can expect a visit from us three days from now. Right where you are now. From there we'll go to neutral ground and figure out the best way to work this out."

The caller rang off, leaving the general strangling the phone in his hands.

"WHAT THE HELL is a special forces chopper doing here?" Barrabas asked, his field glasses tracking the unmarked black chopper that sailed at treetop level toward General Hamelin's redoubt in the woods.

It was daylight but Barrabas wasn't worried about being seen. He was crouched in the observation post they'd set up a few nights before a half mile away from the general's property line.

Camouflage netting and a few slight alterations to the thick brush had made the SOBs' post undetectable from Hamelin's haven, night or day. An array of automatic weapons, shotguns, grenades and surveillance equipment was spread out along the perimeter of the clandestine post.

Beside him Liam O'Toole worked the Maxilux M image intensifier attached to his SLR camera. Made for long-range target acquisition in the field, the long scope was mounted on a tripod that gave O'Toole a wide arc. He'd been using the unit to photograph the general's discreet guests who'd been arriving night and day since Barrabas made the phone call to spook the general.

By now there was a virtual covert convention taking place. It looked as if Hammerhead Hamelin was calling in his troops. But definitely not American ones.

The whump-whump-whump of the rotor blades faded as the black chopper passed behind Hamelin's house, then touched down on a strip of lawn.

"There's your answer, Colonel," O'Toole reported. "The chopper's dropping off special forces, from the look of 'em." His camera kept clicking away as the chopper dropped off its human cargo, who crouched and ran for the house.

"Not ours," Barrabas said. "Jessup and company would have given Lee the word if any of our teams were in the area. And Goliard would have done the same if it was a Belgian chopper."

"Maybe we can't trust Goliard after all," O'Toole said.

"It's his funeral," Barrabas said. "But I don't think he's crossing us. He's with us all the way on this."

He'd spoken at length with Henri Goliard. Along with looking into the deaths of the Americans, Locke and Anderson, the Belgian antiterrorist officer had been investigating the massacre of a group of drug and arms smugglers on the Dutch border. That attack had all the earmarks of an ESI hit, despite the cover story splashed all over the media about open warfare breaking out between rival gangs of traffickers.

Goliard was convinced that some of his own people had gone over to the other side. He, too, was ready for a behind-the-lines war.

"Just keep shooting for now," Barrabas said. "I'll run it past Goliard before we make our move."

Liam O'Toole nodded. He continued photographing the men who disembarked, the pilot and the faded markings of the chopper.

Farther along to the right of O'Toole were Alex Nanos and Claude Hayes, positioned back to back, watching to make sure no one approached the observation post.

Billy Two was on the left flank, lying flat in the tall grass, his face the color of the earth, his eyes piercing like a hawk's as he scanned the surroundings.

Lee Hatton was driving through the Belgian countryside in a cream-colored Citroën, serving as communications relay between Jessup and the SOBs. She was ready to pick up the SOBs at a moment's notice whether they radioed or signaled her from one of the pickup points they'd arranged along the road.

The recon was going well.

Barrabas meant to know his enemy inside and out, especially since that enemy had a small and deadly army at its command.

"She's off again," O'Toole announced, as the chopper lifted off and swiftly soared in the direction from which it had come.

"Give me the film," Barrabas said.

O'Toole nodded. He rewound the film, unloaded the camera, put the roll in a small black container and handed it to Barrabas.

"Now we find out who our friends—and our enemies—are," Barrabas said, dropping the film into his pocket. He backed slowly out of the brush until he was out of range of Hamelin's house, then jogged into the woods, heading for the main road where he would soon hitch a ride with Lee Hatton.

THE TOP ACTION MAN in Belgium's Escadron spécial d'intervention was no longer dressed as a waiter. Instead, he wore a black suit that was cut close to his lean figure. That, combined with the darkness in his eyes, made him look like an undertaker who was about to drum up some business.

"It is as I feared," Henri Goliard said, tapping his finger on one of the glossy photographs spread out on the long trestle table in the SOBs' safehouse overlooking the Meuse. He had arrived only a short while earlier, after reviewing the film that Barrabas had dropped off for him in Brussels.

Goliard was all business. The car outside carried a couple of stern-looking men, who obviously weren't along to provide conversation for the Belgian. They were professional security men whom he personally trusted and believed he would need.

"I know this man," Goliard said, tapping the photograph again. This time his fingers curled into an eagle's claw as he struck at the image of the monkish man with the receding hairline.

"Who is he?" Barrabas said.

"Bernhard Vallance," Goliard said. "He's one of my best men. Or rather, he *was*," he corrected himself.

Barrabas nodded. "Unless Vallance is on official business for the ESI."

"He's not," Goliard said. "An operation such as this, involving a man of General Hamelin's stature, would have to be personally approved by me. Vallance has obviously cut me out of the loop."

Barrabas nodded.

"That means he's no longer working for me," Goliard said. "He's working against me."

The Belgian security man lifted another photograph, this one of a man with much darker hair, looking younger than Vallance and somehow haughty as he'd stepped from the helicopter.

"And this man," Goliard said, "is Maurice Sordett. He's with the French—GIGN. You know their full name—it's a mouthful: Groupement D'Intervention de la Gendarmerie Nationale. He was seconded to one of our units for a while. Assisted us on some of our operations."

"What unit?" Barrabas asked.

"The one headed by Bernhard Vallance," Goliard said. "But Sordett is not with us anymore. At least he's not supposed to be. He is, I suspect, working with the Realm."

Goliard also identified the chopper as one that was used by the ESI special units. And the pilot was attached to ESI.

Barrabas saw that the man was struggling with the evidence in front of him—evidence the Belgian had long suspected existed. But now that he was bringing it out into the open, it was a different matter. Admitting to yourself that someone had betrayed you was always difficult. Admitting it to someone else was even harder.

But Goliard met the truth head-on.

"It appears that you are not alone in dealing with traitors, Barrabas," he said. He tugged on his trim beard, combing it with his fingers, then shook his head from side to side.

"Then you and I should work together," Barrabas said.

"That is why I came here as soon as I saw these photos. We're ready to help you out in any way we can."

"Fine," Barrabas said. "Let's start with the pilot. Was he in on it?"

"No," he said. "He claims he thought it was a sanctioned mission. Vallance had used him in the past and he believed this was another legitimate but hush-hush mission. He's supposed to be on standby in case Vallance needs him."

Barrabas picked up the photograph of the pilot. "He's a good man, then?"

"Appears to be. But in this business, appearances don't mean all that much."

"Right." Barrabas studied the pilot's photograph. For a moment he felt as if he were back in the Middle Ages, plotting intrigues against princelings, allying himself with warlords. But such acts were necessary when fighting a medieval concept like the Realm.

"Well, then," he said, "let's make sure that Vallance needs him."

THE LEATHER-CLAD BIKER whipped down the road, a black shadow against the coming dawn. He rode hard and fast, ricocheting along the winding curves that cut through the forest.

The woods embraced châteaus and farmhouses and modern estates, the thick forest enveloping them with the lush green growth of centuries.

It was usually a region of quiet. But today the morning stillness was broken by the grind and growl of the iron horse rapidly approaching General Hamelin's grounds.

Wind buffeted the black-helmeted rider on the streamlined BMW, but it didn't bother him. Clad in leather jacket, oiled jeans and leather boots, the Osage rider was invulnerable to the high-speed chill.

The motorcyclist roared past the general's house for one last recon before he went into action. It was separated from the road by a white fence and stone walls. Sitting back on the high ground, the sprawling L-shaped cabin looked more like a frontier barracks or stockade than a haven. But then, the formidable retreat was suitable for a man who'd never retreated in his life.

TWO MILES AWAY, in a staging area flanked by woods, Nile Barrabas slapped a clip into the Heckler & Koch MP-5 SD3, the silenced submachine gun that served as the standard tool of the covert trade. Friend and foe alike would be working with the finely machined German weapon. He had several more magazines for the H&K in his web belt, and he was carrying a Browning Hi-Power for backup, a familiar weapon that spoke his language.

Barrabas wore a loose-fitting black shirt, the sleeves rolled up past his elbows. Thick veins and scars crisscrossed his forearms. Ceramic plates bulked out the

Kevlar body armor across his torso. Stretched taut across his silver-streaked hair was a faded khaki bandanna, its ends hanging like tails down his back.

His face wasn't daubed for camouflage. When he went into battle today it would be face-to-face with the general, with no disguises.

He was standing in the dark shade of a barn beside a long wooden rack full of scythes, iron-toothed rakes, spades and forks. Behind him was a hitch and a harrow coupled to a tractor and several smaller pieces of machinery. It was a working farm.

Today the workers were off. They'd been ushered from the site by a plainclothes squad of judiciary police that Henri Goliard had dragooned from the Groupe de répression du terrorisme. The GRT often worked in tandem with Goliard's ESI units. With many of his own personnel under suspicion, Goliard had been more than glad to bring them in on this one.

"I don't think it'll work," Goliard said now.

"Is that right?" Barrabas said. "You're not exactly dressing for a day at the office."

"I want to be ready just in case it goes down." The bearded ESI man was also in combat gear, with body armor bulking up his blue windbreaker, and a silent cousin of the Heckler & Koch submachine gun draped from a sling around his shoulder.

A half dozen similarly clad ESI men were milling about in the shadows, their boots softly scuffing the hay-strewn earth as they talked quietly among themselves while they waited to go into action. Some spoke French, others Flemish. But all were Belgian commandos whom Goliard trusted implicitly, drawn from ESI units across the country.

At one end of the barn, also concealed in shadow, were two Ford Transit recon vans. Reinforced with antiriot grilles, they were loaded with radio equipment and plainclothes GRT teams. Both vans were stocked with a variety of Remington 870 12-gauge shotguns and Belgian FN 7.62 mm NATO sniper rifles to provide extra firepower to the GRT teams already en route to the target area.

"We're taking a lot of risks here," Goliard said.

"Risks worth taking," Barrabas reminded him, recognizing the second thoughts that were working on the ESI man. It would be so easy to abort the operation and let the powers that be conduct their typical plodding investigations, hoping they would break up the Realm with their slow maneuvers, impeded as they were by transfers, retirements, endless interrogations and secret reports. But Barrabas's way was bound to have immediate effects. By igniting the sparks at General Hamelin's retreat, they were forcing the Realm to show its hand once and for all.

"I suppose you're right," Goliard said, nodding. "But it seemed so much clearer last night."

Barrabas looked at his watch. Soon, he thought. Soon there would be no turning back.

The seconds grew heavier. Slower. The time that remained was critical. Would Goliard be tempted to call off his participation? Barrabas wondered. Come what might, Barrabas was going ahead.

"If it doesn't work out as you say—" Goliard began.

"There's a backup plan if we need it," Barrabas said. "But it'll work. Hammerhead Hamelin always makes the first move. He's so intent on surprising the opposition that his surprises are predictable."

"You think he will . . ."

"I know he will," Barrabas said. "Hamelin shoots first and thinks later. No matter what kind of war he's in."

"If you're right, then you've sent one of your men on a suicide mission."

"It won't be his first," Barrabas said. "Besides, it was his choice."

The SOB chieftain thought back to the planning of the raid on the general. Initially he had been going to make the approach. But the Osage had protested vehemently when he outlined the plan, saying that it would be Barrabas's last ride if he went.

"And you?" Barrabas had asked.

"I'm a better rider," the Osage had responded. "And flier. Hawk Spirit has shown me flying away after the mission."

Barrabas had studied the Osage mercenary's face for a moment and said, "Yeah, but was your body still attached?"

Billy Two had nodded.

And so Barrabas had agreed to the change. It wasn't totally because of Hawk Spirit, though he had long ago decided that Billy Two's inner voices were worth listening to. Another factor was the marshaling of the allies available to him. Barrabas was needed more here, riding herd on the Belgians, than he was on the BMW that Billy Two had made an extension of his body.

It wasn't a matter of bravado. Barrabas wouldn't have asked one of his men to do something he wouldn't do. It came down to tactics. What was best for the operation? That was the deciding factor.

Besides, there were no easy roles in the game they had to play. Barrabas would face the fire soon enough.

The SOB chieftain inhaled the country air, feeling his blood start to race. "It's time," Barrabas said.

THE LONG-HAIRED SOB MADE his final approach, screaming down the road on the BMW. Midway across the frontage of the general's land, he hit the brakes and slid to a stop, scorching gravel in front of the gate.

He revved the engine, sending the BMW's throaty howl over General Hamelin's green lawn and garden. Announcing his presence.

It didn't take long for those inside to respond. Curtains fluttered in a row of windows along the front of the rustic wooden retreat. The motion spread from window to window, as those inside took up their posts.

All of them took a look at the messenger in black.

Billy Two spun the bike around in a small circle, steadily twisting the throttle, kicking up dust, dirt and gravel in a murky cloud. The exhaust plumed from the chrome pipe like the hiss of a dragon.

He tugged on the handlebars, raising the front wheel off the ground, doing a madman's pirouette before finally coming down hard on both wheels, aiming the bike for the gate.

The wide-shouldered Osage straddled the seat, his black-visored helmet a mask, his long legs balancing the bike. He announced himself again with a twist of the throttle, drowning out the sounds of morning with the angry roar.

A rifle barrel poked out of the window closest to the front door.

Whyyyph.

The shot hit the biker in the chest with a loud thwack. He tumbled back. But his body snapped forward a moment later in an unguided fall. He grabbed the handlebars.

Two more silenced rounds knifed through the air. Then, unhorsed, the rider fell to the ground, the bike collapsing in front of him.

The front door crashed open as half a dozen White Brigade commandos, all heavily armed, scrambled from the wooden fortress, rushing to their fallen quarry.

They had delivered their message to the messenger. Like many a general before him, Hamelin was laying down the terms. No deal. No talk. The only winners were the ones left standing after the smoke cleared.

Now the general's men were coming out to claim their first victim and pull him out of sight.

The man in the lead was scarecrow thin, his long legs pounding on the dirt driveway, his jeans flapping against his shins as he ran. His automatic rifle glinted.

He reached the fence ahead of the others. Then they all piled against the wood, scrambling to unbar the gate. They flung the gate open and poured out.

Still in the lead, the tall man raced toward the fallen biker, holding his rifle in one hand. He was about ten feet away when he made a strange unnatural sound.

That was when Billy Two came back from the dead. He sat up, cradling the H&K submachine gun in his arms and calmly triggering a burst.

A trio of slugs ripped through the man's chest, kicking him back at an angle. His momentum caused his legs to keep moving forward, sliding into home a dead man as his feet thunked into the BMW's frame.

The "dead" biker continued firing at the advancing White Brigaders who were shocked out of their shoes and into the next life. At best they'd expected to find a wounded man. Not someone who swiveled a silenced SMG at them, whipping the air with a 9 mm lash that cut their legs out from under them. Three of them were dead before anyone could start to return fire.

But Billy Two was not about to be overrun. He crouched behind the armor-plated motorcycle and continued firing. The armor plating offered a shield from the lead fusillade just as the ballistic helmet and Kevlar and ceramic plates beneath his leathers had kept him alive when the snipers first unseated him from the BMW.

Automatic fire ripped from the woods to the left as the SOBs rained lead down on the general's men.

Suddenly the White Brigaders had no more desire to face down the "dead" Indian. Instead they triggered their SMGs, unloosing full-auto blasts toward the woods and toward the biker as they returned to the safety of the house.

During the confusion Billy Two slung the SMG over his shoulder and righted the BMW. He roared up the driveway after the fleeing gunners. Just before he would have ridden into their midst, he tugged on the handlebars, lifted the front wheel and rode on the back. He aimed the upright bike straight ahead, then jumped off. Once Billy Two was out of the line of fire, the SOBs poured lead up the driveway.

The bike crashed through the running men, then collided with the front steps. Then the extra padded seat went off. Filled out with strips of C-4 cushioning, the armored bike was a bomb. As soon as it neared the front door, Liam O'Toole pressed the button on a hand-held radio detonator.

The loud explosion blasted through wood, glass, flesh and blood, literally blowing the doors off General Hamelin's hardsite and blowing some of the enemy soldiers' brains to the sky.

CHAPTER TWELVE

Smoke streamed from the front of the house. Debris littered the opening.

The motorcycle blast had struck just as reinforcements were gearing up to pour out of the house. With that avenue of escape in flames, the White Brigaders moved back to the windows to return fire—just as Lee Hatton pulled the trigger of a Heckler & Koch GS3 sniper rifle with a 20-round box magazine.

The full-auto burst of 7.62 mm NATO rounds scythed through wood and windows, cutting down the defenders like blades of grass. Two of the gunmen dropped from sight, heads shredded instantly. Another hurtled backward, knocked off his feet by a metal fusillade. Flashes erupted from the shattered windows as more White Brigaders fired blindly at the SOBs.

Off to Lee's right another H&K GS3 opened up as Claude Hayes drilled the splintering face of the house with a burst of full-auto fire. This second wave of projectiles slashed through the windows, striking home at the inhabitants.

Lee slapped in another box magazine and flicked the selector on the pistol grip to semiautomatic. Then she paced her shots one after the other along the windows, as if knocking down a row of ducks in a shooting gallery.

The H&K rifles in their camouflage casings swiveled from left to right, nestled on bipods balanced on the dew-covered ground, as the two SOBs shot at any sign of movement behind the windows.

They had scrambled closer to the house, setting up at prearranged sites, during the commotion caused by Billy Two. Now, stretched flat in the high grass, they laid down a heavy metal rain.

"ANY DOUBTS NOW?" O'Toole asked. The red-bearded ex-Army captain picked up the Remington 12-gauge shotgun for his house call on the general. He was a walking armory of grenades, Starflash and CS shotgun shells. He carried a short-barreled MP-5 for in-close fighting.

Like the others, he had been moving closer to the house, circling around from the rear. He and the man he was talking to were still concealed by the fringe of greenery.

"I never really had any doubts that Hamelin had gone into business for himself," the CIA man said. "But I did have my doubts that we'd get the chance to put him out of business. Unless we brought in an outside force."

Mitchell Rhodes, the local CIA action chief who'd brought the SOBs to Belgium, was on the scene as an observer. An extremely armed one. Behind him in the woods was a three-man team of CIA shock troops, stretched out in a skirmish line. They, too, were observing the action, through sniper scopes aimed at the house. In green khakis Rhodes and his men were nearly invisible from a distance, blending in with the shadow of the woods.

"I just had to see it all in living—make that dying—color," Rhodes explained. "For a report that'll never see the light of day."

"I like the caliber of your witnesses," O'Toole said, glancing back at the woods, where Bennett, the stocky scar-faced Agency operative, was gesturing for the other CIA ops to spread out.

Nearly undetected, Alex Nanos passed quietly through the brush and trotted up to the Irishman. The Greek SOB's face was streaked with green and earth camouflage, the colors of covert warfare. "It's time to pay our respects," he said. Like the Irishman, he carried an armory of grenades and magazines for the H&K submachine gun.

Rhodes looked down at the house. Most of the activity was at the front, where the SOBs and a team of sharpshooters provided by Henri Goliard were keeping Hamelin's men busy.

"We'll be here if you need us," Rhodes said.

O'Toole nodded, then gestured toward the house. Covered by Rhodes's team, he and Nanos circled through the woods until they were in range of the clearing behind the general's farm.

BULLETS SLICED through the ranch-style house in a nonstop torrent, drenching the interior with metal and blood. While the White Brigaders scrambled for positions throughout the house, trying to find targets to return fire, General Hamelin stormed through the shambles of his house.

"Vallance!" he shouted, thundering down the corridor toward his office at the back. "Where the hell are you?"

"Right here, General," Vallance said. The soft-spoken commando looked up from Hamelin's desk, dropping a sheaf of papers as the general walked in.

He seemed as unconcerned about being discovered as he was about the living hell enveloping the farm.

"You've been snooping while your so-called commandos are getting chewed to pieces."

"That's right, General." Vallance nonchalantly continued to probe the general's desk. It was obvious he'd already scanned behind bookshelves for a safe, then prowled through the room before turning to the desk and its locked drawers.

"Fiddling while Rome burns," the General said.

"This isn't Rome, General," Vallance replied. "It's but a province, ruled by a barbarian—who used to follow orders." He turned around quickly, the SMG slung around his chest whipping through the air before falling back against his chest.

He was armed for war but he was acting like a bookkeeper.

"Dammit, Vallance, what the hell are you doing here? I demand an answer."

The Belgian ESI renegade looked him in the eyes. "It's simple, General. You see, I'm looking for your parachute. Where is it?"

Hamelin closed the gap between them. "What are you talking about?"

"The parachute you keep in case you ever have to bail out of the group—proof that the Realm exists."

"I don't have one."

Vallance laughed. It was a dry merciless cough. "General, I have one. I expect a man in your position has to have the same. Names, places, records, connections—something you can bargain with. You didn't exactly volunteer to join the group. It took women, wine and numbered accounts. A share of the power. But you took them. So you must have some nice bits of evidence stashed around here in case things went wrong."

The Belgian nodded toward the front of the house, where the outlaw commandos were firing wildly at the invisible sharpshooters pinning them down. "And things don't get much more wrong than this. So, I repeat the question, General. Where is the evidence you've gathered against the Realm?"

Like a human volcano about to erupt, Hamelin faced the wiry and no doubt quicker man. He wasn't about to back down. It wasn't in his constitution. That was both his strength and his weakness.

"I'll have you shot."

"Relax, General, it's not what you think. We're not cutting you out of the picture. We've got a chopper ready to come in here and take us away. I've also got a few crews riding the roads, disguised as tourists, in case we have to hitch a ride."

"Terrorists," Hamelin said. "Not tourists."

"Suit yourself," he said. "Whatever term fits, General, we're all in this together. We're all of the same stripe. Now show me where the goods are and we'll get the hell out of here."

Hamelin noticed the glint in the other man's eyes. It was just a flicker. As if he were looking into the future, a future without General Hamelin.

The general reacted instantly, swinging his ham fist overhead, straight down on the commando—just as Vallance was reaching for the MAT-49 submachine gun slung in front of him.

The magazine housing was folded forward and clipped to the barrel. It took Vallance only a second to swing back the housing and make the 9 mm submachine gun ready for action.

But Hamelin didn't give him that second. His fist clubbed into the side of Vallance's head, sending him sprawling. He tumbled over the desk, not from the force of the blow, but to avoid the crushing follow-through.

Hamelin reached for his sidearm, aiming the .45 Colt automatic at the commando just as Vallance succeeded in freeing the MAT-49 and aiming it.

Both men held lethal looks in their eyes, knowing that death was just an eyeblink away.

"Stalemate," General Hamelin said. "For now."

"Defeat." Vallance shook his head. "And it's forever. Where can you turn to now, General? Your people won't want you back. And the Realm doesn't suffer traitors."

"Traitors! Coming from you that sounds rather strange."

"These are strange times, General. You're with us to the end. It's up to you to decide when the end is. You have no choice but to come with the White Brigade now."

"White Brigade, my ass," Hamelin said, as scream by scream, bullet by bullet, plank by plank, his Belgian fortress was coming apart at the seams. Just as his life was. Hamelin shook his head. "How about Yellow Brigade?"

Vallance shrugged, still holding the submachine gun.

But Vallance's extra firepower wasn't a deciding factor for the general. Not yet. One shot from the Colt .45 could kill Vallance just as dead.

Hamelin stared at the man. He knew that no matter what Vallance said, no matter what offer he made, his fate was already sealed. The White Brigade detachment hadn't come here to save him—at least not solely for that. If things went bad they were to eliminate him and recover his parachute, as Vallance preferred to call the evidence the general had gathered on the Realm. Hamelin had a parachute all right. But he wasn't about to give it up. There was still one victory he could salvage.

The sound of the battle grew louder.

It was obvious that the force besieging the house was neither a White Brigade faction nor an underworld splinter group looking for money. It was a covert team and it was here in force, here for the duration.

It was also obvious that Vallance's squad was getting the worst of it.

"What now?" Hamelin said.

"Looks like it's time to fly, General," Vallance said, backing away from Hamelin toward the door. He moved his left hand slowly, reaching for a small handheld radio, while keeping his right hand on the MAT49. "I'm calling in the chopper, General. If you want to be on it, bring a parachute."

Vallance backed into the hallway.

Hamelin quickly moved from where he'd been standing, expecting a flood of bullets from the MAT-49 to come streaming through the walls. He held his automatic steady in his hand, ready to fire.

THE BLACK CHOPPER SOARED over the green plateau, flying just above treetop level as it headed for the general's house.

From the air the heavily armed men could see the layout of Hamelin's stronghold, besieged from several points. Sporadic firing poured from the windows and from the holes the White Brigaders had bashed in the walls.

Sharp yellow flashes of automatic fire came from inside, as smoke grenades thumped against the house, enveloping it in billowing clouds.

The chopper crew saw the jeeps and vans spread out across the serpentine road, the barricade reinforced by linked metal tongs nearly a foot long, zigzagging across the road like metal stalagmites. The hollow spikes created an impassable barrier for any wheeled vehicle.

The Blackhawk helicopter knifed through the air and circled the farmhouse. The grass shivered in the rotor wash as the chopper dropped into the clearing.

Painted a flat black, nearly impossible to see with the naked eye on night missions, it had just the opposite effect during the day. In all of its menacing glory, the armor-plated Sikorsky chopper was a powerful psychological weapon.

Able to carry a crew and eleven passengers, it was also a formidable ally often relied upon by Army Airborne divisions, special forces units, antiterrorist squads and renegades like Bernhard Vallance.

"Gather the troops, Sordett," Vallance ordered, as soon as the chopper he'd radioed for touched down.

His second in command nodded, then dashed through the house, tapping several of the White Brigade defenders on the shoulder, leaving others to stay at their posts. By the time he moved to the rear of the house, only a skeleton crew manned the windows. Some of them were destined to be real skeletons soon enough as they fired at an enemy they couldn't see.

Sordett raced to Vallance's side with about a dozen men, their faces covered with smoke and blood. They gathered in the rear corridors and the kitchen.

Peering out at the chopper, Vallance radioed the pilot. "Give us sixty seconds," he said. Then he turned to Sordett. "We'll give the general one more minute to make up his mind."

Sordett nodded. "He's already made up his mind," he said. "Otherwise he'd be out here with us."

"There's always a chance we can bring him with us," Vallance said. "If not, we destroy him and his hideaway, and leave no trace."

Vallance gestured to a cadre of the White Brigaders, who hurried down the hall outside General Hamelin's office.

"Still there?"

The man guarding the hall nodded.

At Vallance's order, the men spread out along the walls. He shouted to the general above the din of gunfire. "Hamelin! What's your answer—"

A bullet chewed through the wall. Two more shots rang out as the Colt .45 barked from inside the room.

Vallance nodded.

Like firemen hosing down a blaze, the White Brigade assassins opened up. Automatic bursts ripped through the wall, splintering the wood, thudding into the floor and ceiling, clanging off the metal desks inside.

The endless fusillade riddled the walls.

"All right," Vallance said. "Destroy the room." Two men reached for grenades to toss inside.

LIAM O'TOOLE EMERGED from the clouds of smoke sifting through the house, rounding the corridor just as the White Brigade chopped through the walls with automatic fire.

A few of them turned scowling, grasping at spare magazines to shoot at one of the attackers.

''Lighten up,'' O'Toole said, swinging the barrel of the combat shotgun their way and pulling the trigger. The Starflash muzzle blast sent a stream of white-hot sparklets toward the enemy. The stun grenade hell created a blinding tunnel of white.

Some of the gunners recovered quickly, managing to fire a few shots. O'Toole retired out of sight and dropped the shotgun on the floor.

Alex Nanos stepped around the corner of the hall and opened up with his MP5. The Heckler & Koch barrage cut down half the gunners before they knew what hit them.

O'Toole spun around the corner again and backed up the Greek's assault with a lethal spray from his own Heckler & Koch machine.

The remaining White Brigaders fled toward the back of the house.

''MOVE IT!'' Vallance shouted, nearly pushing one of his men off his feet as they streamed from the back door. They jumped from the porch, clearing the steps and landing on the run.

Sordett was first to reach the Blackhawk. As he neared the chopper the cabin door slid open and a hand reached out for him. The instant he threw himself inside he realized something was wrong.

The chopper was full.

The Blackhawk hadn't come to pick them up—it had come to deliver more attackers.

Sordett broke loose from the hand that gripped him, teetering on the edge of the cabin, torn between getting his balance and going for his gun.

Then one of the passengers solved the dilemma for him. White hair visible beneath his khaki bandanna, the man stepped forward and snapped his right foot into Sordett's jaw. The powerful kick sent him flying.

Nile Barrabas jumped from the Blackhawk, bending his knees as he landed, springing forward. He saw the fallen and dazed Sordett grasping for his submachine gun, a river of blood pouring from his mouth.

Barrabas aimed his Hi-Power and pulled the trigger. Sordett jerked once as the 9 mm round blasted his right shoulder, knocking him over the border of consciousness he'd been straddling. As he lay still, Barrabas scooped up the man's SMG and flung it back into the chopper.

Bernhard Vallance had instinctively slowed down as he approached the Blackhawk, letting the throng of White Brigaders pass.

Something was wrong. Alarms went off inside his head as he tried to figure out what that something was. What had registered in his mind?

Then he saw Sordett fall.

Several dark-clad shapes jumped from the Blackhawk. ESI commandos, he thought. Real ones, not renegade factions working for the White Brigade. He raised his Heckler & Koch SMG.

Then he saw a familiar face—Henri Goliard, the commander of the ESI, who had trained him, had launched him on his covert career.

The bearded commander stood there in the cabin. "Vallance!" he shouted. "Drop your weapon!"

Vallance paused. For a moment the old Vallance was there. Listening to him. Caught out at last. Caught like a criminal, like the men he used to hunt.

But then Vallance shouted. And as he shouted the real Bernhard Vallance returned, drowning out the ghosts of his past. He raised the SMG.

Goliard tracked him at the same time.

There was a mutual hesitation. But both men finally fired. And missed.

Vallance was on the run and had fired just as Goliard dropped to the floor of the chopper.

Vallance corrected his aim, triggered another burst. One of Goliard's men did a dance back into the cabin of the chopper. Then he staggered forward and fell headfirst out of the chopper. He landed lifeless on the ground.

Meanwhile Vallance's men, caught out in the open but not defenseless, fired at the troops who appeared from the Blackhawk.

Vallance shot a burst at the ESI commandos who'd run for cover.

Bullets kicked up the earth all around him, singing through the air around his head, thwacking into the wood behind him. His men fought furiously, unleashing a blizzard of automatic fire. Some fired from the house, others from the running herd by the helicopter.

It was madness. Chaos. And in the chaos, Vallance managed to break away, pulling out his transceiver as he headed for the woods.

He radioed to the "tourist" cars waiting by the road. He summoned them into the fray while he ran for the haven of the woods, coming closer and closer as he pounded across the field.

THE WHITE FORD VAN STOPPED at the roadblock and the driver stuck his head out the window at the approaching GRT man in blue.

Several other drivers had turned back at the roadblock, relieved that the Belgian GRT team was there to police the area and keep them safe.

The driver of the van nodded as the security man explained the situation. Then he backed up and started to make a three-point turn.

He didn't complete the maneuver.

When the van was broadside to the roadblock, the side door slid open. A four-man kill team poured lead from inside the van, cutting down the security man where he stood. Then, kneeling inside the van, they expanded their field of fire, slicing two more men into ribbons before the GRT team realized they had a fight on their hands.

A second van of hitters pulled up and joined the fray as the White Brigade "tourists" shot the hell out of the barricade—keeping the GRT team from pursuing either of the vans as they slowly backed into the woods to the point where Bernhard Vallance emerged, bloodied and panic-stricken.

He dived headfirst into the van.

NILE BARRABAS KICKED the door to Hamelin's office. Already shattered and cracked, it came clear of its hinges and fell flat on the floor.

O'Toole and Nanos stood in the hall, covering the room from two angles. No one was visible.

Barrabas stepped forward, the barrel of the Browning Hi-Power leading the way. He moved slowly. He wasn't in a hurry to get killed. And there was no need to rush, since the house was now under their control.

Lee Hatton, Billy Two and Claude Hayes were covering the front of the house while Goliard's ESI teams worked their way through, checking for survivors among the blood-soaked renegades sprawled everywhere.

There was still fighting going on outside, but Barrabas was interested in the main quarry, General Hamelin.

The thick metal top of the overturned desk was pockmarked with bullet holes. Behind the desk, his legs sprawled on the floor, sat General Hamelin. A blood-soaked trench ran from his left arm to his shoulder where a bullet had lodged. The stocky officer was breathing hard as he leaned against the wall, his eyes closed. A layer of dust and grime had settled over his face and uniform. The right side of his face was black-and-blue. Either something had dropped on him during the volley of fire or he had banged his head in falling.

As Barrabas approached, the general's eyes snapped open. They were clear and hard, as if he'd just wakened from a long sleep. He looked up at Barrabas.

"Who the hell are you?" he said. Despite the wounds, there was still a lot of strength in him.

"I'm the man who put you here, General," Barrabas said. "With your back against the wall, and heavy time staring you in the face."

"You wouldn't have a name, would you?"

"Barrabas."

"Colonel Barrabas," Hamelin said. His eyes widened, as if he were relieved in a way that he'd been taken down by someone of Nile's caliber. "I've heard of you. You and I covered a lot of the same ground, way back when.''

"I know a lot about you, too, General," Barrabas said. "We *were* on the same side at one time. But we've gone down different roads since then.''

Hamelin nodded. He looked at the emptied Colt .45 on the floor, then at the spare clip about ten feet away that had been knocked out of his hand sometime during the chaos.

"Don't try it, General," Barrabas advised. "Not just yet.''

Hamelin looked up at the white-haired warrior, decoding his words and seeing the chance he was being offered. "I see you're a sporting man," he said.

"Wouldn't be here now if I wasn't. But it's not much of a gamble, General. You wouldn't have a chance against me. No, the man you're going up against is yourself.''

"What are you talking about?"

Barrabas looked down at the general. "Like I said, General, I know a lot about you. And about the Realm. And the White Brigade. I'll take them down just like I took you down. For as long as it takes, I'll be after them. But you can help if you want.''

Hamelin laughed. "What's in it for me?"

"Your name, General. Way I see it, all you have left is your reputation. And we don't have to take that away. You can still go out of this a hero, General.'' Barrabas paused, then said, "Or you can just go out of it.''

Hamelin looked up at him. Silently. He was looking at another world, a world of the past.

"Right now the world at large, your friends, your family think you're a hero. They think you're still

Hammerhead Hamelin, the man who fought for his country back in Nam.''

"Yeah," Hamelin said.

"I see no reason to change their minds, General."

"You mean I can walk away from this a hero?"

"I said nothing about a walking away. I said 'go out.' We don't have a sword you can fall on, but—" He looked over at the clip for the Colt. "You can use that."

"If?"

"If you tell us what you can. Give us names. Proof. Anything you got."

Hamelin sat there. Shot up. A far cry from the general he once was. Now he was a murderer caught red-handed. But he could regain that luster to his name, he could keep his reputation intact.

"They were going to kill me," Hamelin said.

"You don't sound surprised."

He shook his head. "The operation was going sour. Too many bodies were turning up. Too many leads. And then you came on the scene. The Realm wanted me out of the picture. They wanted me silenced. There weren't too many places for a compromised general in their organization."

"Why'd you do it, General?"

"I believed in them," Hamelin said. "At first. It sounded noble. It sounded worth risking everything for. Worth dying for. Like the days of old.... A quest. Then, bit by bit they reeled me in—with other things...."

Barrabas nodded. "I know what you mean. There's always a part of us that wants to fight for king and crown. And sometimes we don't see that the man behind the throne—a man like Auguste Bayard—is just a killer and not a king."

Hamelin looked surprised. "How much do you know about this?"

"Enough to get this far, General," Barrabas said. "And now I'm hoping you can help us get the rest of the way."

Hamelin nodded. "What you're looking for is right in here," he said, leaning forward and resting his hand on the edge of the desk.

"The drawers?" Barrabas asked.

"No, not them," Hamelin said, laughing. The effort caused him to cough wetly as blood flecked his lips. "Even if Vallance could have opened the drawers, he'd have come up empty. It's the desk top itself."

General Hamelin gripped the edge of the desk, dug his fingers into one of the metal border strips, pulled it off. Then he pressed a smooth section of metal that was revealed beneath. A spring-loaded tray slid out from the false-topped desk. Shielded by the fire- and bullet-proof desk, the thin drawer contained photographs, maps, papers. An organizational chart of the Realm's hierarchy. And a journal.

"Everything I know is in there," Hamelin said. "There's a lot more to it than what's there, but it's what I got a handle on."

"Looks like you were planning for the future," Barrabas said, scanning the contents.

Hamelin nodded. "I never retreated. From anything. But hell, I knew in this game you always had to be ready for whatever comes. I thought this might happen one day. Thought somebody like you might come along, and I could . . . try to explain."

"Yeah," Barrabas said. "I'm here now, but I've got to be going. This place is going to be haunted with spooks from every agency in Europe any second now." He gathered up the materials from Hamelin. "All that's left now is deciding how you want to play this."

"The only way," Hamelin said.

Barrabas nodded. He picked up the spare clip for the Colt .45 and headed for the door. Then he spun around and tossed the clip to Hamelin. As the stocky war-horse snatched it from the air, the SOB chieftain said, "Thanks, General," and left the room.

As Barrabas walked down the corridor, he heard a loud bang, a dull sigh, then the sound of a body falling to the floor.

One more hero was gone.

CHAPTER THIRTEEN

Spinning tires rolled along the cycling lane, creating a comfortable rhythm as the slender rider pedaled down the slight incline. He moved his legs spryly for a man who had aged thirty years in the past two days.

In that short time his blond hair had become gray. Hanging out from beneath his tweed cap, it blew in the wind.

He smiled as he coasted around a sharp curve, hardly looking like a man who was being hunted by at least a half dozen European police and intelligence agencies.

But then, they were looking in Belgium for a man named Bernhard Vallance, a name that no longer belonged to him. And he was in Holland. His passport identified him as Jules Mabran, a retired jeweler from Amsterdam on a bike holiday, a common excursion this time of year.

Patches of sunlight warmed his face as he coasted in and out of the shade from the trees lining the bicycle lane.

He'd already overtaken several other cyclists as he worked his way up the bike route that skirted the Netherland's eastern border with Germany. They'd paid him little notice, nor had he given them the chance. A closer look would have shown that he wasn't winded at all, that the blue eyes behind the glasses were those of a sharpshooter, that the gray hair was a wig.

Then again, a closer look might have revealed the 7.65 mm automatic carried in a rig under his left shoulder.

But he'd been lucky so far. Though he was on the run, Bernhard forced himself to act casually while he slowly worked his way to the sanctuary waiting for him at a small wood frame house just outside the town of Venlo in north Limburg province.

It had all been set up beforehand. In the event of a blowup like the one at General Hamelin's, a safe-house was waiting for him. There he would find money, food and, more important, someone to shepherd him on the way.

Vallance had set up similar sanctuaries in the past for White Brigaders who'd had to go underground after completing operations. They'd all worked out perfectly.

The Realm looked after its own.

By midafternoon, the gray-haired cyclist reached his destination. He pedaled off the main road, went up a steep hill, then coasted down a country lane. He rode past his turnoff twice to check it out. Then, satisfied there was no ambush, he pedaled down a narrow car path toward the house.

It was on low ground, with long sheafs of yellow grass sprouting around the front porch. The garden was slightly overgrown, and much of the wood siding was poorly kept. The place looked lived in.

He leaned his bike against the porch, then walked slowly up the steps, still maintaining a casual air. Half expecting a squad of police to jump out of the woods, he kept his right hand inside his jacket in case he had to shoot his way out.

Just as he was about to knock, the door swung open.

"Entrez-vous, Bernhard."

Vallance stared for a moment at the man in the doorway, who'd obviously been watching him every step of the way. He hadn't expected a man of this caliber to serve as his shepherd. When the shock wore off, Vallance laughed. He dropped his hand from the holster and stepped forward to embrace the other man, clasping him on the shoulders.

That was when the other man kneed him in the groin.

The impact lifted Vallance onto his toes. For a crucial moment, the pain from the sledgehammer blow whited out his brain. The other man put Vallance in a headlock, then flipped him head over heels.

With a sickening crack, Vallance's neck snapped as his body flopped onto the floor. Mouth open and eyes wide, Vallance looked up at the expressionless face of his executioner.

Still holding Vallance's head in his hands, the "shepherd" twisted one more time, crushing his windpipe, then dropping him to the floor.

"Vogue la gallère, Bernhard," he said. "The ship sails on."

THE AIR OF A CATHEDRAL hung about the regal gray stone building on avenue René-Coty between Cité universitaire and place Denfert-Rouchereau on the southern edge of Paris.

It was a fitting atmosphere. At times the man who lived there acted like a modern-day Cardinal Richelieu pulling the strings of commerce and government from his rooftop courtyard.

Spirelike antennae and satellite dishes cast shadows upon the terraced rooftop gardens. Auguste Bayard sat beneath a canvas pavilion where he could look down upon the smog and the majesty of Paris, seeing while not being seen. It was a habit of decades he was not about to break, not even in his "retirement" from public service.

Bayard was a firm believer in the divine right of kings—as long as he was king.

Whenever he spoke he delivered his pronouncements as if they were final, absolute commandments that came to him from on high. And though his covert cabinet was composed of high-ranking counselors and ministers, as far as he was concerned their duty was more often than not to listen to him.

Listen and obey. Those were the cardinal rules of the Realm.

As a matter of form Bayard tolerated his cabinet members' protests and appropriated their best suggestions for himself, taking the credit if they seemed of merit. After all, that was the kingly way of ruling.

It was the way he had ruled his intelligence fiefdom for years. Back then he had had an entire covert apparatus at his beck and call. As a premier spymaster he had derived his power from the worldwide surveillance capacity that gave him information about friends and enemies alike, information that he exploited ruthlessly. And it didn't hurt that he had a covert action arm to strike at his enemies for those rare times when they didn't listen to reason.

Bayard still used the same tactics. But now his power stemmed from a worldwide private intelligence network funded by multinational corporations and foundations under the Realm's control. The backbone of the network was Liège Industries, an electronics combine that manufactured and launched commercial satellites for clients all over Europe and Africa.

As chief executive officer of Liège, Bayard had used his contacts and his insider knowledge to line up customers both willing and unwilling. Liège had quickly outstripped its main competitors, those half dozen American companies that had filled the void when the United States government reduced its access by commercial clients. It was one of the most profitable businesses controlled by the Realm.

But there was an even greater benefit. While Liège provided their clients with communications satellites, those same clients unknowingly provided Liège with critical information.

Their information was Bayard's information.

Their knowledge was his.

And so their power was his.

Bit by bit, Bayard had increased the reach and the power of Liège until it was an invisible anchor in the covert chain, infiltrating several other industries through a maze of holding companies.

The holding companies did the dirty work of bribery, entrapment, blackmail and headhunting, all of these untraceable to the power behind the throne— Auguste Bayard, who now sat on a Parisian rooftop, sipping tea with a premier killer of the Realm. A man about to become marshal of the Realm.

To someone with a cynical mind, the man who chatted so easily with Bayard could be taken as a sociopath, a man who had made killing his entire life. He excelled at the art of murder and had also proved himself adept at Bayard's attendant intrigues.

The man was hardly a saint, but then saintlike qualities were not yet in demand of the Realm. Later, perhaps, when Bayard had assumed total control, the marshal could become a saint. It wouldn't be the first time histories had been erased.

Bayard had already altered history a number of times—burying dossiers that identified some of France's most glorified Resistance fighters during World War Two as collaborators who had actually worked with the Gestapo, selling out many of their own compatriots to the Germans.

In return for Bayard's not exposing them, the supposed Resistance heroes were most grateful. They threw their support and their funds into the United Realm of Europe movement, which, for all practical purposes was the United Realm of Auguste Bayard. Once he was in command of the Realm the others would see that he was the fittest to rule.

If necessary, men like the marshal would help them see.

Bayard talked with his young warlord about his impending maneuvers for several minutes before standing.

"Come," he said. "It's time to show our hand. To our friends and our enemies."

Bayard gestured toward the stairwell that led down to the room where the rulers of the Realm waited.

"GENERAL HAMELIN IS DEAD," Frederick Albrecht said. "Our key American ally and his apparatus have been eliminated. Perhaps even more frightening is the matter of Maurice Sordett. We must assume he is dead or in captivity. Either way we've lost one of our best men and now our entire organization is at risk." As the Dutchman spoke he looked directly at Auguste Bayard, laying the blame at his feet.

As a former high-ranking officer in the Dutch Korps commandetroepen, the headstrong and solidly built Albrecht saw no need to bow to Auguste Bayard. As a man whose wealth and upbringing nearly matched the Frenchman's, the Royal Netherlands Marine Corps veteran often considered it his duty to oppose Bayard just for the sake of appearances.

Auguste Bayard nodded slightly, recognizing the complaints of a subordinate.

Like the gargoyles ringing the outside of his Parisian mansion, Auguste Bayard had been sitting there without moving while the Dutchman spoke—as if he were one of those solid strong creatures who were said to come back to life occasionally and speak with mere mortals.

Bayard had let the Dutchman speak on until even the other members of the Realm were tiring of him. Only Albrecht's chief aide sitting beside him seemed entranced by his words.

"Thank you, Frederick," Bayard said. "For telling us what we already know. A number of times, in fact. But that is one of the reasons I called you here today—to discuss our course of action. The future of the Realm is at stake. Sordett was a valuable asset to the White Brigade. A great loss. And a great danger. He will be attended to."

"And Vallance poses an even greater danger," Albrecht said. "He knows even more than Sordett. It's a fatal mistake to have a man like that on the loose. He's liable to do anything."

Albrecht's argument scored points with the other rulers of the Realm and their retinue gathered around the table. Statesmen and would-be king alike, they were all seeing their castles crumbling as the doom-saying Dutchman spoke.

Naturally each of them saw his place in the Realm as of the utmost importance. No matter who ruled the organization, the others would have sufficient status and power—if the Realm's plans went through. Once the Americans were pushed out of Europe the power vacuum would have to be filled by men like themselves, men capable of taking hold of the reins of empire.

But lately the Realm had been suffering too many setbacks, setbacks almost gleefully recounted by Frederick Albrecht. His litany of catastrophe had been aimed squarely at the man at the head of the table. Though the mahogany round table was nominally a table of equals, around which sat the knights of the Realm, Auguste Bayard clearly sat at its head, looking down at the peers of the Realm to his left and right.

The Italian representative was nodding in cadence with Albrecht's complaints. A straightforward military man like Albrecht, he often supported the Dutchman at these summits.

Hubert, the Belgian Realmist, looked back and forth from the Dutchman to Bayard, ready to support whoever emerged as the winner of the argument.

Both the British and German peers of the Realm looked indifferent to the proceedings, while the Dutchman painted an apocalyptic picture for them all, a masterpiece of gloom and destruction.

The Realmist from Portugal, a veteran of Grupo de operações especiais, the special operations force attached to the Polícia de segurança pública, thoughtfully watched the quiet give-and-take between Albrecht and Bayard. He suspected them both, but that was because he suspected everyone in the covert trade. Philip Emanuel had thrown his considerable support behind the Realm on several occasions, but he had also held back now and then, dissenting from the inner council's demands in an almost cavalier manner.

Very compact, elegantly dressed, Philip looked more like a businessman than anyone in the room. His jet-black hair was cut short, his mustache immaculately clipped and combed. Often silent, he preferred to let others speak and make their case, often telling him more than they intended to reveal. To Philip there was no such thing as too much intelligence, which was why he patiently listened to the Dutchman discuss the Hamelin disaster.

Albrecht's portrait of ruin centered on Vallance. And, indirectly, on the man who should be held responsible for the fiasco. "All we know of Vallance is that immediately after escaping from the Hamelin Inferno he went into hiding and broke all contact with the Realm."

Bayard smiled. "As he was supposed to do in such circumstances," he reminded them. "The moment his backup team spirited him away, he went underground. Or would you want him to come to the Realm before it's safe, leading his hunters to us?"

"It's not wise to have such a man on the loose," Albrecht responded. "He should have contacted one of the sanctuaries by now, so we would know his status."

Bayard nodded. "A dangerous situation," he conceded. "But you'll see, Frederick, it will all work out. For now, let's move on to other matters. To lessen our need for dealing with men like Hamelin and arms-smuggling rings, we are putting the finishing touches on acquiring a major armaments corporation based in France, with subsidiaries worldwide. The current owner is almost ready to come in with us. With just a little more persuasion..."

The discussion moved on to other Realm business. The Realm was involved in as many legitimate businesses as underground ones. And no matter who controlled them they always had problems to be worked out.

The heads of the Realm had gathered in Paris in a conclave of covert chieftains, intent on ironing out the problems of their multinational companies as well as determining damage control for their recent covert catastrophes.

They were equipped to deal with both fronts. Along with their roles in the Realm they all had respected positions in business and politics. Aside from their various illustrious military, intelligence and business careers, they were men of privilege and power. As well, they shared something more—a quest for kingship, in practice if not in title. They were peers of the Realm. In time each one of them would rule the Realm. They would take back Europe from the Americans, whom they saw as an occupation force. A benevolent force, but an occupying power just the same.

To many of them the presence of the United States had been needed forty years ago. But things had changed since then. They now saw the United States as a towering shadow looming over them, a shadow that not all of their countrymen could see. It took a special breed of visionaries to see beyond that shadow, to remove that stranglehold from their own dominion. Only when Europe took its role as a superpower in its own right would it be able to free itself from the tyranny of the Eastern and Western titans.

The winds of change that blew from the Soviet Union through Eastern Europe weren't enough. Neither was the plan for a united Europe by the year 1992. What the Realm power lords needed was a means to put concentrated political power into their own hands.

The first step had been the unofficial network built by the European intelligence groups during the late seventies and the eighties. As the terrorists organized, so did the counterterrorists.

Special operations forces from many countries trained with one another, learned from one another, sharing intelligence and techniques, and lending discreet support during covert operations. The links between the services had widened.

At first the public rejoiced, but when too many cases of excessive force surfaced, they pulled away, once again rolling out a bloodred carpet for the terrorists.

So the joint covert operations went further underground.

And the White Brigade was born, an international organization of small close-knit groups that conducted cross-border raids, carrying out nearly untraceable hits on terrorists before returning to their own country.

From the very beginning the movement was bankrolled, spearheaded and guided by Auguste Bayard, who stamped his own ruthless but effective code on the organization.

Terrorists were no longer apprehended; they were simply eliminated. While it seemed to the public that terrorist outrages went unpunished, it was frequently just a matter of the punishments being unseen, unheard, unrecorded.

Soon a lot of other White Brigade activities went unrecorded, as Bayard led the organization away from its original goals. The freewheeling operatives adapted techniques used by their opponents—entrapment, murder, blackmail, looting. But those sins were all forgiven because it was for a good cause—The United Realm of Europe. Bayard had gradually created the feeling that the White Brigade's acts were sanctioned by a pan-European movement and they were the shock troops of a new order, when men like them would rule for the good of all.

And so patriots had become distorted mirror images of the men they'd originally set out to hunt. Terrorists of the Realm.

Bayard had cloaked it all in a semimystical, semiheroic organization that only the most worthy could join—and never leave. That was the subject he returned to after a half hour of more routine business had been discussed.

"Now we must all agree on our course of action from here on in," Bayard said. "It is true we have had a small setback in one of the provinces—"

"Not since World War Two has there been such a small setback," Albrecht said. "The action was loud enough to be heard around the world. Everyone is wondering what is going on."

"They'll know soon enough," Bayard said. "When we make ourselves known." He glared at the Dutchman, an ever-present thorn in his lion's paw. "The attention was unavoidable, Frederick. It appears there is a major group moving against us."

"Who?" the Dutchman asked.

"I believe they are Americans," Bayard said.

"We have enemies all over the Continent trying to strike at us," the Dutchman said. "What makes you think it is the Americans who are after us now?"

Bayard shrugged. "We're picking up bits and pieces from our contacts in the community, but nothing definite yet."

"Whoever they are," said Victor Amadeus Constantine, "they have acquitted themselves well."

Bayard nodded. "They obviously know of us. And it appears they know how to deal with us. We must be prepared to encounter them in the open from now on. For too long we have restrained our power, keeping to the shadows. Now we must declare war upon them."

The Realmists looked at one another. Until now the Realm had been a slowly building dream, a pleasant one at that. Now it was crossing the boundary. Now it was taking yet another step to coming out into the open—into open warfare.

As they pondered Bayard's last statement, a group of attendants bustled into the room, pushing before them a silver serving cart. These trusted soldier servants usually came in at some point during the summit meetings with choice wines, meats and breads to sustain the Realmists.

And the Realmists usually ignored them.

But today one of the servants was hard to ignore. He stood behind the serving cart positioned just to the right of Auguste Bayard, staring down the table not as an inferior, but more like someone on an operation, a look the men knew well. Gradually they recognized him as a low-level aide to Bayard who always seemed to be in the background of Realm affairs, acting as a courier, driver or bodyguard, often shepherding some of the mistresses of the Realm.

"And of course," Bayard said, "in wartime, we must all be prepared to make sacrifices occasionally."

He turned and nodded to the man standing behind him. The man lifted the cover of the serving tray.

And there, on the tray, the head of Bernhard Vallance stared back at the Realmists. The neck was cut evenly with the blanched skin looking like a collar. Drained of blood, waxen, looking almost shellacked, the monkish visage of the White Brigader gave mute testimony to Auguste Bayard's ruthlessness. It also served notice to friend and enemy alike that the cult of the severed head was still alive and well in the Realm.

The men around the table drew back instinctively from the gruesome head. But no one was overwhelmed by the barbaric spectacle. In their long clandestine careers many of them had seen worse.

Only the Dutchman started to speak. "I'd expect this technique from Idi Amin, not someone who fancies himself a modern-day Charlemagne—"

"Charlemagne took his share of heads," Bayard replied, pinning Albrecht with another regal glare. "Most of his conversions to the church were made at sword point. A technique I strongly recommend."

The Dutchman looked away, suppressing the urge to speak, aware that he was in the presence of a man about to take control of the Realm. That control might result in his own head being placed on a platter one day. Bayard had engineered the spectacle for its shock effect—his way of showing what happened to those who didn't follow his dictates.

The mantle of equality was about to be discarded—though inwardly, none of them could be surprised. No one had any doubts about Bayard's ambition.

As if the severed head were an honored guest, Bayard turned and regarded the man who used to be one of his strongest field commanders. Just as the busts that hung in seventeenth-century halls echoed the days when warlords displayed the heads of their conquered enemies, so the severed head of Bernhard Vallance showed what happened to those who became enemies of the Realm, whether through betrayal or cowardice.

"It is all a matter of balance," Bayard said. "On his last mission, Vallance had two objectives. To neutralize the force harassing Hamelin and, if necessary, to eliminate Hamelin and any evidence he could bring to bear against us. Vallance failed at both, apparently thinking his life was more valuable to the Realm than his mission. It wasn't."

Bayard scanned the faces of the peers as he continued. "As a result of Vallance's failure, a commander in the ESI, Henri Goliard, was able to overrun us and destroy a good number of our people in the bargain. We know Hamelin is dead. The newspapers have sung his praises loudly. But we don't know what, if anything, the good general left behind—thanks to Vallance's flight before the operation was complete."

He paused, then looked back at the severed head of Bernhard Vallance. "He should have died at his post. As a matter of balance, we have taken care of that for him. Gentlemen, from now on, to maintain this balance, we must act swiftly and ruthlessly. The war has begun."

Bayard nodded at the man standing behind him, who covered the head and pushed away the cart, then returned to where he had stood.

Bayard gestured toward the man behind him. "I would like to introduce Kaspar Ulrich to you," he said. "Some of you know him from his other roles, for Kaspar has been many things for us. But he has also been something not all of you have known—my personal envoy, carrying out a number of delicate tasks for me. All of them quite successfully."

Kaspar Ulrich bowed slightly, a long lock of hair falling across his forehead. In the company of all these esteemed men he looked like a brigand, a hood of the Round Table. But he was more than a match for any of them and they all knew it.

Philip Emanuel shrugged. "What you are saying is that Kaspar, like many of our high-ranking KGB friends, has merely been posing as chauffeur all along. A driving force in the organization, rather than just a driver."

"Until now he has intervened for us several times behind the scenes," Bayard said. "At this point I wish to make it clear that he is marshal of the Realm. He will do what must be done. As you saw, he silenced Vallance. He will do the same for Sordett, as soon as he is able to find him. Help him in any way he asks. From now on, his voice is mine."

KASPAR ULRICH WAS one of the last to leave Bayard's elegant mansion on René-Coty. While the others went out through the ornate main door, Ulrich left via a subterranean passageway that connected to the catacombs beneath the French capital.

Nearly two hundred miles of tunnels ran beneath Paris, many of them lined with bones and skulls from the days when they were used as a cemetery. The dark and dank underground tunnels were two thousand years old. Originally used as quarries, then as hiding places for revolutionaries, the catacombs also served as burial chambers over the ages. Many of the long corridors had become boneyards where skulls and skeletons sat undisturbed in niches carved in the walls.

Some tunnels shrank gradually into hidden arteries that were little more than crawl spaces. Others branched out into large caverns that had served as underground headquarters for Parisian brigands during medieval times and as bunkers during World War Two.

Many of the limestone corridors interconnected and formed endless mazes, often leading to dead ends. Others ascended to different exits throughout Paris. Many were self-contained thoroughfares known only to a few.

Parisian lovers of the mysterious, tourists and students haunted the underground corridors, many entering at place Denfert-Rouchereau because the government had shut down most other entrances.

The catacombs were a second home to the action branch of the Realm, the White Brigade, who had literally gone underground to evade the surveillance concentrated on Bayard's Parisian mansion. The corridors served as intricate escape routes and underground caches for the Realm. They could emerge anywhere in the city, apparently striking at random, then vanish into the underworld.

Kaspar Ulrich walked down a lantern-lit corridor, secure from the other corridors. He was carrying the head of Bernhard Vallance. He made a number of turns before stopping in front of a gap carved in the wall.

There he placed the head of Bernhard Vallance. The Belgian White Brigader stared back at him with the guilt-inspiring eloquence of the dead.

As Vallance took his rightful place in the hierarchy of spirits of the Realm, Kaspar Ulrich couldn't help feeling like a hard-core cultist. Then again, he told himself, it was only natural. After all, he was in the largest cult of all, the cult of intelligence.

Kaspar Ulrich glanced once more at the head, which despite its pallor looked majestic, an oracle hinting at the future of the Realm.

Ulrich backed away from the grisly trophy, already thinking about how to capture Sordett and the others. After all, it would not do for Vallance to be lonesome for long.

CHAPTER FOURTEEN

"Where the hell are we?" Sordett asked.

"Hell's close enough," Barrabas replied. "But actually you're in purgatory now." Barrabas paced in front of the chair in which sat the bandaged and bloodied White Brigader.

Sordett's purgatory was actually a high-tech dungeon in a Belgian safehouse on the North Sea coast, just south of Ostend. The complex resembled a seaside resort. But it was a very private one. Most of the "vacationers" were intelligence operatives.

Guests of the state, like Maurice Sordett, also stayed here. The length and manner of their stay often depended on how they reacted.

The upper floor of the main building where Sordett was being kept had a superb view of the water. There several security men carried out their work in an almost tropical atmosphere. Because of its pastel color, open-air balconies and sun decks, the building that housed the intelligence station was known as the Country Club.

The lower floor of the main building was white, sterile and soundproofed. In one of the lower suites Sordett had had his injuries attended to and had been dosed with tranquilizing drugs. Then he had been transported to a small white room.

The interrogation room was sparsely furnished. It contained a dull green government-surplus desk and a couple of old wooden chairs.

Sordett wasn't handcuffed. In his injured state he was hardly a threat, although Barrabas kept his guard just the same. Leopards and assassins didn't change their spots easily. In tight situations they might always revert to what they'd been trained to do.

"Only you can determine what happens now," he said to Sordett.

Sordett tilted his head to one side with mock attention. "I've got nothing to say except that I believed I was on a sanctioned operation that turned out to be a tragic mistake. I was recruited under a false flag."

"Absurd. No one will believe that."

"It'll play in court."

"This is as close to court as you get," Barrabas said.

"I see." Sordett had obviously been prepared for that and didn't appear shocked. But even so the light in his eyes went a shade dimmer.

"And don't hope for a dramatic rescue by your former comrades in GIGN. You've been disowned. And the White Brigade won't know where you are until we tell them."

"You might as well paint a target on my back."

"If it comes to that, we'll let you choose the color," Barrabas said.

The French commando nodded. He fell silent for a while, then said, "What do you want from me?"

Barrabas stopped pacing and sat on the edge of the desk. He looked casual, unconcerned, as if the life or death of Maurice Sordett meant nothing to him.

"I want everything you know about the White Brigade operations. Everything you can tell me about the Realm. And I want it all without having to pull teeth for it. When you're done talking, we'll start in on the questioning."

Sordett was in pain. His shoulder had been shattered by the 9 mm slug Barrabas had drilled him with at the battle at Hamelin's place. His jaw was black and blue and he'd lost a number of teeth in the scuffle. But he sat up straight, feigning relaxation, as if he were attending a movie premiere instead of an interrogation.

"Your answer?" Barrabas asked.

Sordett made a dismissive gesture with his hand.

"Wrong answer," Barrabas said. "I've got no time to waste on you. Especially since your value has gone down considerably in the past twenty-four hours."

"That is how bargains are made," Sordett said. "Knock down the value of the other side. Increase your own."

"Yes," Barrabas said. "But sometimes it's true, and not just a bargaining technique. You see, Maurice, we don't need you anymore."

"So you say."

"No," Barrabas replied, "so General Hamelin says. Or said. Before he died he told us a lot. And he left physical evidence that gave us several links to Auguste Bayard that we're checking out."

"So why do you want me?"

"To help us break those links," Barrabas explained. "We know we hurt the Belgian faction of the White Brigade. We've got some leads to a faction in Portugal and France. And we also know the White Brigade set up a smuggling network in Holland called the Bank."

Sordett raised his eyes, genuinely surprised. "You know about that?"

"Hamelin dealt with them extensively. They laundered cash, transferred arms and drugs, appropriated

NATO codes and encryption devices.'' Barrabas had assembled a profile of the group from information the CIA had gleaned, along with sketchy details provided by Hamelin. But he was still lacking the most important details. Names. Places. Strengths of the Bank.

"If you know all that, what's left for me to give you?"

"Corroboration," Barrabas said. "It'll take us time to double-check all the information. We'll get it eventually. But you can save us time. And you can save your neck."

"The Realm has lots of friends in Amsterdam," Sordett said. "It could be very dangerous for you." He smiled at the thought.

"I also have friends in Amsterdam," Barrabas said. "They've been dangerous for years and they're still at it."

"Maybe both sides should meet."

"That'd be a hell of a party," Barrabas said.

Sordett laughed, a smile cutting through the mask of pain. "And you want me to send out the invitations."

Barrabas studied the weathered face of the commando. A high-ranking member of the White Brigade, Sordett was privy to a lot of its secrets and connections. Despite his nonchalant attitude, he had to be considering his chances. And in any negotiation there had to be give-and-take. Barrabas didn't want to steamroller him with harsh tactics unless necessary.

"Let me think about it," Sordett said.

Barrabas nodded. "I was hoping we could do this the civilized way," he said. "Rather than bring in the headshrinkers."

"That's a nice thought," Sordett said.

Perhaps the last rational thought he would have, Barrabas thought, if they had to go the drug route. The intelligence community thoroughly endorsed the concept of better spying through chemistry. The covert chemists had developed a wizard's brew of concoctions that could easily open up a man's head. Unfortunately, they couldn't always close it once the secrets were spilled.

It was a last resort. Barrabas preferred to have the man cooperate of his own free will—while he still had one. One thing in Barrabas's favor was that Sordett knew the score. He'd been in the trade long enough to know he had a zero chance of living in the hands of his former comrades, who would move quickly to silence him. He also had zero chance with his current jailers unless he cooperated.

Sordett sighed loudly, releasing his resistance and his resignation all at once. "People kill for the kind of information you want."

"Or die for it," Barrabas said. "Cooperate and you may walk out of this."

Sordett nodded. "It's worth taking a chance. Considering that I'm already dead as far as the Realm is concerned. Give me a ticket out of here and I'll..." He paused as he carefully selected his words. "I'll collaborate."

Barrabas nodded. Collaborate. As if Sordett were dealing with an occupying power. As if the Realm had been invaded. Well, if that was the way he wanted to think of it, Barrabas wouldn't argue the point. The important thing was that Sordett had chosen to keep his brain unscrambled by chemicals and to volunteer information.

"Fine," Barrabas said. "For starters, tell me everything you can about the Dutch ring and its connections to the Realm. I also want to know about Lili Kavroleira and where she stands in all of this."

"She doesn't stand," Sordett said. "She lies down. She is part of a ring whose specialty is snaring the high and mighty."

"Is she voluntary?"

"Lili lost any say in the matter years ago. She does what she's told."

"And who tells her?" Barrabas said.

Three hours later Barrabas emerged into the haze of the hot afternoon that was baking the white sand of the Belgian coast.

He walked down the beach toward Liam O'Toole, who sat like a tame bear in the sun. Beside the Irishman was a book of poetry, a cooler with a can of soda and an automatic pistol. A tweed cap shaded his eyes as he stared out at the whitecapped horizon.

Lee Hatton was bodysurfing in the water, attentively guarded by Alex Nanos.

Nearby, Billy Two and Claude Hayes were sprawled on the sand, concentrating on cheating each other in a poker game. They were using a French deck of cards bearing a photographic lineup of shapely female nudes.

"You might as well fold now and get it over with," Billy Two said, fanning his cards, then waving their backs toward Hayes.

"Careful with those things," Claude said. "You might knock my eyes out."

"Come on, Claude, your bet."

"All right," he said. "I'll raise you two dollars and a tail feather from Hawk Spirit."

"Throw in your immortal soul and you've got a deal," the Osage replied.

Barrabas stopped watching the high-stakes game and returned to O'Toole. As he drew nearer, O'Toole sat up. "What's the verdict, Colonel?"

"The verdict is guilty," Barrabas said. "But with extenuating circumstances."

"Such as?"

"The Don Quixote syndrome. Sordett went looking for one windmill too many. He saw his involvement in the White Brigade as a quest, and he got caught up in it."

"Did he turn around?"

Barrabas nodded. "Sure as hell did. Umpteen hundred degrees worth. He pointed us toward the Dutchmen, Captain. So you might as well enjoy the scenery while you can."

"We're not going to be here much longer?"

"That's right," Barrabas said. "And I suspect once we get back, this place won't be around much longer, either. The way I see it, the White Brigade is going to knock it off the map."

O'Toole nodded toward the Belgian safehouse manned by Henri Goliard's ESI support staff. "Did you tell that to our hosts?"

"They'll know when they have to know," he said.

Barrabas strolled toward the water, hooked two fingers into his mouth and gave a piercing whistle that panicked a flock of gulls. When Hatton and Nanos looked his way, he signaled for them to come in from the water.

A few moments later they had grabbed a couple of beach towels and joined the other SOBs on the sand.

Nanos quickly toweled himself off, then turned to Lee. "Need any help?"

"Not this century."

"Okay, people, listen up," Barrabas said.

Nanos suddenly found himself thinking of another kind of action. "We in business again, Colonel?"

"You could say that."

"What's on the agenda?"

"For starters," Barrabas said, "we're going to knock off a bank."

THE BANK WAS HEADQUARTERED in the heart of Amsterdam. Several narrow canal-side houses and houseboats served as the main staging and holding areas for the smuggling network. In addition to the well-appointed houseboats and seventeenth-century houses, the Bank had several barges, freighters, sightseeing boats and powerboats at its service.

The CIA and the Dutch and Belgian intelligence services were aware of the network and had tolerated it because it had been useful to them. The Bank provided information and links to the underworld. Like most organizations that worked both sides of the street, the Bank informed only on the competition— other smugglers and arms dealers who were out of favor. In exchange it was allowed to carry out its own business discreetly.

Until Maurice Sordett's capture and subsequent revelations, few outsiders realized just how powerful the Bank had become. It had started as a small but efficient smuggling operation. After being infiltrated by the White Brigade, it had mushroomed into a huge underworld apparatus involved in murder, money laundering, drug and arms trafficking, and anything that could turn a twisted dollar.

One of the latest operations involved withholding a nearly limitless supply of diamonds from the market to create an artificial market demand for diamonds. Taking advantage of some of the long-standing contacts between the Netherlands and Africa, a group of South Africans were mining diamonds covertly and transferring them to the Bank. Drawing upon its black market expertise, the Bank disposed of the gems by using its own cutters or by delivering the stones to jewelers owned by the Realm. In the diamond capital of the world, such largess was easily disguised.

The man who brokered the Bank's diamond deal and many other criminal enterprises was Adolphus Norburg. A native Dutchman known as the Banker, Norburg had served his apprenticeship by embezzling from numerous firms while working as a young broker. After a short stretch in prison he applied his talents on the black market and quickly made a fortune. He was groomed every step of the way by White Brigade infiltrators, who handled him so well he was never quite sure when control of the network slipped from his hands. But as long as he lived in the right style, he wasn't about to complain. And owing to the number of armed men around him, he was unlikely to voice those complaints aloud.

The Bank thus continued to be guided by the White Brigade, although it still looked as if Norburg was holding the reins.

The intelligence on the Bank had been growing over the years. It was like a subterranean culture that had never been exposed to daylight—not until Barrabas got the information from Sordett.

Armed with several key names and addresses, Barrabas passed the word to Walker Jessup. In turn the Fixer used his CIA and NSA contacts to provide a blueprint of the operation. Jessup was able to hand over detailed layouts of the buildings and houseboats controlled by the Bank, along with photos and covert histories of staffers working them.

Now all that remained was to find the right wreckers to tear it all down.

TEN O'CLOCK AT NIGHT was still early in Amsterdam. The narrow canal-side streets echoed with footsteps of lovers moving in tandem with their reflections in the water, of friends walking in the cool night air and, here and there, of staggering drunks.

Nile Barrabas walked alongside the Herengracht canal with his arm around a beautiful woman, his hand casually tucked into her jacket pocket.

Lee Hatton rested her head on his shoulder as if they were sharing a whisper or a private joke. She wore a beret that shadowed her eyes and high heels that announced her presence.

Anyone who looked at them would first see the woman, and only then the man accompanying her. He wore a black denim jacket with the collar turned up and a biker's cap with a brim shielding his eyes. He looked like a man able to take care of such a woman.

They had been walking for nearly half an hour from their drop-off point, hoping to make their appearance as a couple look all the more convincing. They'd strolled over bridges, down streets lined with parked cars and bicycles and along canals congested with moored houseboats, barges and powerboats.

The atmosphere changed as they reached the Herengracht. The Gentlemen's Canal was home to the Amsterdam elite, with exquisite seventeenth-century houses outdoing one another in gabled splendor. The canal-side houses were refined, the streets elegant. Carefully spaced shade trees lined the quay beside narrow three- and four-story buildings capped by ornate spires and gables. The facades of the houses were alight with windows that peered down at the water. Their rooms were like high-ceilinged railroad cars. Some houses abutted their neighbors; others were separated by narrow alleys.

These homes had once been the luxury quarters for traders, the Dutch East Indies merchants who had the world come to them in their ships. Now some of them were home to traders of a different sort.

Barrabas and Hatton slowed as they neared the headquarters of the Bank, where three moored houseboats bobbed in the water. The boats were parallel to three staid houses, boxlike but sleek, with bright paint and homey features that made them seem pleasantly livable. The boats and houses belonged to the Bank. The houseboats were often used as floating vaults for contraband, and could go to the customers on occasion.

"A kiss might be nice," Lee said.

"Why?" Barrabas smiled.

"Because we're being watched."

"It might be nice anyway," he said, as he looked up at the windows and saw dark shadows moving behind the lights.

Barrabas kissed her, savoring the feel of her body against him. He was also grateful for the feel of the 9 mm automatic in her pocket.

They were being careful. Like many genuine lovers who roamed the streets, they had to take precautions in case someone spotted them.

Although Barrabas had studied the layout of the Bank's operation in photos and blueprints, and had driven through the area earlier, he wanted to feel the actual street beneath his feet. He needed to get a sense of the distances between the houses and the canal, and identify the cover the banker's men might use.

"Mmm," Lee said. "Enough. I think we've convinced them." She backed away slightly, but Barrabas still held her pinned with his arm.

"Just to be on the safe side," he said, kissing her again. He pulled away from her a moment later and they continued up the street. Their brief embrace would have been more noticeable if other couples hadn't been strolling in the night. Those lovers might have shared potent moments, but none as loaded as his and Lee's, Barrabas thought.

CLAUDE HAYES TROD WATER in the dark and murky canal.

Like a doctor with a stethoscope, the ex-SEAL listened to voices inside the houseboat's rear bedroom. One voice belonged to a woman who'd been recruited from the Walletjes district to spend an evening aboard and in bed. The party girl's voice was strident.

The night was ending too early for her. She'd obviously expected to crash in the plush confines of the houseboat. But now that the party was over, the man was giving her the boot.

Hayes, still treading water, heard the woman call her host a bastard, a cheat. She'd expected him to pay the fare for the night, not just for a couple of hours. Now she would have to get back to the red-light district in the old quarter of Amsterdam.

She pleaded to stay, but the man would have none of it. In a gruff voice that left no room for debate, he cut her argument short. Hayes heard a slap, then a thump. It sounded as if the woman had been hurtled across the room.

After just enough time to dress, she left the bedroom in a huff, swearing at the client who'd changed the terms on her after she kept her part of the bargain.

The man laughed in a low churlish voice. He was a guard, one of several who stayed aboard the houseboat to protect the Bank's vault. In addition to usual contraband, another package of South African diamonds was arriving tonight.

That was one of the reasons the hooker got pushed away.

She was lucky, Hayes thought. Soon she would have had to vacate the premises in a much harsher manner.

Hayes breathed slowly and kicked, his flippers dragging softly through the water. He wasn't worried about being detected. Designed for shallow water, the closed circuit scuba gear didn't produce any air bubbles to go to the surface.

Hayes was all in black, the color of the night, invisible in the dark water as he held on to the side of the hull with rubber suction grips. He'd also attached a stethoscopelike object to the houseboat, which amplified sounds from inside.

He and Alex Nanos had wired the houseboats to enable them to monitor the conversations inside, coordinating their actions with the land-based team through the UTEL units they'd brought with them for their swim in the Herengracht. The underwater communications devices, with headphones, lung microphones, receiver and a transducer unit, could instantly connect them with the ground team working the back streets, as well as the CIA powerboat that was cruising the canal about three hundred yards away.

The boat was piloted by Bennett, the man who'd literally gone through fire for the Agency, his fierce countenance still scarred after major repairs. The CIA action man in Belgium had attached Bennett to this operation, not because there weren't qualified operatives in the Netherlands, but because he was a man they all could trust.

With his scarred face, Bennett was immediately recognizable. But if all went well, Bennett would hardly be noticed at all.

Not with the fireworks that were going to light up the canal.

Both Hayes and Nanos were specialists in underwater demolition. They'd shaped a number of charges on the houseboats to effect maximum damage when they pulled the switch.

LIAM O'TOOLE SAT in the sturdy crook of a tree on the far side of the canal. He had a perfect line of fire on the trio of houses used by the Bank as well as on the houseboats. But his mission wasn't the boats—just the houses.

At another time he might have felt like a leprechaun, sitting in a tree while the canal flowed around him, carrying with it the well-lit reflection of the mansions flanking the Gentlemen's Canal.

But tonight wasn't a night for magic. It was a night for business. An operation was going down, and whether the SOBs walked away from it or not depended on the Irishman taking care of that business.

He was concealed from both the houses behind him and the target houses across the canal, thanks to the planners of the city, who had so thoughtfully groomed the cobblestoned area around the canal. Thick lush shade trees whispered in the wind all around him, while he prepared to produce another kind of whisper—with the silenced sniper rifle resting in his arms, the same color as the leafy boughs around him.

Despite the name of the organization, the Bank, the people inside the headquarters were not tellers. They were killers, most of them recruited from the underworld or from the ranks of renegade intelligence agents working for the White Brigade.

BILLY TWO WAS HOUSE HUNTING.

Creeping silently across the gabled roof of the Bank's main house, he was hunting with a crossbow, the laser-sighted weapon just one element in the silent arsenal he carried.

He had ropes, garrotes, a knife, a cross bow and an H&K silenced submachine gun. He also had a miniature receiver with a headset to tell him when to go into action.

If that didn't work, he had something more intangible working with him tonight as he prowled the gabled aeries of Amsterdam.

Hawk Spirit.

The Osage's job was simple. And it was most complex. Taking down the Bank could have been one-two-three. The SOBs could have destroyed the houseboats and the mansions easily. But Barrabas wanted to take down the bigger organization that controlled the Bank from afar—the Realm. And to do that, they needed the Banker alive.

Billy Two had drawn the assignment to keep Adolphus Norburg alive—and to silence the gang of White Brigaders assigned to protect him.

As MIDNIGHT APPROACHED the streets cleared, except for two lovers—two lovers who had strolled beside the canal earlier in the evening.

They had been watched then and they were being watched now as they strolled along the canal where the houseboats were moored.

The watchers were inside the trio of houses facing the canal. The lights were out in most of the windows. But the rooms fronting the canal were nonetheless occupied by armed men who had shown an intense interest in the street.

On a night when diamonds were coming in, anyone's presence had to arouse suspicion. Exactly what Barrabas was counting on.

By focusing on the street, the White Brigaders were identifying themselves to Liam O'Toole, who was perched across the canal watching through his night vision scope.

It was a killing view.

By ONE O'CLOCK in the morning the Bank appeared to be closed. Most of the house lights were out and only dim lights shone on the houseboats. Quiet had fallen over the Herengracht except for the sound of water lapping against the brick sides of the canal.

But despite the quiet and the lateness of the hour, the Bank hadn't closed down. Like its legitimate counterparts, it stayed open for special clients—like the man who appeared on the cobblestoned street ten houses along the canal. He'd come out of the alleys and he was carrying a pack slung over his shoulder.

The diamonds had arrived on schedule.

The courier looked like a second generation *kabouter*, descended from one of the hippies who had founded their own Shangri-la in the middle of Amsterdam, sleeping like gnomes in Vondelpark or living in mild anarchist communes in the abandoned factories and apartment blocks.

His long brown hair draped past the epaulets on his khaki jacket. But he wasn't of the peace-and-love variety of hippie. He looked all business, and he looked strong enough to carry out that business. He'd buried his share of men during his rise through the underworld.

Two gunmen followed the courier, keeping to the shadows while they provided backup for him. Though several deliveries had been made before without problem, there was never any guarantee that things would go smoothly.

After all, the man was carrying a glittering fortune.

FROM THE MOMENT he stepped into the street, the courier was watched by the underworld army gathered at the Herengracht headquarters.

White Brigaders and Norburg's henchmen alike carefully watched the progress from Norburg's second floor headquarters in the middle house of the three.

Other eyes, too, watched the courier emerge.

From a black surveillance van parked at an angle about one hundred yards from the Bank property, Nile Barrabas and Lee Hatton had a clear view of the street through long-range scopes.

"This is it," Barrabas said as he watched the courier approach from the other side of the Bank.

"Time to play lovers again," she said.

"Every job has its fringe benefits."

The dark-haired woman nodded, then pulled away from the night vision scope that was flush against the tinted bubble window of the van.

She checked her H&K P7M8 one more time. The compact 9 mm automatic had a squeeze-grip cocking mechanism. Easily concealed, the small pistol packed a lot of power with its 8-round magazine.

Barrabas was carrying his Browning Hi-Power with a 13-round clip, counting on the accuracy and firepower of the 9 mm autoloader to help him through the night's work. But he didn't plan to wade into a free-fire zone with just the automatic.

"Don't forget your purse," he reminded Lee.

She was already ahead of him, picking up the long leather handbag that carried an H&K submachine gun and a couple of spare clips. It also had room for a small Webley Schermuly antiriot pistol and several 38 mm smoke and CS cartridges. It wasn't the most stylish handbag in the world but it was large and functional, carrying everything they needed for a proper date.

They weren't using silencers tonight. The bulky sound suppressors would have been difficult to conceal. Besides, silence wasn't their overriding concern. Tonight's hit was meant to be heard around the world—and around the Realm.

Once the hit went down it was going to go down loud and fast.

Barrabas picked up the small transceiver and spoke two words to Bennett, the CIA action man whose floating communications center was nestled on one side of the canal near the spot where the courier had arrived. "River deep," Barrabas said.

"Mountain high," came Bennett's response.

Barrabas switched off the transceiver, then moved to the back of the van. Bennett would signal the other SOBs in turn. The hit was on.

Though they could have hit the Bank at any time, this was the best moment. The Banker himself, Adolphus Norburg, would be present with most of his henchmen. The hangers-on and the women would have been sent away while the diamond transfer was taking place.

That left only the guilty, the hard-core bankers, on the premises.

Lee Hatton lifted the handle on the back door of the van. The greased door silently opened. She and Barrabas slipped out of the van. She closed the door softly.

She shivered. Whether it was from the cool night air or nerves before battle was hard to tell. It was only natural. It was her bodily instincts kicking in, telling her to think twice before wading into the water.

Barrabas closed his hands around hers, grasping them tight. "Ten minutes from now we'll be riding away from here, just a couple of tourists wondering what the hell all the noise was."

"A lot can happen in ten minutes."

"It sure as hell can," Barrabas said. "Let's make it happen right."

He wrapped his arm around her shoulder and they strolled out into the cobblestoned street. His other hand was coiled around the Browning pistol grip in his left jacket pocket.

They walked slowly down the street, gradually drifting to the center of the road. Then they began to move erratically from the middle of the street to the cars parked along the canal.

Barrabas laughed, adding a drunken spin to his voice. It echoed down the street. The two of them careened toward the White Brigade headquarters, making sure they were loud enough to be noticed.

They had one thing going in their favor. They'd made sure they were seen before, the first time they walked past the Bank. Their reappearance would keep the White Brigaders off balance for a critical few moments while they tried to figure out if the two lovers were legit.

Neither Barrabas nor Hatton dwelt on the flip side of the coin. The White Brigaders were looking out for their own. Anyone who walked into the middle of an underworld transaction was going to be scrutinized most carefully.

As the lovers neared the houseboat into which the man with the diamonds had vanished a few moments before, the courier's two backup men stepped from the shadows. The first was tall and businesslike. He moved straight toward them like a shark. The second hung back, looking up at the Bank's guards in the houses.

They spoke Dutch. It was clear from their tone that neither of them liked what was happening.

Barrabas ignored the tall man's order to stop. Instead he and Lee meandered toward the houseboat, standing between the backup men and the houses.

"I don't like this," the tall man said.

"It's just a guy and a girl," the other man said. He looked up at the house, then at the lovers strolling toward them.

"They picked a hell of a time to go for a walk," the tall man said. "And a hell of a place." Then he barked out a command to the late-night lovers.

Barrabas stopped, as if he'd suddenly noticed the other man's presence. "What do you want?" he asked, in the belligerent tone of a drunk.

"I want you gone," the man said.

Barrabas straightened to his full height, facing the man with a challenge in his eyes and dropping his drunken pose. "You won't be the first," he said.

The eyes of the SOB chieftain burned into the gunman, seeing his past and future in that one steady gaze. Bloody all the way.

Like a predator staring at his quarry, the gunman locked his eyes on Barrabas. But the killing gaze was deflected by the battle-hardened eyes of Barrabas, who'd walked streets like this a dozen times before.

The tall man went for his piece. He cleared a long-barreled revolver from inside his black overcoat in a jerky motion. A thin smile came to his face, making him look like a wild-eyed cowboy.

Barrabas didn't draw his weapon. He turned to his left and pulled the trigger of the Browning Hi-Power in his jacket pocket. The 9 mm slug burned through leather, then through the tall gunman's hide.

Blood and bone splintered from his chest as the bullet chopped him down like a tree. He fired one shot in the air, his last act on earth before collapsing onto the cobblestones.

A blanket of confusion dropped onto the street.

The remaining backup man thought the attack was a rip-off by someone working with the Bank. The watching White Brigaders wondered if their diamond courier was pulling a double cross, trying to make an unplanned withdrawal from the houseboat vaults.

That heavy silence lingered for just a brief moment.

Then a shot rang out from a second floor window, whining across the cobblestone at Barrabas's feet. The shot would have taken him down for keeps if he hadn't stepped back an instant before.

The long-haired courier emerged from the cabin of the houseboat, carrying a pack slung over his shoulder, an automatic in his hand. He jumped onto the rail and brought his weapon to bear on the street, quickly searching out his targets.

Just as he was swinging his automatic toward Barrabas, Lee Hatton aced him with two shots from the self-cocking 9 mm pistol. The *kabouter* toppled eyeless back onto the houseboat.

It happened in just seconds. The remaining gunman on the street debated whether to join in the fray or run for his life. Finally he decided. He spun on his heels and ran down the cobblestone.

Barrabas let him go, concentrating instead on the second floor window of the Bank, firing two rounds at the glass where the shot had come from. He and Hatton then hoofed it away from the houseboats.

The house lights went out. The White Brigaders poured through the door and toward the shadows in the alley.

ACROSS THE CANAL, Liam O'Toole sighted along the facade of the high-gabled building.

The G3SG/1 H&K sniper rifle had a 20-round box magazine and could fire full- or semiauto. The Irishman had the selector on semiautomatic.

As soon as the shoot-out began, O'Toole blew out the second floor windows, moving left to right, squeezing off round after round with deadly effect. The Lasergage Night Sight LWS 1060 gave him a clear view of the gunmen lined up at the second and third floor windows, who thought they were hidden in darkness.

O'Toole corrected their assumption with a fusillade of 7.62 mm rounds that knocked them into permanent darkness. The ex-Army marksman made every shot count.

With methodical grace, he poured quick but accurate fire into the buildings. Plates of glass shattered and sliced down toward the street in spearlike shards. Two gunmen came with them, hurtling down headfirst into the cobblestones.

O'Toole slapped in another magazine, flicked the selector to full-automatic, then coated the Bank headquarters with a heavy metal blizzard.

Several wild shots came his way once the White Brigade defenders observed the rifle flashes. The bullets sluiced into the water, chipped off the brick edges of the canal and chomped into the bark of the tree.

To avoid getting hit, O'Toole dropped from the bough and moved behind the tree.

Right now he was the number-one attraction on the White Brigade's hit parade. But that would change any moment now, the Irishman hoped, as another barrage of lead thwacked into the tree, biting off strips of bark and spitting them into the air.

THE TWO BLACK-CLAD SHAPES had knifed through the dark water of the canal, their flippers propelling them just under the surface as they sped away from the houseboats. Unreeled behind them was an umbilical cord of wire-bound primacord designed for underwater use.

Safely out of range of the houseboats, they broke the surface, then swam silently to their command detonation post. By gouging out bricks from the side of the canal wall, they'd created footholds, handholds and a niche for their hell box.

After hooking up the wire to the small blasting machine, they waited for a signal.

They didn't have to wait long. The first shot was echoing in the night when it was followed by a second. Then came the Irishman's steady rain of sniper fire.

Alex Nanos gripped the side of the canal, ready to push off into the water. "This is it, Claude," the Greek said. "Give them our best."

"Loud and clear," Hayes said. Then he pressed the hell-box plunger, triggering an immediate blast through the detonating cord.

The cord ran along the bottom of the canal, then branched out into a trident shape, each fork leading to the plastic explosive charges they'd planted on the hulls.

The houseboats blew simultaneously. The muffled blasts shredded the bottoms of the boats, ripping out the hulls and smashing the boxlike crafts with the force of a tidal wave.

They rocked against their moorings, lifted out of the water for a moment before groaning back down. Suddenly weighted by the flood of water surging through the sundered hulls, the vaults of the Bank began a steady descent toward the canal bottom.

Suddenly finding themselves watching over flaming, sinking wrecks, the gunmen on guard duty scrambled for the deck, some grabbing weapons, most knocked senseless.

A thickset man scrambled from the middle houseboat, carrying a shotgun. Standing atop the tilting roof, he blasted one round aimlessly into the street, then aimed at the alley where Barrabas and Lee Hatton had sought cover. Suddenly he pitched forward, bouncing face first on the roof of the houseboat, then sliding into the water.

Blood streamed from the shotgunner's chest where Liam O'Toole had sniped him.

Barrabas stepped out of the alley, scanned the building. Rifle barrels sprouted through the jagged windows. He sprayed a burst of full-auto fire from the Heckler & Koch subgun.

While the 9 mm slugs forced the gunners from the windows, Lee Hatton stepped from the alley and thumped a CS cartridge into the second floor window of the middle house. Barrabas covered her while she fired several more cartridges, blanketing the building with a thick cloud of smoke and gas.

Panic spread with the stinging gas and smoke billowing through the rooms. The gunners who'd been looking at the trashed houseboats a moment ago, now had their own house to look after. They streamed from it as from a house on fire.

CLAUDE HAYES EMERGED from the floating wreckage, bobbing up and down among a splintery assortment of hull-length boards. Beside him the Greek appeared. Both swam toward the edge of the canal, wending their way through the debris.

The houseboat was on its way to the bottom.

And the well-heeled rats were deserting it.

ONE OF THE FIRST OUT of the Bank building was Adolphus Norburg, hustled between the strong arms of two White Brigade enforcers.

They'd acted the moment the battle started, getting him away from the second floor and waiting for further developments. When the Bank began to come down around them they guided the Banker toward the exit.

As soon as they emerged into the alley, one of the enforcers hurtled into the open, spun around and aimed a submachine gun at the front of the alley.

But there was no one there.

He motioned to the Banker, who stepped out into the alley. The second enforcer followed. Then the trio headed down the alley.

They saw and heard no one.

Until an Osage Indian fell from the sky, landing on the shoulders of the lead gunman.

Billy Two used the impact to slow his descent from the nylon line with which he'd rappeled down the three-story building. As he jumped away from the man's shoulders, he snap-kicked the back of the man's head.

The gunman fell forward. Billy Two matter-of-factly elbowed Norburg in the face, sending the Banker sprawling backward into his second guard.

The remaining White Brigader regained his balance by flattening out against the wall. But before he could level his automatic at the Osage, Billy Two let out a war cry, jumped over the fallen Banker and hammer-fisted the gunman's wrist against the wall.

The gun dropped.

So did the White Brigader, after the Osage kneed him in the rib cage. There was a loud crack and the man collapsed.

Adolphus Norburg groaned and looked up at the black-haired guerrilla fighter through dazed eyes. Billy Two reached down for him. The Banker tried to sink into the earth, pleading in Dutch to the Osage, who appeared to him as a barbarian.

Billy Two smiled. "No speakum Dutch," he said, lifting the paymaster up by the collar, noticing the blood all over his silk shirt. He pushed him back against the wall.

Disconcerted by the smile, still panic-stricken, the man said, "English?" Then he turned at the sound of footsteps and saw the man in the black jacket coming down the alley. The same man had strolled by the Bank before with a black-haired woman. He carried a submachine gun.

"English will do just fine," Barrabas said.

"What do you want?" Norburg asked, turning. "The diamonds?"

Barrabas shook his head. "No."

Norburg looked at the weapon. "Don't kill me."

"Relax. You just won the lottery."

"What do you mean?"

"We need someone alive," Barrabas told him. "Someone who can help break the real bank down in Paris."

"Bayard?" Norburg said, his face turning pale. "You're going against Bayard?"

"You got it," Barrabas said. "Let's go." He led the way, nosing the Heckler & Koch in front of him as they headed back down the alley.

Billy Two hustled the Banker along, practically picking the stunned man off his feet.

"It's Nile," Barrabas announced as he reached the mouth of the alley.

"It's about time," Lee Hatton said, standing guard.

They made a dash through the smoke and the madness as CS-laced White Brigaders continued to stagger from the buildings. Some of them moved toward the team of SOBs as they neared the quay. Barrabas triggered a full-auto burst, kicking up the cobblestones and sweeping the enemy back.

Billy Two picked up the Banker and flung him headfirst into the water. He landed with a loud splash, then came up kicking and screaming.

Suddenly a hand clamped over his mouth and pulled him under the water. Alex Nanos and Claude Hayes towed the startled man toward the CIA powerboat that was idling nearby, waiting for them and their precious cargo.

Adolphus Norburg kicked and twisted—until Nanos rapped him on the side of the head. Then he moved along like deadweight.

After firing more lead into the cobblestones, Barrabas, Billy Two and Lee Hatton dived headfirst into the canal to help safeguard the withdrawal they'd just made from the Bank.

CHAPTER FIFTEEN

Erika Dykstra brushed her bright blond hair down her left shoulder as she sat on the edge of the bed. The brush whisked quickly through her hair before getting tangled at the ends. She worked it free and repeated the motions.

Each movement was carefully studied by her select audience, Nile Barrabas, who had entered a short while ago through the iron-gated courtyard at the back of her seventeenth-century Begijnhof house.

The house had been around nearly as long the Dykstra clan had been involved in the smuggling trade.

But this morning, Erika hardly looked like an empress of the black market. She wore a cream-colored silk chemise that seemed just a shade too short for her long legs and a bit too tight for her full bust. The silk undergarment was one of the legitimate items carried by Dykstra Imports, one of several subsidiaries of the Netherlands Import Management Company. Erika had put it on before admitting Nile Barrabas to her home shortly after dawn.

A morning chill flooded the room and coated the parquet floor with an icy sheen. It matched the icy bridge that spanned the gulf between them.

Barrabas sat on the slanted sill in the recessed window. Now and then he turned to look at the skyline of Amsterdam behind him, although he was interested in a more imposing view.

Sometime friend, sometime lover, Erika Dykstra had a long history with Barrabas. It was a history she'd thought had come to an end the last time he vanished from her life.

Her skeptical blue eyes measured the SOB chieftain. Her eyelids moved rapidly, like shutters changing screens every few moments. Hate, love, lust and curiosity flashed from her haughty expression.

Despite her caution, she was curious about what brought him back to Amsterdam. It showed in her eyes and in the movement of her body.

Barrabas savored the symphony of curves that rippled beneath the silk. Erika wasn't a wide-eyed girl, nor was she ready to collect a pension. She was at that magical age when her ripe figure still sparked daydreams and the experience radiating from her blue eyes showed that she'd toured a world most hadn't seen.

A world once shared by Nile Barrabas.

"You still think you can just walk in here any time and I'll drop everything for you?" she asked.

Barrabas nodded. "Yes." He tried to mask the smile fighting to emerge.

"I do have a life aside from you," she said. "There could be someone else. Did it ever cross your mind that maybe there's someone who commands my interest more than a...a *tourist* who strolls through now and then?"

"No."

She whapped the hairbrush on the bed, spending some of the fury that had been bottled up inside ever since he left her a couple of missions ago.

"Dammit, Nile, you're such a bastard."

"From head to toe."

"You're the most frustrating man—"

"Absolutely the worst."

She shook her head, furious that he was agreeing with her.

Barrabas shrugged. He'd never made any pretense about their relationship. It was pure and simple. Well, he thought, perhaps not so pure.

Erika recited the litany then. "We've got a screwed-up past and no future."

"Just the here and now," Barrabas said.

"Every time you come here, you throw my life out of gear—and then you take off again like a sightseer. Is that what you're doing here today? Have you come to see the sights?"

"I like the sights I'm seeing right now," Barrabas said. "But actually I came here to see some fireworks.

Her eyes flickered. "Are you in trouble?"

"More or less. Haven't you been reading the papers?"

"The Bank on the Herengracht—" She caught herself in midsentence, not really wanting to know any more details than he was free to tell.

Barrabas nodded.

"Are the others with you?"

"Here and there. Quartered around the town for now."

"And you're looking for sleeping quarters?"

"Yes."

"I don't know what to think," she said.

"I think you're here right now and so am I. That's what I think."

Erika glided away from the bed. "I think you're right," she said, dropping all the inhibitions and caution that had chilled their conversation since he'd arrived at her villa overlooking the Amstel River.

Barrabas embraced her, his lips prowling the side of her neck as she turned her head. Her blond hair fell like silk over her light skin. He ran his fingers through her hair, then down her back, his hands coating her body.

She rippled against him, twisting from left to right. The straps of the chemise dropped down her shoulders, revealing her breasts.

She unbuttoned his shirt hurriedly, her hands eager to snatch him back from the past they'd lost. Though some doubts remained in her mind, her body was in charge now and her body said yes.

Because like every other time they came together, this time could be their last.

Barrabas lifted her onto her toes, pulled her to him in a hungry grasp. Then they finished undressing in a lust-filled walk to the bed.

He hovered above her for a moment, looking down at the body that enflamed his and into the eyes that had entrapped his soul for decades.

An hour later Erika was asleep and Barrabas was sitting by the window on a tilted-back chair, his feet propped up, the heady smoke of his cigar streaming out the open window.

He was thinking about what it would be like if he retired from the trade and could spend all his time with her.

It would be horrible, he decided. There would be no moments like the one they'd just shared. Love was rare and he didn't want to flood the market. Otherwise entropy would creep in.

Nile Barrabas kept alive by staying on the edge, not in a soft bed with a beautiful woman.

He was glad to see her, but that wasn't the only reason he'd come. The Netherlands Import Management Company had a long and glorious covert history. He'd first encountered it back in Vietnam when Erika and her brother, Gunther, were mining the black market trade, smuggling out Vietnamese artifacts, gems and even people, many of them CIA operatives who'd been exposed and marked for death.

The Dykstra firm also handled a number of arms shipments for the CIA and CIA clients, expanding their reach throughout the covert arena. By staying clear of drugs, the smuggling outfit had stayed in the good graces of police and intelligence services.

It helped matters that Gunther Dykstra had been a member of the Whiskey Company, the Marine Close Combat Unit the Netherlands used for antiterrorist operations. Although he had a reputation as a wild man, he was a dependable businessman whose business just happened to be smuggling. It wasn't exactly a criminal enterprise. Nor was he preparing to enter a monastery.

It was known that while he would cut corners, Gunther wasn't a cutthroat like so many others who worked the trade. His territory was somewhere in between, a gray corridor patrolled by spooks, con men and thieves, switching roles from operation to operation.

Though he was streetwise enough to plot the course for the smuggling network, more often than not Gunther was content to be the brawn while Erika was the brains of their operation.

Erika suddenly stirred and rolled over. Her arm fell onto the empty space beside her. Her hand patted the bedspread softly at first, then with more and more force. Finally her eyes snapped open and darted wildly around the room before settling on Nile.

"You're still here?" she said, in the voice of someone who'd just seen a miracle.

"For a day or two," he said. "Until I can set up a few things."

"I see," she said, taking her robe from the bedpost. "You mean what's happened so far has only been a warm-up?"

Barrabas shrugged. "It had to be quick, and it had to be loud," he said. "Otherwise they'd get even more powerful. They'd win over some people who so far have been sitting on the fence."

"Who're *they*?" she asked, donning the robe.

"The Realm."

She laughed. "That's just a fairy tale."

"It's grim," Barrabas said, "but it's no fairy tale."

He elaborated on the Realm and the White Brigade, revealing just enough details to convince Erika of the threat they posed. After sketching in the powers behind the throne, Barrabas mentioned the amount of matériel diverted from NATO bases—much of it supplied by the United States.

"Aside from that," Barrabas continued, "the Realm has subverted some high NATO officials, bought a general or two, and opened up links to the Soviets, who are also scheming to get the United States out of Europe. The Realm is prepared to sell the Soviets American codes and code-breaking equipment. Or to wield that threat to push Uncle Sam out of Europe."

"Why tell me this now?" she asked.

"Because I want you and Gunther to know what you're up against when the Realm comes calling."

"The rough stuff is Gunther's department," she said. "Maybe you should talk to him."

"Yeah," Barrabas said. "That's what I figured. Where can I find him?"

"Where else?" she said. "In the clouds."

"Do these clouds have an address?"

"He's at a place called the Bookhouse Café. Don't laugh! It's true. He bought it about three months ago."

Barrabas couldn't help laughing. It was hard to imagine Gunther Dykstra anywhere but in his sixties' nightclub on the Leidsepleine or one of the raunchier clubs he haunted in the Walletjes district.

"The Bookhouse, huh? Where is it? And since when did Gunther get culture?"

"Since he wanted to meet a different kind of girl."

"What kind is that?"

"The kind who doesn't swing upside down from chandeliers," she said. "You know, those lovely girls he staffs his club with. The ones so fond of shedding their clothes and dancing on bearskin rugs. Surely you've seen them when we've gone there."

"Never noticed," Barrabas said. "Must have been the company I kept."

Erika smiled. She gave Barrabas Gunther's new address.

LIAM O'TOOLE DRIFTED through the first floor of the Bookhouse, which turned out to be a secondhand bookstore with some new titles toward the front. One entire wall was devoted to an assortment of international magazines and newspapers to fuel discussions in the café upstairs.

For a moment, the Irishman felt a bit envious of Gunther. Then he realized he preferred walking through a bookstore to living in one. And though it would be nice to settle into a more sedate life for a while, the source of his poetry was the life he led with the SOBs. Retiring from war would kill his work.

Still, it was pleasant to savor the atmosphere of the shop. He glided up and down the aisles, listening to the soft folk music that emanated from speakers in the walls. That was one plus for the shop. It wasn't playing piano concertos as so many others did, as if they were churches instead of places dedicated to the spreading of knowledge.

O'Toole did notice one major flaw. The poetry section was severely lacking. There wasn't a single copy of his chapbook, *Warmongrel*. Other than that, O'Toole liked what he saw.

The Bookhouse fiction shelves held a bizarre mixture of British, American, French and German novels, both in their original language and translated into Dutch. A global village, Dykstra style.

Barrabas, too, was wending his way through the shop, checking it out as a front for the smuggling operation more than as an actual bookstore.

Gunther had done well.

The woman who ran the shop was a bohemian type, looking every bit like an import from a Manhattan beatnik bar circa 1956. She was obviously the real thing and had selected the right kind of stock to attract a wide clientele.

It was a good place for Gunther to do business, Barrabas thought. The café upstairs was a natural place for just about anyone to visit. And Gunther could conduct his covert business from the offices on the third floor, accessed via a staircase cordoned off on the second floor.

"What do you think?" Barrabas asked O'Toole. "Has Gunther gone intellectual on us?" He shook his head as if to dispel the alien thought. "It's hard to picture him soaking up all this culture."

O'Toole laughed. He was holding several books. "If he reads these, he's got it," he said. The top two books—*I, Jan Cremer* and *Jan Cremer Rides Again*—were by Jan Cremer, the Netherlands' answer to Jack Kerouac and Henry Miller.

"Either he's really expanded his horizons," Barrabas said, "or he's got a hell of a place to win friends and run guns from. Let's find out."

O'Toole nodded and headed for the cash register, where he paid for the books and an *International Herald Tribune*.

They went upstairs to the café and soaked up some afternoon sun and coffee at a window table overlooking the Kalverstraat.

After they paid their bill they approached a curtained alcove beside the cash register. A young blond woman with a streak of silver running through her braided hair moved from behind the cash register to cut them off. *"Verboden,"* she said.

"Dat begrijp ik niet," Barrabas replied, feigning ignorance, as if it were the most normal thing in the world for him to be here.

The woman looked exasperated and was about to call for help when Barrabas spoke in English. "Sorry," he said. "We're friends of Gunther's from America. He said to call on him when we could."

"He's not expecting you?" she said, switching easily to English.

"Gunther likes the unexpected."

She smiled. "Maybe you do know him," she said. "But even so, I shouldn't let you go up. There are so many dangerous people about these days."

"Lady, if we came to hurt him," Barrabas argued, "we wouldn't stop to ask your permission, would we?"

"No, I guess you wouldn't. Go ahead."

She waved them on.

Barrabas noticed her furtive smile. No doubt she had already signaled the third floor that visitors were on their way.

When they reached the top of the stairs a glass door swung halfway open, revealing the pug-nosed profile of a large bodyguard. Inside, at the far end of the room, sat Gunther Dykstra hunched over a chessboard. Though his eyesight had always been perfect, he was sporting a pair of glasses that made him look positively scholarly.

"Herr Professor," Barrabas said.

Dykstra looked up from the board, a white knight in his hand.

The bodyguard who had opened the door had a piece at his fingertips, a SIG-Sauer P-226 automatic pistol. Though it was holstered, it would have taken only a fraction of a second to become operative.

Gunther whooped and rose from behind his desk. "Barrabas!" he thundered. "How the hell are you?"

"Alive and kicking," Barrabas said, as he and O'Toole slipped into the inner office of Gunther Dykstra, smuggler, black marketer and, apparently, chess master in training.

The bodyguard, whose hand had fallen away from the holster, quietly closed the door.

Dykstra practically sprinted across the room to pump Barrabas's hand. "Nile," he said, "good to see you."

"And you," Barrabas said, clasping his shoulder. "Hell, in this racket it's good to see anyone who's not taking a shot at you."

The blond-haired Dutchman took Liam's hand next, letting out a mock growl as he squeezed the Irishman's massive mitt. The two of them contested steel grips for a moment before they both broke up laughing.

"The bard of the battlefield," Gunther said to the Irishman. "And how's my favorite old druid doing?"

"I'd be doing a lot better if you carried my latest book in your shop."

"Sorry. We must be all sold out."

O'Toole held up the books he'd picked up in the shop downstairs. "At least you're carrying this rogue's stuff."

"Ah, yes," Gunther said, studying the name on the top book. "Jan Cremer. A great writer. So I hear. I plan on reading him soon."

Barrabas laughed as he and O'Toole dropped into the soft-cushioned chairs facing the Dutchman's desk. "Same old Gunther," Barrabas said. "Thank God. For a moment there I thought you'd become a college professor."

Gunther swept his hand around the room, the gesture taking in the chessboard, the leather-bound books and tasteful prints lining the wall behind him—trappings of a world previously alien to him.

"All this comes with the territory," Gunther said. "It's mostly for appearance's sake, but to tell you the truth, it's a lot more peaceful than living in the nightclub day and night. I don't know how I survived there."

"It's a nice setup here," Barrabas said. "You seem to be doing well."

"Booked solid, brother." Gunther reached into the bottom drawer of his desk and took out a bottle of *oude jenever* and a trio of shot glasses. As he poured a slow-detonating gin for each of them, he said, "Before you tell me what trouble you've brought me this time—although I have an idea—let's have a drink."

"There's always a first time," O'Toole said, grabbing his shot glass.

Barrabas tossed down the innocent-looking but loaded Dutch gin and suddenly remembered a hundred nights in Amsterdam, spread out over the years, in the company of Gunther and Erika Dykstra. The Dutchman was a hell-raiser and Erika was a hell of a woman. Outside of the SOBs, they were the closest thing to family he had.

"Now, my friends," Gunther said. "What are you about?"

"We're about to go to war." Barrabas filled Gunther in on the Realm and the White Brigade.

Much like his sister, Gunther was unbelieving at first. "The Realm is the world's worst-kept secret," he said. "It's just the dream of some crazy French king and his so-called royal court. Hell, you can buy a half dozen countesses in the red-light district alone."

"That's what you're supposed to believe," Barrabas said. "A dream. But it's a bad dream about to come true unless we put them in the dark where they belong.''

O'Toole spun the empty shot glass on the table. ''Once word started to get out about the Realm, they put up a smoke screen around them using their contacts in the media to make their activities look like foolish but noble pursuits.''

''But there's nothing noble about murder,'' Barrabas said. ''And that's what they're into right now. They're starting a purge—much like some other crazy dreamers called the SS did years ago. No one believed it would ever happen.'' He outlined the covert campaign of terror and entrapment waged by the White Brigade so far, and the direction they were going.

Gunther nodded. ''You think we can stop them? If they're really that powerful?''

''We already let them know what we can do the other night.''

''On the Herengracht?'' Gunther asked. The look in his eyes hinted that he already knew the answer. A man in his business knew the ins and outs of the covert battlefield.

''Yes,'' Barrabas said. ''We put the Bank out of business. They were working for the Realm. And so now the Realm has to look around for another smuggling network.''

''I think I know where this is heading.''

''Right,'' Barrabas said. ''They'll probably be contacting you soon.''

''They already have,'' Gunther said. ''Last night, as a matter of fact, one of their emissaries came around, making inquiries. They wanted me to do some work on the wrong side of the street.''

''What did you tell them?''

"I told them they could kiss my Royal Marine ass." Gunther laughed and pounded his hand on the table so hard the shot glasses danced.

"They'll be back," Barrabas said.

"What makes you so sure?"

"Right now there's about three hundred police and intelligence ops putting the heat on all the other rings but yours. The CIA and company are really going to town on this one. The Realm will have to come to you."

"And when they do?"

"Tell them you've reconsidered," Barrabas said. "Cut a deal with them with prices so steep they'll believe you."

"And then?"

"And then we can track any shipments they send through your ring. We can stop the shipments, destroy them or trace them to the Realm."

Gunther nodded slowly. "And then?" he said again.

"And then those same intelligence people will probably give you a get-out-of-jail-free card for another ten years or so. Along with a substantial bounty."

"Good," Gunther said. "If I'm still alive I'll be able to spend it."

"If any of us are alive," Barrabas said, "we'll help you."

CHAPTER SIXTEEN

Pierre Duval had survived nearly as many wars as Nile Barrabas. It showed in the weathered lines of his face as he sat on the terrace and watched the convoy of cars roaring into his paved courtyard.

Chances were that he would live or die depending on the actions of the man in the lead car, the former Special Forces colonel whom everyone was touting as their last hope against the Realm.

Duval had claimed the title for years. Perhaps that was the problem, he thought. Too many years had passed. Too much waiting, not enough fighting.

Despite the danger the man represented, Duval's eyes were calm, his breathing easy. There was a season for everything. Even for war.

As he watched the coarse-haired colonel stride across the courtyard, Duval was sure the season had come.

He went downstairs to meet him.

BARRABAS HAD ARRIVED at Duval's Parisian headquarters on rue St. Louis-en-l'Ile a full day before the rest of the covert chieftains would gather for a summit meeting.

Like the residences of the retired presidents and diplomats who'd settled on Ile St. Louis, Pierre Duval's fortresslike mansion blended old-world charm with high-tech security devices. The paved courtyard's ivy-covered walls and galleries were well protected by servants and guards.

Duval, though retired from the SDECE, still lived close to the center of power in Paris. The Palais de Justice and headquarters of the *police judiciare* were located on the nearby Ile de la Cité. Many of his contacts were within walking range.

The SDECE had been reorganized and renamed DGSE, Direction générale de la sécurité extérieure, but many of Duval's associates were still active and loyal to him. And some of them still considered themselves SDECE men.

With all the manpower and funds at his disposal, Duval might as well have been the acting head of an intelligence service. Duval Associates International included a private think tank under its corporate umbrella. Known in the trade as an information boutique, it was a clandestine matchmaker and vetting service, and advised corporate and political powerbrokers.

The think tank served another covert function. It infiltrated the Realm at every opportunity, placing Duval's people in key positions. His spies' information allowed Duval's private security company to gather more armaments in the war against the Realm.

Duval's enmity with Auguste Bayard had continued long after they both left their respective French intelligence services. While Bayard became the power behind the Realm, Duval commanded the opposition forces.

Soon their intrigues would break out into open warfare. That outbreak was heralded by the arrival of the SOBs at his well-guarded enclave.

"THANK YOU FOR COMING ahead of the others," Duval said in flawless English, stretching out his hand as he met Barrabas at the courtyard entrance.

"I figured we should have our own summit," Barrabas said, clasping his hand. "Tomorrow when all the heads meet, there may be more words than action. I wanted to see if we could do business together."

"Are we soldiers fighting a lost cause?" Duval said. "But you and I think alike. Perhaps we'll find a way out."

He glanced curiously at the three cars that had passed through the iron gates. The SOBs had left two of the cars and stood beside the middle one, a dark Citroën that held two passengers.

Duval had been prepared to receive Barrabas and his SOBs. Walker Jessup, the Fixer, had specifically said there would be six of them, when he set up the meeting. Not eight.

"More friend of yours?" Duval asked.

"Not exactly friends," Barrabas said. "More like calling cards."

"Who are they?" Duval asked.

"Maurice Sordett," Barrabas said. "Late of the White Brigade. I thought you'd like to talk to him."

Duval's weathered face brightened. "I was hoping to share in the intelligence from his debriefing—but I didn't expect a chance to see the renegade myself."

"You'll find he's become very cooperative," Barrabas said. "He's finally realized we're about his last friends on earth."

"Perhaps because you're the only ones who aren't trying to kill him," Duval said.

"As long as he keeps his end of the bargain, we won't."

"And his companion?" Duval asked, nodding at the Citroën.

"Adolphus Norburg," Barrabas said. "Otherwise known as the Banker. He, too, is willing to talk. I thought you'd find him useful in helping to unravel Auguste Bayard's empire."

The silver-haired intelligence veteran looked stunned that Barrabas could so casually offer him such a prize. He was aware of the importance of the gifts Barrabas had brought him. They were proof positive that Colonel Barrabas still knew what he was about. His reputation was deserved.

With Sordett's knowledge of the military capacity of the Realm and the Banker's input on the Realm's financial dealings, Duval would finally be able to topple the man who'd been his sworn enemy for decades. "I'm forever in your debt," he said.

Barrabas smiled. "Not forever. Perhaps just a day or two. Until I ask you to return the favor."

Duval nodded, granting the favor before it was asked. He enjoyed working with forthright men. They weren't common in the intelligence business.

The two strolled through the brick-bordered gardens that stood like islands in the courtyard.

Both men needed each other. To successfully invade the Realm of Auguste Bayard, Barrabas needed Duval's backing. While the SOBs could wield the weapons of war against the White Brigade troops, it was Duval who controlled access to the corporate battlefields where a more subtle warfare was being waged.

By combining forces they could attack on both fronts.

After conversing for a while, Barrabas and Duval walked back toward the cars.

Barrabas nodded toward O'Toole. The Irishman opened the door of the Citroën, then ushered the two men out. Both Sordett and Norburg were happy to step into the light.

"Welcome to the enemy camp," Barrabas said. "You're in the heart of it now."

Sordett looked evenly at the former SDECE headman. He nodded curtly like an equal.

For a split second Duval studied Sordett as if he were a specimen under a microscope. Then, softening to the realities of the situation, he returned the nod. In that short time his gaze had acknowledged the good Sordett once had done, the damage he'd caused and his chance to win redemption.

The Banker was another creature entirely. A cipher. A computer. He worked with facts and figures. The facts were simple. He had to do what he was told if he wanted to live. The figures were the secret bank accounts he wished to keep. Norburg looked cautiously around, as if trying to sniff out some hidden danger, some unseen trap.

"Don't worry," Duval told him. "If the time arrives to get rid of you, you won't see it coming. You won't even know it is happening. I promise."

Norburg stepped back, then looked around for some sign of compassion. But the men around him had a limited supply. Though they would bargain with him, they wouldn't pretend they enjoyed it.

"Monsieur Duval will see to your needs while you're here," Barrabas said.

Even as he spoke a half dozen of Duval's men stepped into the courtyard, ready to escort Sordett and Norburg away.

"Give him your full cooperation," Barrabas continued. "Hold nothing back. And one more thing—hope we win. If this war goes against us, you'll be on the front lines."

Both men silently nodded, accepting the bargain. Either they were in all the way or they were six feet under.

THE NEXT DAY the covert chieftains and their retinues arrived at Duval's headquarters. Mitchell Rhodes, the CIA covert operator, had Bennett in tow, whose reputation as one of the CIA's best action men was enhanced by the scarred face. A few other CIA operatives had come along for the powwow, including a man who apparently worked in the role of a journalist who'd been keeping track of the Realm.

Henri Goliard, the Belgian ESI man, was accompanied by several hard-looking men. They were all seasoned operatives he could trust from the covert group code-named Diana.

The host's private army was stationed inside and outside the mansion. Many of the men who stood guard for Duval were older than usual for that kind of duty. But they were experienced. They had the look of men who'd trekked across their share of battlefields in their old SDECE days. Because of that service they now enjoyed trekking across the finely carpeted mansion, still servants of the same master.

War-horses in tweeds, Barrabas thought, still willing to go to war if necessary. He noticed a couple of them sizing him up as he approached Duval, who had just broken away from a spirited conversation with Henri Goliard.

The SDECE man was standing by a copperplated fireplace mantel flanked by built-in bookcases and a pair of armed guards posing as servants.

Barrabas glanced at the two old soldiers who were studying his every move. "Those old war-horses weren't recruited from butler school, were they?"

Duval smiled. "Everyone has a place in our organization, whether they are old war-horses or young colts," he said. "That's the secret of loyalty in this game. My people know I'll take care of them from cradle to grave."

"And sometimes they get sent there ahead of time."

"True," Duval agreed. "But to keep on living, sometimes we have to risk death. But I believe you know that."

"Everyone in this room knows that," Barrabas said. "And they're all taking a hell of a risk tonight. If the Realm launched an all-out attack on your place right now, there'd be damn few of us left to go against Bayard."

"That's why I've doubled security tonight," Duval explained. "And what about your people? Are they still in the area?"

"They're around," Barrabas said.

"I haven't seen them."

"That's the idea. If your people haven't seen them, then the White Brigaders won't, either."

"Ah, there's your man, Jessup," Duval said, looking across the room. "It appears he's finally winding down. By now I imagine he's told each and every man here that only he can pull this operation off and that everyone else is counting on him."

"He does lay it on thick," Barrabas said, watching Walker Jessup move from group to group, chatting with the clandestine headmen. As the common denominator among the crowd, he'd been the pivotal man in getting them all together. Jessup's words, like those of an oversize Solomon, carried a lot of weight with the covert controllers. He'd worked with all of them individually and had never burned any of them.

The Fixer drifted closer to Barrabas and Duval, then stopped to speak with a stone-faced man in his early thirties. Solidly built and elegantly dressed, he looked like a gunman in a tuxedo.

"That's the reporter you praised so highly yesterday," Duval said to Barrabas. "The one you said I should meet."

"Yes, Francis Rollins."

Duval nodded. "I'm familiar with his work," he said. "Or at least the material that appears under his byline. But he doesn't look like a reporter. Is that just a cover?"

Barrabas shook his head. "No. He's real enough. He can write his own material if he has to. Hell," Barrabas said, "he's no Miss Manners but he does know a lot about etiquette. And about court manners—particularly in the Realm. His briefing gave me some new avenues to explore—and hopefully to close off. I'm sure he'll do the same for you."

Francis Rollins, well-known as a reporter and society columnist in Europe and the United States, had cultivated a reputation as a jet-setter. To many he was more interesting than the people he wrote about. This gave him carte blanche to ricochet from site to site, to mix with society. His affairs were legendary. But it was his less-known work that had made him a legend in the intelligence world.

He killed with a pen just as easily as he did with a sword.

Rollins was attached to a CIA research division known as Science and Sociology. Because of the initials, S&S, the operatives were known as the Sword and Sorcery unit. They were tasked with studying world leaders and discovering everything they could about them, separating fact from rumor. They also kept tabs on would-be world leaders like Auguste Bayard.

Although glib columns about world leaders and high-society types appeared regularly in newspapers and magazines under the Francis Rollins byline, the real profiles he wrote were for a much more restricted audience.

Rollins's CIA-oriented profiles outlined the weaknesses and strengths of Realm backers, described their habits, vices and fears and suggested ways they could be threatened, befriended or bought off by Company dirty tricksters. They also detailed their schedules and haunts to provide a field guide for assassins.

Rollins had been following Bayard for years, writing favorable articles about the United Realm of Europe movement and carefully giving the impression that he just might be able to be cultivated by them. It wasn't the first time a journalist was co-opted by the people he was studying.

Rollins forwarded his damaging information to men like Mitchell Rhodes—and soon Pierre Duval.

The S&S man's work paralleled that of Duval. Duval's think tank had funded a so-called ancestral heritage foundation, which meticulously detailed the illustrious family trees of modern French royal families. Bastards included. From the foundation he'd obtained much information on Bayard and the Realm. Information that was now coming out into the open for the first time.

Duval called the meeting to order, after moving the covert chiefs into a smaller room, where they sat around a table illuminated by a large medieval-looking chandelier.

"And now, gentlemen," Duval said, "we must all lay our cards on the table. And our souls. Normally we are a secretive lot, but not today. Not if we wish to succeed in our struggle."

The silver-haired SDECE man spoke of the trail he'd been following for so long. For years he'd tracked Bayard's network of corporations and contacts in the intelligence world, the marriages that wedded the high and mighty to his cause, the attempted takeovers of companies in the vital communications and armaments industries. He also spoke of the ring of swallows like Lili Kavroleira that Bayard had set up to entrap those who resisted his legal maneuverings.

The Frenchman held nothing back, setting the tone for the summit.

The others responded in kind. As the meeting wore on, Henri Goliard of the ESI, Mitchell Rhodes of the CIA and Francis Rollins of the Sword and Sorcery unit poured out chapter and verse on the Realm, recounting every bloody fact known to them.

It was clear the Realm was a criminal kingdom that outshadowed the P-2 conspiracy, Propanganda Due, that had toppled the Italian government a few years earlier. The P-2 lodge had taken control of several Italian banks, infiltrated the Vatican and owned outright more than a dozen generals and intelligence chiefs and several political figures. In the process it created a shadow government inside Italy, one that ruled the country until its leaders were finally unmasked.

With a net that reached out across the European continent, the Realm was considerably more advanced, controlling a much larger organization than P-2. Its recruitment had increased at an alarming pace as the monarchist juggernaut steadily consolidated its power.

The price paid to enter the Realm was steep. Official secrets were the coin of the Realm and they were payable in advance. Political espionage enabled the Realm to pull the strings of candidates and influence the lawmaking machinery. Military and industrial espionage gave its operatives access to key officers and inside information on pending government contracts.

The Realm was forming a ghost government behind the scenes. Deals were made with kickbacks to cutthroats, pardons were signed in blood.

The machinations of the Realm and the White Brigade even put NATO at risk. So-called secure vaults in army bases and embassies had been penetrated by traitors working for the Realm. In some cases the data transmission lines from the communications rooms had been spliced into or replaced so that both coded and decoded signals could be diverted to listening posts. In other cases the encryption codes as well as the actual designs of encryption and decryption machines used by the military were diverted to the Realm.

There was little that was guaranteed secure anymore. NATO plans, Western operations against ComBloc countries—all of them were up for grabs as long as the Realm held that crucial information and technology.

The information on Bayard, the Realm and the White Brigade poured out as every intelligence and action man assembled in Pierre Duval's mansion added what he knew. It was the most complete dissection of Auguste Bayard ever attempted, revealing a foul creature indeed—a would-be king who'd sold his soul and his country for a crown.

But along with descriptions of the powers of the Realm came the hard intelligence against it.

The information Barrabas had obtained from General Hamelin provided crucial links to Bayard's organization. So did the taps the NSA had placed on the general just after the SOBs began their harassing operation.

General Hamelin had responded to the SOBs' pressure by placing a call to a broker in Paris to discuss his stock in Liège Industries, the communications conglomerate controlled by Bayard. Obviously speaking in code, Hamelin had told the broker he was thinking of dumping his stock and getting out of the corporation. He had asked the broker to advise him.

The broker had called back a day later with some hard advice. He'd told Hamelin he didn't recommend getting out of Liège Industries—unless the general wanted to lose everything. Good news followed that very clear threat. Some advisers would visit the general soon to help him steer the right course, the broker had said.

Subsequently Bernhard Vallance, Maurice Sordett and the contingent of White Brigade commandos had arrived at Hamelin's place. Barrabas and the SOBs had taken care of them, discovering the evidence that linked the subversion, murder and conspiracy directly to the Realm.

There was other damning evidence, much of it garnered from Adolphus Norburg, the Banker, whom the SOBs had deposited in the secure arms of Pierre Duval for further debriefing on the financial killings engineered by Bayard's smuggling network. Maurice Sordett, formerly of the White Brigade, had provided information on Realm commando attacks ordered by Bayard and on trafficking in privileged information.

"The evidence against Bayard is ironclad," Barrabas said, summing up the evidence. "We've got enough to prove his guilt now. But if we take him to court, chances are he'll buy his way out of a prison term."

The SOB chieftain looked around the room at the clandestine council, then said, "That means he has to be convicted the covert way. In other words, he has to die for his convictions. If anyone thinks otherwise, he'd better leave now."

No one left.

"Good," Barrabas said. "Now it's up to us to decide how we can take him down. Since the White Brigade is the military arm of the Realm, I suggest we form a counterforce to neutralize them—the Barrabas Brigade. So far my people have made a number of limited strikes against the Realm. But for what's coming up, we need some troops and we need you to produce them."

Mitchell Rhodes nodded. The CIA man had stood by while Barrabas's men risked their lives in the operation. Now he was willing to risk the lives of his own people.

Henri Goliard was also in agreement. The Belgian special forces man knew they were on a war footing—a civil war, in fact—with many of his ESI commandos on opposite sides. The war had to be ended now, before the covert apparatus ran amok.

Pierre Duval had his own army to draw on. He, too, nodded his acceptance.

"We'll be fighting on two fronts," Barrabas continued, "Military and economic. For the military action, we're going to use Maurice Sordett as bait. The White Brigade is keen on silencing him once and for all. Their operatives have been making discreet inquiries about his whereabouts. At the same time, Pierre's surveillance has noted a large contingent of Portuguese White Brigaders preparing for an operation. The Portuguese are a crucial link in the chain. They're the real money holders in the Realm. No matter how loudly Bayard calls the tune, it is often the Portuguese who decide if the White Brigade is going to dance."

"Philip Emanuel is a cautious man," Pierre Duval said, "but a dangerous one. He has the backing of the monarchists and mercenaries in Portugal. If he commits himself fully to Bayard's plans, we will have a hell of a battle on our hands."

The men were familiar with Emanuel's reputation. As a veteran of Grupo de operações especiais, he had a long string of covert victories to his credit. When he switched loyalty to the Realm, he delivered a top commando operation into their hands.

"We're going to make sure that battle is on our terms," Barrabas said. "So far we've kept the location of Sordett's safehouse a closely guarded secret. Soon we'll let that secret slip out—and when Emanuel's White Brigaders come in for the rescue, we'll give them a royal reception.''

Barrabas paused for a moment, gauging the reaction of the select representations in the room. It was positive. They realized they'd come to a point of no return, a point where drastic measures had to be taken.

"The other front is a corporate one. With Pierre's help I'm going to place one of my people inside an arms company facing a violent takeover from the Realm. We want him to become their next target. Apparently, to entrap vulnerable chief executive officers, the Realm uses a sophisticated call girl ring. And I've got just the man for the job," he said.

Barrabas had Nanos in mind. He was already preparing for the role of a Greek financier who'd just taken controlling interest in an arms corporation. According to Pierre Duval it was only a matter of time before the current CEO came running to him. The CEO had approached Duval once already, when the Realm started making overtures. Now he was running out of time.

The Greek SOB would have the time of his life, Barrabas thought. The call girl ring had already taken down several intelligence operatives, a general or two and a CEO. If ever a man was born for this task, it was Nanos.

He wouldn't be alone, though. Lee Hatton was going to go in as Nanos's wife. After all, Nanos had to play the part of a vulnerable married man—what better way to set the trap than to have the Greek with the roving eye attached to a jealous wife?

Barrabas kept most of the details to himself. The rest of the council didn't need particulars.

One by one he looked at the hard faces of the counterterrorist chieftains. Thanks to the raids in Belgium and the Netherlands, they knew what he was capable of. But what were they capable of? he wondered. Could they sustain a prolonged attack against the Realm? Could they move outside of channels long enough to do the job, or would they get spooked halfway through? And could they withstand the inevitable counterattack? Their very survival depended upon the answers. If they didn't move against the Realm now, they might not have another chance.

It was all so civilized now, so quiet in Duval's sedate mansion. But that would change soon. Chances were the next time Barrabas saw these men they would be going to war.

"Remember one thing, gentlemen," Barrabas warned. "We are gathered here to bury the Realm once and for all. No one else can do it. And make no mistake, Auguste Bayard is going to pull out all the stops to get his crown. It's up to us to make sure it's a crown of thorns."

CHAPTER SEVENTEEN

Gilles Pontaillier saw the hangman coming.

From his top-floor office suite in the Parisian headquarters of Manufacture d'Armes de Pontaillier, the CEO of the armaments corporation had a spectacular view of the Seventh Arrondissement, one of the most exclusive neighborhoods in the French capital.

That view was spoiled by the appearance of the hangman who had telephoned minutes earlier and told him to drop everything. There was business to discuss. Realm business.

The fiftyish executive had dropped everything. He had no choice. The company guards, the armored doors, the secure rooms—nothing could keep the hangman out. He had one of the most powerful weapons known: information. Information on the private life of the very married Gilles Pontaillier.

The hangman's well-tailored suit sat well on his lanky frame. He carried a slender black attaché case and swung it in a chopping pendulum motion as he walked. He walked as if he were a product of the nearby Ecole Militaire. Besides the military bearing there was an arrogant air about him, as if he owned the fashionable quarter, or soon would.

But Gilles knew differently. He knew that Kaspar Ulrich had not attended the military school. Ulrich was a product of the underclass, who had learned the language and mannerisms of those more highly placed socially. Though he spoke that language well enough, he gave the impression that it was foreign to him, a second language he could readily discard.

Pontaillier's security men had followed Kaspar Ulrich, photographed him and studied him at every chance, but had discovered very little about him. For all they knew he could have been French, Belgian or German. Sometimes he spoke with a heavy German accent, sometimes with a Flemish one. His French was flawless. Whatever his origin, his allegiance was clear. He was a creature of the Realm, a gatekeeper, who was ushering Gilles Pontaillier in.

Pontaillier sighed as he waited for his fate to catch up with him.

Kaspar Ulrich had been haunting Pontaillier with phantoms for weeks now. Time was running out. Unless he cooperated with the Realmist henchman, he knew he would soon become a phantom himself.

Shrieking winds sliced through the white curtains, billowing them like parachutes. Just a moment ago the wind had provided pleasant relief from the afternoon heat baking the smoggy city. Now it seemed mocking, foreboding. It was almost as if the elements were turning against Pontaillier, telling him he'd made a wrong move. He was in for a thunderstorm by the name of Kaspar Ulrich.

"God help me," Pontaillier said, resting his head in his hands.

What he did next could decide his future. It was a crucial moment. He couldn't put off the Realm much longer. Bayard was growing impatient with his stalling tactics.

From the start Pontaillier had fallen under the spell of the personality cult of Auguste Bayard. He'd been allowed into the charmed circle of the messianic monarchist. By the time he realized it was a cult of the king, it was too late. By then Gilles was hypnotized by the Czech actress, Lili Kavroleira. It was she who lured him to the doorstep of the Realm. And Kaspar Ulrich was the ogre waiting behind the door.

The first few times Pontaillier had seen Ulrich, the man had identified himself as a chief officer of Liège Industries, a troubleshooter for Auguste Bayard. But it was obvious he spent little time huddled away in corporate offices.

Pontaillier watched the approach on the security monitors that covered every inch of the building. It didn't take long for Ulrich to sweep through. He chose the stairs rather than the elevator, bounding up with rapid steps.

Manufacture d'Armes de Pontaillier, or MAP, had been in the munitions business for centuries, providing revolvers, shotguns, carbines, cannons, submachine guns and tank guns to military and police agencies right up to World War Two. During the past twenty years the Company had shifted its emphasis and expanded into high-tech warfare, producing surface-to-air and air-to-air missiles, remote control drones for reconnaissance and attack, night vision devices and helmets, and intelligent mines that could be programmed to destroy a variety of targets depending upon their signature.

Along with the high-tech weaponry, MAP still produced conventional weapons, making it ripe for takeover by the Realm. The Realm could divert factory runs or produce duplicates and sell them on the underground market. The Realm could outfit freelance terrorists and enlist them in its cause. If scandal arose, it could sever all ties with Pontaillier just as quickly as it had formed them. And the company would be left in ruins—along with Pontaillier's good name.

The architect of that ruin was now approaching.

When he reached the top floor Kaspar Ulrich strolled past the security guard without a word. He ignored the receptionist in the outer office and walked down the hallway posted with signs forbidding visitors to go any farther. Such restrictions didn't apply to Kaspar Ulrich. Very few rules of the ordinary world applied to the black-haired, black-hearted ambassador of the Realm.

He had told Pontaillier over the phone to instruct his subordinates not to interfere with his passage. His orders were all carefully thought out, designed to show Pontaillier who was in control.

Kaspar Ulrich stopped at the door to Pontaillier's inner office. His snakelike eyes bored down on the CEO's executive secretary. She pressed a button on her desk, and the lock on Pontaillier's door clicked open.

Though he looked like many a brash young executive who'd stepped into this room, Kaspar Ulrich wasted no time in breaking that illusion. He'd come to negotiate a different kind of business.

"Don't get up," he said, crossing the room. His eyes pinned Pontaillier to the chair as he lifted the attaché case and placed it in the middle of Pontaillier's desk. He flicked open the clasps, then raised the lid.

"I've brought you something."

"You are too kind," Pontaillier said.

Kasper lifted a packet of photos from the case and handed it to Pontaillier. As the Frenchman took it he knew it was the most potent explosive that Kaspar could wield.

Gilles Pontailler opened the packet. The photographs were cold to the touch, sending ice crystals streaming toward his heart. They were strong enough to blow apart the corporation from top to bottom. He examined the first few photographs. They were very sharply focused, very professionally printed. And very pornographic.

Suitable for one of the bolder magazines or seamier tabloids.

They showed the fiftyish executive in all his glory, in the very capable hands of Lili Kavroleira. The Czech actress had played one of her best roles to date. She had convinced him that she was interested in his company—not his corporation. Sex with her was magic. Black magic, he realized now.

He'd been easy prey for such a beautiful woman. Brown hair with blond streaks, ripe figure with a vein of wickedness rippling through it. It all seemed so transparent now—the entrapment had been as naked as the two of them had been in her love nest in Paris. Had he really been that much of a fool? At least if he had been a fool, he'd fallen for the best, he thought. Even now he felt a yearning for her. She had brought him to a new plateau—the one from which Kaspar Ulrich now seemed so eager to push him.

"What do you want?" he asked Ulrich, pushing the photographs away without looking at them all.

Kaspar dropped into a contoured chair and draped his arm over the back. "All you can give," he said.

Pontaillier looked at Kaspar's ruthless face, then at the candid photographs. The beautiful actress was just as ruthless, he realized. In truth, she was the one who had captured him. Kaspar was merely tightening the noose.

The Frenchman crumpled into his chair. He knew he had everything to risk—his company, his family name, his wife, his homes. And these people, these desperate, crazy and dangerous people, had nothing to lose.

Gilles Pontaillier's family fortune was exactly that, tied inextricably to his family. His members were spread across the country, confident that he was managing everything. Pontaillier had grown into the position despite the early expectations of his family that it would be too much for him, that he was too much of a wastrel, a playboy unsuited for such a challenge.

In the end he had proved them right.

That proof was captured in the glossy photographs.

Kaspar spread out the photographs as if they were a deck of cards. "Ah, yes," he said. "They came out very well. See for yourself. They're quite remarkable."

Pontaillier stared straight ahead.

"I said see for yourself," Kaspar repeated.

Pontaillier sighed. He was middle-aged, stout, no match for this slender killer. Pontaillier had no doubt of the danger Ulrich represented. He'd seen his type before. Much of the company business was with intelligence types, covert officers who used the exotic weaponry he could supply. And in some of their faces he had seen a similar look. Those men were always at war even when they wore civilian masks like Kaspar Ulrich's.

Ulrich singled out a particularly revealing shot of Pontaillier, obviously sated, and Lili Kavroleira wrapped up in a bondage pose. It had been her idea, Pontaillier remembered. She'd provoked him into it.

"This is . . . this is awful," he mumbled.

"Awful?" Kaspar shrugged. "Different, perhaps. Experimental. Decadent. True, some people may see the private life of Gilles Pontaillier in a different light. You may be branded as a pervert in the eyes of the public, your family, your children. But we must have our discipline, mustn't we?"

Pontaillier remained silent.

"Keep looking," Kaspar urged. "You haven't seen the best yet."

"I have no desire to." Kaspar shrugged. He pushed aside several more photographs to reveal yet another bondage shot. This one was with a different woman, a blonde. It was much harsher. Whip marks stained her back.

Pontaillier felt a cold sensation sweep through him. "Who is this?" he asked.

"She is no one," Kaspar said. "Actually, she is someone just like you. Someone we own."

"But I didn't do that to her—"

"Appearances are everything, Gilles. It is the same room, the same love nest you so often visited. She is prepared to swear it is you and to press charges if necessary."

Gilles shook his head.

"Now," Kaspar continued, "the question is this. Do you want these photographs released? Or do you want to cooperate and show that you are a trusted member of the Realm?"

"I'm not in the Realm."

"Then you are in a most dangerous place. Cooperate with us and you might even be able to pluck the heartstrings of your precious Lili again."

The idea sent a spark flickering through Pontaillier's eyes. Kaspar smiled as he noticed the reaction, which he'd expected. "What do you say?" he asked, mimicking the tones of a friend who wanted to smooth things over.

"There's nothing I can say... yet."

Kaspar's hand knifed through the air with blinding speed onto a photograph of Pontaillier's face. He could have struck Pontaillier himself just as easily. "Decide," he said. "And do it now."

"It is not my decision alone," Pontaillier protested. "The company is not totally under my control. Other interests must be consulted—I can't just do whatever the Realm wants me to. These things have to be considered—"

"Consider this," Kaspar said. "If the photographs do not ensure your cooperation, the next inducement will. My dear Pontaillier, you might not want to find out what the next inducement is."

"But there are too many complications—ownership of the stock, the directions of the company—"

"Uncomplicate it," Kaspar said, rising from the chair. "I will be back shortly. By then, you must decide... or we will decide for you." He spun on his heels and left the office.

Pontaillier followed him, closed the door, then walked around his office as if it were a prison cell. He finally stopped by the window and looked down on the genteel bustle of the Seventh Arrondissement.

He'd always enjoyed the view, considering it one of his well-earned privileges. But that would soon change if he gave in to the Realm.

Ten minutes after Kaspar Ulrich left, Gilles Pontaillier picked up the phone. He clung to it like a lifeline as he called the one man who could help him, a former intelligence man Pontaillier had known for decades and had grown to trust. He was one of the company's most valued customers, Pierre Duval.

Pontaillier had made previous attempts to enlist Duval in his cause and had actually approached him several times. But he'd never told him all of the specifics, always pulling back each time as if he couldn't bear to admit his failings to someone else, let alone himself. But now there was no other choice.

PIERRE DUVAL FELT like a psychiatrist ready to hear a patient's confidences as he studied the nervous executive sitting across from him at the table in the conference room where the anti-Realm summit had taken place.

Except for the discreetly armed men silently watching the courtyard, Duval's mansion had been quiet when Gilles Pontaillier arrived late in the afternoon. He'd come by a circuitous route, apparently having traveled randomly through Paris before finally hailing a taxi.

The cabbie was actually one of Duval's drivers, who, after a concerted effort to lose any tail, brought the CEO into the safe harbor of the former SDECE man.

Though he'd sounded urgent when he called, Gilles Pontaillier wasn't quite ready to open up.

"Here you may feel free to talk," Duval assured him, looking across the smooth table at the corporate man—who even now was probing the room for shadows.

"It's difficult," Pontaillier said. "And it's quite personal. Scandalous..."

Duval nodded. "We are all vulnerable at times. We've all made some mistakes. And when you first contacted me some time ago, I knew it would be 'personal,' as you put it." He reached across the table and patted the man's hand. "Believe me, you are not the first man to fall since Adam."

Pontaillier took a deep breath, then handed the packet of photographs to Duval.

Duval scanned the packet of photographs quickly and dispassionately. As he shuffled through the mild bondage scenes involving Pontaillier and Lili Kavroleira, he let a smile come to his face. "Ah, Lili," he said. "Up to her old tricks."

"You know her?"

"Very well. There are not many of us in this business who do not know her."

Pontaillier looked surprised.

"It's an old trick," Duval explained, "as old as spying itself. And naturally our friends in the Realm combined them both." He discussed the honey trap, how both the Soviet bloc and Western countries used women to entrap politicians, businessmen, embassy guards, anyone who was vulnerable to their charms.

It reassured Pontaillier. "Then there is a way out?"

Duval shook his head, cautioning him. "Not so quickly," he said. "There's never an easy way out of a situation like this—unless you can pose a greater danger to them than they to you. And at the moment,

Gilles, you present very little danger to anyone—except to your family and your corporation.''

"So what can I do?"

"You can string them along until someone else can spring a deadlier trap on them."

Pontaillier nodded. Then he urged the SDECE man to continue looking through the photographs. "There's something else you should see."

Duval riffled through the remaining photographs, casual and relaxed, until he saw the blond woman, who had obviously been whipped for real. It was not stage blood that crisscrossed her back. "Did you do this?" he asked.

"No! I swear, I was just . . . they made it—''

"Relax. I didn't think you would do such a thing. But I wanted to be sure." Duval shook his head as he looked at the photo. "The poor girl means nothing to them. They may kill her just to have something to pin on you. She may have as much value to them as the price of a bullet—or a blade. Or she may be one of their most faithful courtesans. It is hard to say exactly. All we know for sure is one thing. The Realm has plans for you. That means they'll put you on the leash soon."

Pontaillier bowed his head. "They already have," he said. He told Duval about Kaspar's visit, his demands, the Realm's plan to use Manufacture d'Armes de Pontaillier as its own private armory and his own belief that they wouldn't let him live much longer—even if he did go along with them. "That is why I've come to you, Pierre. Can you help me?"

Duval shook his head.

Pontaillier was stunned. He looked around the room in disbelief. Then, his eyes accusing, he said, "Don't tell me you're with them, too—"

"Hold on, my friend," Duval said. "No, it is nothing like that. It's true that *I* can't help you, personally. Or overtly. It would be too obvious if I suddenly intervened in your company. If Bayard learned of my involvement he wouldn't take the bait."

"But I don't understand."

"There's another group I'm working with," Duval explained. "They have earned my trust. They are the ones who can pose the most danger to the Realm and to Auguste Bayard. They may help you."

As if he were a penitent who had just caught a glimpse of heaven, Pontaillier's eyes lit up with the spark of salvation. "Thank God," he said.

"Don't thank anyone yet," Duval warned. "They may help you, but it won't be easy. *You'*ll have to help *them* take over your company."

"What?"

"On the surface, only on the surface. On paper it will appear that your company has been taken over, or that someone is attempting to wrest control from you. That part will take time to be worked out. In reality you will retain full control. But by the time anyone can unravel the truth, it will be too late."

"I don't follow you," Pontaillier said.

"It's quite simple. The group we bring in will orchestrate matters so they appear to control your company. That will make *them* the target of the Realm. And then, when the Realm strikes the target, they will find that it strikes back."

"And I?"

"You will either live or die depending on how well you play your part," Duval said, leveling with the harried executive. "It's a dangerous game we're playing. But your chances are better with this group on your side."

"Who are they?"

"They're a small group that knows how to get things done," Duval said. The SOBs, he thought to himself. They were as good as their name. But he didn't want to spell out too many details to a novice like Gilles Pontaillier.

"Are they police?"

"No."

"Military?"

"Yes."

"Whose?"

"Their own," Duval said. "Very much their own. And fortunately for us, they are at war with the Realm."

CHAPTER EIGHTEEN

Alex Nanos slipped his arm through Leona Hatton's as they strolled through the tall hedges in the maze-like garden behind Monsieur Hubert's château. The well-kept castle south of Brussels had become Lili Kavroleira's base of operations.

And Nanos was soon to be operated upon.

He, like every other man at the elite gathering, had noticed her several times. And though he couldn't be sure, he thought she had noticed him. She'd always stayed on the edge of the crowd, her eyes darting at him now and then.

Whenever his gaze met hers, he understood how she had brought so many men to destruction. The brown-haired siren had a way about her that was hard to resist, even if you knew what she was all about. Drop dead beautiful, he thought.

"Don't get us lost, Alex," Lee said, as the Greek maneuvered them through the garden maze. The green-tiered shrubbery led toward a pavilion where graceful fountains flowed.

"Just checking out the company we're keeping," he said.

"Sure you're not just checking on Lili again? Remember, she's supposed to come to you. For once in your life you should play hard to get."

The Greek nodded. "Just looking around," he insisted.

As they emerged from the outer gates of the garden and moved under the brightly colored pavilion, Lili Kavroleira appeared.

"What a coincidence," Lee said, studying the brown-haired beauty. "There's the vamp now."

Lili wore a black silk dress with a wide collar that would have been conservative on anyone else. She wore it with an air of innocence, as if she were unaware of the looks it elicited from otherwise reserved men.

But the dress had been tailored to accentuate the actress's curves. Its collar had an arrow-thin gap in it that immediately snagged a man's eyes and directed them lower to the well-filled bust. Teardrop-shaped slits on the sides of the dress showed an expanse of skin.

"She looks like a career girl," Nanos said.

"For a career of sin, yes," Lee agreed.

"You sound jealous."

"It's part of my cover."

"Well, let me do my part then," he said. "You know, it's actually romantic here." He gestured back at the château, his thickset arm encompassing the manicured gardens, the party lights, the soft chatter of the chic guests from Paris, Mons, Brussels and other power bases of Realm. Then he dropped his arm around Lee's hip.

"Not that romantic," she said, gently pushing his arm away.

Nanos smiled. Though his target was Lili Kavroleira, the woman on his arm deserved special care. Her white gown had spaghetti-thin straps and was cut sharply in front to reveal a coppery expanse of neck and shoulders. Despite the many courtesans at the château, Leona Hatton was not easily overlooked.

The Greek reclaimed her waist with a gentle grasp. "All part of the cover," he said. "After all, we're supposed to be married, Mrs. Kioskouras."

"That's going to take some getting used to," she said.

Nanos smiled, although very much aware they were in the middle of the enemy camp.

Previously they had seen the Belgian's country château only through surveillance photographs of the grounds and of the NATOcrats who were summoned there to plan Realm activities—along with newcomers about to be entrapped into the Realm. Tonight they were walking through the floodlit grounds as guests.

Nanos replayed the meeting with Kaspar Ulrich in his mind, savoring the deception they'd pulled off. When Ulrich paid a second threatening visit to Gilles Pontaillier, the armaments executive had introduced Nanos as a Greek tycoon involved in a buyout of Manufacture d'Armes de Pontaillier. He'd displayed a blizzard of paperwork to Kaspar, showing the Greek had acquired some of the family's shares and most of those owned by the public.

"He is the complication you mentioned?" Kaspar had said, managing to pull Pontaillier away from the Greek for what he thought was a private chat.

Pontaillier nodded, then poured out the cover story the SOBs had prepared with the help of a CIA-owned shipping company.

The company was part of a huge conglomerate based in the Aegean that generated genuine profits and was used as a "home office" for operatives in need of a cover. Like most home offices, the firm had prepared several backstopped identities for its agents to step into whenever needed. The identities would hold up for the length of a covert operation. Mitchell Rhodes had worked out the logistics and helped Nanos and Hatton slip into their identities as Mr. and Mrs. Michael Kioskouras.

Pontaillier had played his part well, convincing Kaspar that the Greek was a man with a roving eye who had won his fortune by marrying an heiress who held a tight rein on him.

The information soothed Kaspar. He treated Pontaillier almost as a trusted accomplice while he arranged for the entrapment of the Greek tycoon.

"I thought it was all a ruse when first you mentioned this kind of problem," the hangman had said. "But apparently not. Our people will check this out. In the meantime, we'll bring Kioskouras to the next affair at the château."

"Which château?" Pontaillier asked.

Kaspar smiled. "The very same one where *you* first met Lili," he said.

"Hubert's?"

"Yes. I'll have Hubert make the arrangements. Between you and me, history is about to repeat itself."

At first Pontaillier had been surprised at how well Kaspar took the bad news. Only when he talked with Nanos afterward did he realize that the Realmist had seen not an obstacle but another opportunity. He would rein control of the armaments company, and the Realm could also expand into Greece by getting their hooks into Kioskouras's company.

Tonight at Hubert's soiree, Nanos was more than willing to get himself hooked by the Czech undercover actress. But despite his natural inclinations, he stayed away from Lili. He and Lee lost themselves in the crowd, appearing to drink freely as the night wore on. Nanos became loud, while Lee played the role of demure but indulgent spouse. Soon they were known by sight if not sound to many of those at the party.

The two of them knew most of the others by sight already. The Fixer had provided them with photographs of known Realmists, possible defectors and potential targets.

The château was just a short drive north of SHAPE headquarters near Camp Casteau, with its large pool of NATO military and intelligence men to draw from. The bureaucrats and behind-the-scenes power brokers came from the civilian NATO community in Brussels. Guests from both areas mingled tonight in the garden or inside the château, listening to the soft music of a jazz trio in a corner of the ballroom.

It was a perfect recruiting ground—and Alex Nanos was ready to be recruited.

After a couple of hours, more than enough time for the Greek to appear to have become intoxicated, he whispered to Lee that it was time for them to separate.

"I'll miss you," she lied, as Nanos went off to get lost, hopefully in the arms of Lili Kavroleira.

It went off like clockwork.

A short time later Lili chanced to brush against him in a quiet corner of the château. Nanos turned as if surprised. He looked down into her sparkling eyes, then, playing the drunken lout, looked a bit farther down.

She smiled, gauging his response and seeing how best to play him. She had worked the same game on all types, highborn and low. All of them fell for her—and many of them never got up again.

"Your wife is a lovely woman," she said, looking across the room where Lee Hatton was being chatted up by Monsieur Hubert himself, and two men who were part of Bayard's inner circle. They would go after her, too, Nanos realized.

"Too lovely sometimes," Nanos said. "Too perfect. Too charming. Sometimes a man needs a bit—" he lowered his head a little "—a bit of danger, if you know what I mean."

She laughed. "You've come to the right place," she said.

She talked freely, acting very much the movie star. Though Nanos had seen her in films, none of them had anything to do with the legitimate cinema. The ones he'd viewed had been turned up by French and Belgian intelligence. Even so, he pretended to be star struck, another man falling under her spell.

A man like Nanos excelled at such a part when with a woman like her.

It was even easier when she reached up and touched the side of his neck. It was just a soft touch, her finger whispering over his skin. But it was enough.

So that was how things were done in her Realm, he thought. Not a quick jump in a back bedroom but a slow seduction.

Her fingers moved away, but the sensual touch seemed to have left an invisible silk thread connecting them. Or would it become a silk noose she would soon string around his neck?

"I spend a lot of time here," she said. "You wouldn't know it now, but it's usually very quiet."

"I'm sure it is."

"Let me prove it to you," she said. She leaned forward. "How about tomorrow night? It'll be quiet—except for the two of us."

Nanos grinned. It was the leer of a man who had stumbled into a wonderful thing, who didn't know the gleaming smile of the woman beside him was actually a guillotine coming down on his neck.

"Can you slip away?" she asked.

"I'm a very slippery fellow," he said. "I'll be here."

The following night Alex Nanos returned as promised. He drove to the château in an armored Mercedes and parked it at the apex of the circular drive, where it was bathed in light from the baroque lamps bedecking the facade of the house.

Positively medieval, he thought, as he headed to the ornate entrance to announce himself as Michael Kioskouras, the suitor about to be suckered into the Realm.

Monsieur Hubert was conveniently in Brussels attending some NATO affairs. At least those were the appearances. There was no sign of the Belgian turncoat. The only ones present were the house staff—the film crew, Nanos thought—and the Czech actress.

The butler ushered him inside to where Lili was waiting.

"Ah, Michael," she said. "So good of you to come."

He took her hands in soft welcome, then raised them to his lips.

Lili was in more subtle costume tonight. A black cashmere wrap clung to her body and gave him the desire to do the same.

"My pleasure, I hope," he said, still playing the buffoon. After all, he was supposed to be the patsy.

She smiled, then took him for a tour of the château. "You and I have a lot to talk about," she said. "We're kindred spirits."

The tour began in a long library lined with volumes and binders and manuals related to Hubert's NATO work. As Nanos discovered with a few subtle movements, Hubert's desk and file cabinets were locked tight. Bursting with the secrets of the Realm, he thought.

Then she took him through the museumlike château, pointing out tapestries, paintings and armor that had been in the family for generations. Together Nanos and she played out the pretense that they could really be interested in such objects at a time like this.

Along the way they consumed several goblets of wine to help them appreciate the aged splendors of the château. They were light-headed by the time they arrived at the real destination of the tour, a bedroom designed to showcase the splendors of Lili Kavroleira. It was decorated in soft leather and satin and had a baroque four-poster bed fit for a fairy princess—or a wicked queen.

Lili Kavroleira fell somewhere in between.

The seduction began when Lili put down her goblet with a soft thunk on a bedside table—a signal that there was a sweeter wine to taste. The auburn-haired Czech beauty stepped forward like a velvet trophy of the hunt, although Nanos was very much the quarry here.

Nanos wrapped his arms around her and kissed her, allowing his hands to glide over her cashmere curves. Still holding her, he twisted slowly around, discreetly looking for the camera lenses that would be embedded in the wall. There would be three or four such lenses, he realized, positioned to catch him from every angle. They would film in light or dark. And the microphones would provide stereo sound, play by play.

He'd seen this room before. On the blackmail films that turned up in intelligence files.

Lili sighed, then gasped theatrically as she melted into his arms. It was all very calculated but it was still very effective. Another man would not have recognized the professionalism she showed. But Nanos knew her background.

Since her youth Lili had been a prostitute. She was one of the most effective swallows ever to graduate from the Soviets' training camp at Moscow. Instead of boot camp, it was bordello camp. Women like Lili Kavroleira were selected at an early age and inducted into the camps before they realized what they were getting into. Once in the sex service, or the whore corps as the CIA liked to call it, the women were virtually brainwashed and reconditioned to do anything for the state. Stripped down mentally and physically, they were gorgeous slaves trained to cater to any sexual whim or kink.

Swallows like Lili Kavroleira had little opportunity to pursue their own pleasure. Some of them went mad. Some submerged their identities with drink or drugs. Others excelled at their tasks, helping to topple governments in the process. Britain, the United States and West Germany had lost more of their peacetime generals, diplomats and operatives to sex spies than to any other type of adversary.

Lili Kavroleira had done more than her share. After her training, the KGB returned her to her native Prague. She was handed over to the KGB's Czech satellite service, who directed her against Western targets in Prague and Vienna. Czech intelligence saw to it that her career as an actress took off, putting her in the so-called underground films that flourished in Prague. Her underground reputation made her seem subversive, the proper company for Westerners.

Lili had racked up an enviable score by the time she was caught by Western intelligence operatives and threatened with prison or worse. She went over to the West. Unfortunately it was the Realm who had turned her.

And now the Realm was responsible in part for the soft and warm lips pressing against those of Alex Nanos, her most immediate target.

He broke off her kiss and held her at arm's length.

"What's wrong?" she said, feigning hurt that he would break away from her.

"Nothing," he said, staring at the brown-haired woman whose fate was in his hands. "I just want to look at you."

"That's why I brought you here," she said as she started toward the bed.

Nanos held her fast and—defying the habits of years—prevented her from toppling them both onto the soft canopied bed.

Though she was doing her best to entrap him, in reality it was the other way around. She was his target. The Russians had used her, the Czechs had used her, the Realm had used her. Now, if things went right, Nanos would use her.

Lili Kavroleira was living on the border, perhaps too good an actress to realize just how near the edge she was. Surveillance on her boulevard du Régent home in Brussels had shown that she was ready to crack. Increasingly tense and paranoid, she was always looking over her shoulder, perhaps realizing the danger of the games the Realm was forcing her to play.

He pushed her away.

"What is it now?" she asked.

"Call it a slight case of conscience."

"I've got just the cure." She stepped closer and once again embraced him. A soft undulation of curves shifted pleasantly against him.

Once again he broke her hold. "Let's get some fresh air."

"You're kidding," she said.

"No, let's take a walk."

Though surprised, she complied quickly. She would comply with anything that would get the job done. Entrapping the Greek industrialist was her prime concern. If he needed to be humored a bit more before the main event, so be it.

He took her down to the garden where it was shadowy and dark. The thick greenery somehow seemed malevolent at night, a covert arena where phantoms played. The shadows of Nanos and Lili walked side by side until they were halfway through the maze. Then their shadows merged suddenly as Nanos grabbed her.

She looked at him. For a moment fear danced through her eyes. Was this man sent to kill her? Or just to watch over her?

He kissed her, though, disarming and confusing her. Surprised by his fierce approach, she exhaled and stepped back.

His hands swept down her shoulders, his palms skiing down her breasts and gently lifting them beneath the soft cashmere. Then he lowered his mouth and kissed her neck.

She squirmed, made a strange frightened sound and pulled away. The bushes jabbed her as she backed into them and flailed away.

"Now it is my turn to ask what's wrong," Nanos said. "Is your conscience bothering you?"

"No, of course not—"

"Or are you only passionate in certain locations?" Nanos asked. "In certain rooms?"

She froze. "What do you mean?"

Nanos shrugged. "You're an actress," he said. "But you're not the only one playing a part. We all are. Auguste Bayard. Kaspar Ulrich. And Pierre Hubert, who was so kind to vacate his palace tonight."

"But I thought—"

"You thought I was a fool," Nanos said. "That is what I wanted you to think. And them."

The veil lifted from her eyes, like a mist blown away by the truth. She looked at him, hard and cold. She didn't know who he was, or where he stood in the scheme of things. But she sensed that he was a dangerous man.

"What do you want from me?" she asked.

"Something more than your body," Nanos said. A smile came to his face. "Although I can't believe I'm saying that."

"Who are you with? The men you're going against, they're not just businessmen. They're more—they have this thing called the Realm—"

"I know all about the Realm," he said. "And I want in, anyway. That's one of the reasons I've been playing along with their charade. I want to see what my partners are capable of. To see how they would lure me and try to gain a hold over me."

"They're capable of anything you can imagine," she said.

The Greek SOB nodded. "So I've heard. So I've seen."

"And now, here you are, mucking things up. I don't know what they'll do to me when they find out it didn't work, that you didn't . . ."

"Didn't what?" Nanos asked. "Fall under your spell?"

She nodded.

"Oh, but I did. Who could resist you? But I don't want to be an actor in someone's film. Nor should you."

"Spare me the advice," she said. "Next you'll have me believing you're trying to recruit me." Though she acted as if she loathed the idea, there was an undercurrent in her voice and a look in her eye that said she hoped it was so.

Nanos sighed. "Recruit you?" He paused for a moment as if he were weighing the question. "Perhaps that is too strong a word for now. But help you? Yes."

"What makes you think I need help?" she asked.

"The Realm has a lot of pieces on this chessboard," he said. "Sometimes they get swept off the board."

"How do you know?" Lili asked. It was clear her mind had been working on the same track, whether consciously or not. "Never mind," she cautioned. "All I want to know is one thing. If what you're saying is true, why are you telling me?"

"So you know there's a place you can come to if you have to get out quick," Nanos explained. "You can come to me for any reason." He gave the name of a hotel in Paris on place des Vogues where a room had been booked in his cover name. "If I'm not there, just say you're a friend of Michael Kioskouras," he said.

"And who's that?"

"Me."

"Maybe it is," she said. "Maybe it's not. Maybe you're something more. Something dangerous. What if I go back and tell my... my...?"

"Your masters?" Nanos suggested. "Tell them whatever you like. I'll deal with them just like I've dealt with others like them before. Remember, they came to me. They want what I have."

The Czech courtesan nodded. "Just like I'm supposed to have what you want."

"And you do," he said.

She shook her head. She was in desperate straits. But she wasn't ready to jump ship yet.

He'd planted just enough doubt about who he really was. He could be a businessman playing his own game against the Realm. Or he could be something more. She'd met a lot of underworld and undercover types in her career with the Realm. Just because they wore suits or owned companies didn't mean they were legitimate. Sometimes it was the so-called executives who had the most blood on their hands.

Nanos could see that right then he was just one more person she had to figure out. But his oblique warning was real. With the SOBs putting heat on the Realm, Bayard's organization might find itself forced to retrench and sacrifice some of their more vulnerable pieces.

Lili Kavroleira sighed. Swearing under her breath, she spun on her heel and stalked back through the maze toward the château.

Nanos caught her arm. "Wait!"

She snatched her arm free. "I don't know what your angle is, but I've got to get back to the château. And I've got to think of a reason why you bolted from the bedroom. I'm supposed to win you over. If they suspect I'm . . . I'm collaborating with you . . ."

"I told you," Nanos said. "Tell them whatever you want. Whatever you have to." He embraced her once again. This time he looked into her eyes, trying to convince her that he wasn't running a con on her. "I meant what I said. You need out, I'll be waiting. As for your friends in the château—"

He nodded toward the medieval structure, which looked like a jagged crown of stone, its spires scraping the darkening sky. "Tell them we didn't have a chance to get to the bedroom. Tell them you were so beautiful that I took you in the garden."

"They'll believe it," she said. "Once."

Nanos nodded. "I'm sure they will, because it almost happened that way. But it's enough to hold them off for now. They want to get a hold on me for negotiations. They could use our 'tryst' to start putting pressure on me."

"And the next time?" she asked.

"The next time you'll probably know me a lot better."

He took her hand and led her back to the château, walked with her into one of the outposts of the Realm. It was a dangerous game, but it was only starting. It would grow more dangerous the closer he got to the heart of the kingdom.

Because there he would have to face not a call girl, but a king.

CHAPTER NINETEEN

The oceangoing yacht cruised twenty miles off the Belgian coast, rising and falling in the choppy waters of the North Sea. Spray whipped over the sides of the 144-footer as waves slapped the ship over and over like frothy black hands in the moonlight.

For several days the yacht had been a regular sight from the resorts that dotted the French and Belgian coastlines. But the cruise was over now.

Midnight swimmers appeared on the deck. Clad in black diving suits and Emerson closed-circuit scuba gear, the commandos had come to the Belgian waters for one thing—the head of Maurice Sordett.

Sordett, late of the GIGN, late of the White Brigade, was scheduled to become the late Maurice Sordett. The Realm had located him at last at the safehouse on the shore. And now an object lesson was going to be made of the man who went over to the other side.

Pedro Braga, a former captain in Portugal's Corpo de fuzileros, oversaw the preparations of the yacht's shadow crew.

They draped rigging over the side, then lowered three Zodiac inflatables into the water, tethering them to the yacht. Like spiders, half a dozen commandos swung over the side and scrambled down the shipboard webs.

Braga moved back and forth from the wheelhouse to the rigging, helping the commandos transfer into the Zodiacs the hidden cargo they'd stashed on board the yacht.

The crew moved swiftly and silently. Each man had served with Braga before and knew his chances of continued service depended on how well he performed in this raid.

A stocky man in his fifties, Braga had done this kind of work for decades. Before moving up into the Realm, he had worked his way through the military and intelligence services. Though he'd operated extensively in his native Portugal, it was in the Portuguese colonies that he'd made his name by conducting guerrilla raids in Mozambique, Guinea and Angola.

Much like the one he was leading now.

Satisfied they had all their gear aboard the Zodiacs, much of it in dry rubber satchels that could be moved underwater, Braga started to climb over the side of the yacht. He looked toward the cabin where a small sliver of light appeared.

Philip Emanuel stood in the doorway, saluting him.

If not for Emanuel, Braga would never have been in the White Brigade. Though at times he had vague doubts, he'd already been knighted into the cockeyed chivalric order of the Realm. He had no choice but to follow his commitment through.

He returned the salute and went over the side.

The Zodiac lines were cut and the inflatables drifted away from the yacht. Powered by silent engines, they moved toward the distant shore, riding the crests of the waves and sinking out of sight into the dark troughs, while the yacht cruised on and quickly disappeared.

The mother ship was disowning its children. The escape route wasn't by sea. It was risky but it had been planned carefully. The yacht would be well out of

Belgian waters by the time the hit went down. Once they reached the beach, they were to keep on going.

The land-based team would take care of the rest.

So Braga hoped. Kaspar Ulrich was an assassin. Braga had no doubt about that. He'd seen him in action. But as for his ability to lead a military operation, all he had to go on was Ulrich's reputation. The man was vouched for by Auguste Bayard—whose word some people believed to be gospel.

To Captain Braga, Bayard was just one more warlord in the feudal game they were playing. He was like all the other leaders of the White Brigade, each believing his own mentor, Philip Emanuel, could best rule the Realm.

But before that could happen, the alliance had to usher in the covert kingdom. And Bayard was first in line for the throne. To share in the Realm, the Portuguese faction had to commit its troops as well as its money to the cause.

Kaspar Ulrich had masterminded the operation, selecting Philip Emanuel's commandos for the task. In turn, Emanuel had selected Braga.

Braga felt confident. But deep inside he knew that was no guarantee of success. A man like him had to feel confident no matter where he was or what he was doing, including storming the beaches of Belgium.

THE SQUARE SHADOW of the Belgian safehouse stretched across the cool damp sand. Lights were on in the upper windows of the house, where a silhouette could occasionally be seen on the shades. No sentries were stationed on the beach, since that would have made it obvious that the house on the shore was much more than a private resort.

Wooden decks ran from both sides of the house toward the water. A thin slanted roof covered the decks and sheltered the beach furniture, and latticed railings kept the wicker chairs and settees from skipping away in the North Sea wind. Outdoor lanterns hung from the rafters of the roof. At this hour the lanterns had long since been extinguished—giving the black shapes that ran alongside them a welcome cloak of darkness.

A team of swimmer scouts had gone over the sides of the inflatables and swum to shore, emerging from the surf at thirty-yard intervals. They swarmed over the landing zone, secured the beach, then signaled the others with a green flash.

The first inflatable landed fifty yards north of the safehouse. The men hauled the boat ashore, and after hiding it beneath a clump of trees, they spread out in the darkness and joined the scouts in the landing zone.

The second boat dropped off its cargo of commandos fifty yards south.

Brandishing the tools of their trade—silenced submachine guns, knives, grenades, explosive charges—they took up positions along the beach and waited in darkness for the rest of the assault team.

Captain Braga's team came in last. After hauling their inflatable up the beach they dashed to the strike zone, a narrow strip of beach protected by the White Brigade commandos.

It was a simple operation, and a bloodthirsty one.

They were to enter the safehouse and neutralize anything that moved. Once they established that Maurice Sordett was still there under lock and key, they were to rescue him. Part of him actually. The head would leave with the assault team. The torso would stay behind.

Instead of returning to the sea where they could be overtaken, they were to make their escape on land.

Kaspar Ulrich's crews were standing by with a convoy of cars and vans. With a green light from shore, Ulrich's people had signaled the yacht earlier that their crews were in place. Ulrich had played chauffeur long enough to know how to handle that part of the operation.

Once they finished off the safehouse personnel, Braga's team would move uphill toward Ulrich's wheelmen on the main road. Then they would be moved through a network of White Brigade safehouses until they made their way back to their own corner of the Realm.

PEDRO BRAGA SHAPED the explosive charge around the entrance of the safehouse, strapping the Dartcord to the door with masking tape. The pastel-colored door was made of reinforced metal, a good hint that this was not just a holiday camp.

The Portuguese White Brigader glanced back at his men, ensuring they were in proper position. Then he set the ten-second fuse to the detonator and stepped back.

The controlled blast blew the door inward, practically wrenching it loose from its hinges.

One of Ulrich's henchmen sledgehammered it until it thudded down like a ramp into the house.

Two commandos dived inside and hurled stun grenades down the hallway.

In blinding succession, the flash bangs lit up the room like strobes. As the room went nova, the men who'd hurled the grenades flattened out on the floor.

Streaming through the doorway a three-man squad opened up with full autofire, painting the walls with 9 mm sprays. Wood and metal flew as the bursts zigzagged up and down the room. The steady silenced bursts created a pockmarked trail on the walls.

Anyone in the room would have been cut dead. But there was no one there.

The occupants had missed the explosive greeting of the black-clad commandos who'd leapfrogged into the safehouse.

Braga swore, then signaled for two men to follow him down the hall. They'd practiced the assault on a mock target in their home base in Portugal, and studied plans Ulrich had obtained of the building.

The Portuguese commander barreled through the house, stopping at a white metal door that blocked the way to the basement. They blasted it off its hinges, then thundered down the steps.

Braga had strapped a flashlight to his Heckler & Koch submachine gun. Now, flickering over the walls, it illuminated the dark hallways. The beam of light was followed by a 9 mm stream of lead that chomped holes in the walls.

Finding the light switch, the man behind Braga flicked on the lights. A dim yellow pall was cast on the corridor.

Racing downstairs, firing as they went, they stormed along the hall toward the cell where Maurice Sordett was supposedly waiting.

Braga felt a cold sensation in his stomach as he hoofed it down the smoothly painted basement corri-

dor and met no opposition. If Sordett was here, this
part of the safehouse should have been guarded. The
only sound was their own footsteps as they hurried
toward the cells.

He heard a sudden exchange of gunfire upstairs as
his men met opposition on one of the upper floors.
But that wasn't his concern now.

He needed the head of Maurice Sordett.

A QUARTER MILE up the beach a tripod-mounted
ground surveillance radar unit cast an electronic eye
upon the White Brigaders prowling over the sand and
scrub. The last half dozen commandos from Kaspar
Ulrich's land-based team were coming in slowly.

Resembling a suitcase on stilts, the LMT Radio
Professionnelle RB12A was concealed at the edge of
a clump of brush. With a range of 1.2 miles for human-size targets, the radar unit had picked up the
movements of Ulrich's men the moment they appeared on the beach.

A long black cord snaked from the LMT to a position thirty feet away, where Billy Two had dug in with
his M-60. At the end of the cord was a hand-held unit
with a hooded screen that gave the intruders' range
and bearing.

The Osage's machine gun emplacement was sheltered with foliage and had a clean sweep of the beach,
covering nearly every inch of the radar field.

A matching LMT unit was positioned half a mile
away on the other side of the safehouse, manned by an
ESI operative seconded from the Belgian counterterrorist force. Both radar surveillance units were geared
for human-size targets.

The Osage had been sitting practically motionless in the tangled greenery for hours.

He was painted for war, camouflage streaks masking his face as he watched the intruders advance.

ULRICH'S MEN suddenly stopped. They milled around the beach like guard dogs ready to attack. But they couldn't find a target. They scanned the shore and the brush, then moved hesitantly forward.

Ulrich had dispatched them toward the coast to wait for Captain Braga's team to finish up. They were to help escort them away or provide backup fire if needed.

So far the hit seemed to be going as planned. The explosion at the door, the stun grenades, the chatter of submachine guns—everything indicated the hit was moving along nicely.

BILLY TWO SCANNED the horizon, using his most reliable night vision device—his eyes. He picked out the shadows from the darkness as they moved steadily closer.

With the naked eye he could make out general shapes. For a closer look he reached for a hand-held imager and swept it across the beach, identifying shapes as men and their automatic weapons.

Not that he had expected to see innocent tourists walking the beach this time of night, but he wanted to make sure of his targets before he went to war—unlike the team that had assaulted the safehouse and begun spraying everything in front of them with lead.

The Osage had something else to assist him besides his eyesight and the electronic sensor. He had the presence of Hawk Spirit, his battlefield familiar, his instinct. His guide. Whatever it was, he counted on it now, knowing it would tell him when to swing into action.

The Osage exhaled softly and waited for the warriors of the Realm.

"TAKE IT DOWN," Braga shouted.

The man with the shotgun fired two blasts, ripping the lock mechanism from the final obstacle to their quarry. They kicked through the door and burst into the holding area. Paving the way with lead, they fired several controlled bursts as they rushed down the maze of corridors.

Braga skidded around the last corner and stopped beside the lead commando when they reached the barred cell. The commando looked startled, as if he'd been trying to make positive identification of the man behind the bars.

Gunfire echoed within the cell.

A metaljacket penetrated the lead commando's forehead in a spray of red. A second burst ripped into his head. He dropped to the floor.

Whoever was in the cell wasn't a prisoner.

"Get back!" Braga shouted, retreating around the corner. But another White Brigader had already hurried past him to be in on the kill.

It turned out to be his own. A submachine gun chattered, thwacking a burst of 9 mm slugs into his body, then into the wall behind him.

Braga stepped out and triggered a 3-round burst into the cell, but he was at an angle and couldn't see.

The cell door opened. Braga heard voices in French. The "prisoners" were coming after him. He threw himself against the wall.

As the first man came out, Braga triggered the submachine gun. The 9 mm slugs ripped through the man. His weapon hurtled to the floor.

The next man from the cell was more cautious. He whipped his hand through the bars and triggered a blast toward Braga.

The Portuguese man dived to the floor, returned fire, then retreated toward the corridor. He raced upstairs to find some of his men firing outside in the direction of the beach and firing on one of the upper floors.

A steady barrage of fire ripped through a large outer door, tearing it into splinters.

Braga and his men were trapped. It had all happened in seconds. They'd broken into their own prison, and now whoever had engineered the trap was seeing to their execution. Braga had committed his entire landing force to the operation.

And Maurice Sordett was nowhere to be found. Their intelligence about his whereabouts had obviously been a planted leak.

The lightning-fast raid was in shambles. It was impossible to abort it now. Braga and his men were practically prisoners. And judging from the staccato bursts outside the safehouse, the rest of his team was in a thick firefight.

Braga raced over to the ocean-side floor-to-ceiling window. The floor was littered with smashed glass, and glinting shards hung from the window frame. The curtain danced crazily as automatic fire thudded into it and burst through to the inner wall.

Paolo, one of Braga's best men, hurried down from the second floor to report on the slaughter. The blood on his face said it all. They'd been stopped dead up there. The blood of several White Brigaders had turned the carpet red.

"What shall I tell the men?" asked Paolo.

"Tell them to move out," Braga replied.

"It's raining suicide out there," Paolo said. He sounded calm but his eyes were glazed from smoke and fire and the current of fear racing through him.

"There's no choice. Every second we stay here, the worse off we are. Unless we move, we're dead. I'll lead a run toward the beach. You go out the back and see if you can hook up with Kaspar's men."

"If they're not dead already," Paolo said.

"If they're not dead I'll kill them myself," Braga threatened.

Paolo ran toward the door, which now looked as if it had been repeatedly shelled. Chunks of the wall were missing, chewed off by the metal spray pouring inside. He touched the shoulders of two men who were crouched, firing into the darkness, and pulled them away from the door.

As he was about to take them toward the back, a dark-clad shape moved outside the front of the house, knelt and aimed a grenade launcher at the doorway.

Paolo shouted and edged away, swinging his 9 mm submachine gun toward the shape.

HALFWAY DOWN the wooden deck, Nile Barrabas caught sight of the White Brigader in the doorway, aiming at Bennett as the scar-faced CIA op was about to toss a gas grenade into the house.

Barrabas snap-aimed his Heckler & Koch and triggered a full burst of 9 mm hail at the gunman.

Dropping his weapon, the gunman spun around, clutching his sides, blood spouting out of him. Finally he dropped like a puppet.

At that instant, Bennett's gas grenade thumped into the house and exploded, causing the White Brigaders inside to retreat.

Many of them streamed to the back, smashing the windows and diving out the back door. Braga summoned the others and led them out the front. In the smoke and confusion of screams and gunfire, it seemed as if they'd arrived in Hades.

Braga expected some of his men on the beach to help them escape. But there were precious few left. Barrabas and the SOBs had seen to that.

The landing party that had crept up to the safehouse had been watched every step of the way. Hidden beneath the deck, Barrabas and Henri Goliard and a team of ESI commandos waited in the sand for the hit to go down.

Finally the assault team arrived.

Only when the commandos committed themselves to entering the building did Barrabas open up on the assault team. He and his crew chopped them from the left flank, while Goliard and a handful of others fired from the right.

Shocked at being attacked after they'd so carefully "sanitized" the beach, the assault team didn't know how to respond for a few crucial moments.

Consequently they responded by dying. The volley of automatic fire scythed through them before their submachine guns could speak.

At the same time the Belgian ESI ops on the upper floors of the safehouse fired from the balconies, which were practically reinforced bunkers.

The fight had erupted and culminated quickly. Now it was mop-up time—a deadly time, since men about to die had nothing left to lose. They would make a desperate rush from the safehouse.

Barrabas catapulted over the railing of the deck into the sand. He landed in a crouch, then stalked toward the doorway through which emerged panic-stricken men, moving like maddened sharks intent on killing, firing wildly as they thrashed through an ocean of lead. Backed up by O'Toole and the ESI squad, Barrabas stood his ground.

CAPTAIN BRAGA SLICED through the smoke, firing at phantoms. Screaming, he urged his men on. They were dead men for the most part, the majority of them falling to the lethal metal rain.

Some of the survivors followed him out into the night. A handful of White Brigaders even made it to the shore. They piled into the Zodiac they'd hauled up the beach and then scrambled into the surf, piling in and summoning half a dozen gods to help get them the hell out of there.

THE WHITE BRIGADERS behind the house paused in the darkness. Plucked from an inferno, they gathered their wits for a moment. What was their next move? There was no question of joining the holocaust in front of the safehouse.

Originally the plan was to reach the road after the hit, where they would be met by Kaspar Ulrich's people. But there was no sign of Ulrich's crews.

The White Brigaders had gambled and lost. They'd attempted a terrorist-style hit on Belgian territory, and no matter how strong the Realm's connections, there would be no burying this one.

"Drop your weapons!" a voice shouted in English. Then the command was repeated in Portuguese.

The gang members opened up with their weapons, firing into the darkness as they charged up the slight incline toward the boardwalk.

A flare went off. The boardwalk suddenly turned into a white-hot bed of coals as machine gun bursts flashed across the night like shooting stars.

LIAM O'TOOLE FIRED the FN-FAL automatic rifle again at the charging White Brigaders. With this wave of lead, the last of the commandos dropped to the ground.

The Irishman shouted for a cease-fire. The CIA kill team that was dug in under the boardwalk held their fire while the smoke cleared around the tumbled bodies.

The rear of the house had been turned into a bloody backdrop, splashed with dark red paint from the stilled lives on the sand.

CAUGHT IN A NO-MAN'S-LAND between a firefight and freedom, Kasper Ulrich's back-up team had known something was wrong when the flares went up and the sound of battle grew so loud it seemed like the assault team had encountered a small army.

The quick raid had turned into slow death for the attackers.

Ulrich wasn't prepared for such a pitched battle. As the fighting escalated his convoy of cars withdrew. He was sure nothing would make it from the safehouse through all that firepower, and his wheelmen weren't ready to be drawn into the ambush.

But the half dozen White Brigaders with Ulrich, hoping they could turn the tide, stormed over the sand toward for safehouse.

It was a valiant effort by the knights of the Realm, but their dreams of glory were smashed by Billy Two's M-60.

Bring the war right to them, the heavy machine gun chattered, spitting out 7.62 mm rounds from a 100-round belt. Immediately, three of the men fell on the beach.

The Osage tracked the remaining three over a sandy ridge, but didn't shoot even though they were in his range. He wasn't bloodthirsty like the White Brigaders. He was just a soldier and his job was done. He'd held off the backup team.

And there was another factor to consider. Alive, the three survivors would spread fear through the Realm by telling what had happened. Dead, they were just three more bodies on a blood-drenched beach.

THE ZODIAC HEADED out to sea.

Although the craft was seaworthy, the crew was far from it. Captain Braga had been hit in the left shoulder, rendering it useless. A dagger of skin had been ripped from his forehead, gouged out by a wooden splinter when he'd made his escape through the battered doorway. The three others with him were also injured.

But they were alive.

The near-silent engine pushed the Zodiac farther from shore, away from the site of the botched raid and the slaughterhouse that it had become.

But the fighting wasn't over yet.

The inflatable wasn't the only craft on the rough waters. Claude Hayes piloted a 36-foot Seafox through the waves. With a silenced engine capable of doing thirty knots and enough radar masks to penetrate deep inside enemy territory, the special forces attack craft also carried enough manpower to fight a small war.

A one-sided war, at that.

The black ex-SEAL sliced the craft through deep troughs as it stalked the Zodiac. Hayes had an eight-man crew of CIA gunmen aboard, all of them looking hard at their quarry.

"Let 'em know we're here," Claude said.

The gunmen fired a stream of tracers over the fleeing Zodiac, ribbons of flame reflecting in the water as they hissed through the night.

The men in the Zodiac studied their attackers, knowing they could just as easily have been aced by the faster craft closing in on them. Outmanned, outgunned, they had one chance to surrender.

But their leader had other ideas. The stocky man stood in the Zodiac as it pitched up and down, raised his submachine gun with one arm and ripped off a full-auto burst at the Seafox.

Hayes steered into another trough, and the Seafox dropped momentarily out of sight. When it rose on the next wave, the CIA gunners commenced firing.

The volley ripped three of the White Brigaders out of the Zodiac. At the same time two CIA ops launched grenades, one whumping into the water, the other bursting right on top of the inflatable.

Captain Braga was thrown skyward, his body racked by the thunderous blast, his face and body lit by the explosive charge. For a moment he was suspended in the air, a bright and dying knight of the Realm. Then the North Sea took him to a darker and colder realm.

CHAPTER TWENTY

"I want Manufacture d'Armes de Pontaillier," Kaspar Ulrich said. He was sitting behind the desk on the top floor of Pontaillier's headquarters building in Paris.

"So do I," Alex Nanos replied, folding his arms and leaning back in the plush chair facing the desk. "But I think my claim's a bit stronger. You see, I plan on buying the company—not stealing it."

Ulrich shrugged. Though he showed a mask of indifference, Nano's flippant manner had been getting to him. He brushed the lock of hair from his forehead and took out a thin cigar, stabbing the air with it. Finally he flipped open a small gold lighter, lit the cigar and snapped the lighter shut like a guillotine.

"Nice," the Greek said. "If I ever need anyone to burn the wings off flies, you get the job. But when it comes to running the Pontaillier concern, I fail to see what talents you have to lend."

"I have an interest in Gilles Pontaillier's affairs," Ulrich insisted.

"I'm sure you do. I'm also sure that interest won't hold up in court."

"It depends on the kind of court you mean," Ulrich said.

Nanos gestured as though attempting to brush the comment away with his hand. "The Realm again," he said. "The grand court of Europe. I've heard so much about this Realm, about Monsieur Bayard and the great fortunes we can make together. Of course, I am impressed with him. But other than your word, I have no way of knowing you're connected to him."

"Liège Industries retains me as a consultant."

"Liège Industries also retains an army of street sweepers," Nanos said. "That doesn't mean they have the ear of Auguste Bayard."

Ulrich shrugged again. He looked around his fiefdom. Gilles Pontaillier had voluntarily exiled himself to another suite while the two of them discussed the man's fate and that of his company.

"What does it take to convince you?" Ulrich said.

"It's quite simple," Nanos said.

"Enlighten me."

"It takes Auguste Bayard himself."

Ulrich smacked his palm onto the desk. The dull thud echoed in the room. "That's impossible!"

"I thought you were supposed to be a miracle worker," Nanos said. "If arranging a meeting with Bayard is beyond your capabilities . . . well, then—"

"It appears that I'm not getting through to you."

Nanos yawned and looked at his watch. "And unless you do in the next five minutes, we will have no more business to discuss."

Ulrich's face reddened. He gripped the desk and pushed himself back mechanically. The man he knew as Michael Kioskouras constantly kept him on edge. The Greek corporate man would make appointments and never show up. Or he'd avoid committing himself while making Ulrich think he was ready to negotiate. Other times he treated Ulrich as an amusing charlatan.

Rather than playing a buffoon, as he had at first, the Greek had revealed himself—one of his selves, actually—as a formidable opponent. He'd convinced Ulrich that he'd only been hiding behind the mask of a Greek playboy who married wealth. As the battle for the armaments company heated up, the Greek had exhibited a shrewd persona Ulrich wasn't quite prepared for.

But since Alex Nanos, alias Michael Kioskouras, was almost ready to take over the armaments corporation, Ulrich had to deal with him. Kioskouras's company was one of the most powerful in Greece. Since that company was in effect the CIA, it very well could arrange for the buy-out of Manufacture d'Armes de Pontaillier. Any background check the Realmist ran on the Greek's company would show that he was legitimate.

Nanos brushed away the smoke that drifted from the cigar Ulrich was puffing on nervously. "Two more minutes," he said. "Then I must be off."

Ulrich wrung his hands. Subconsciously he probably wanted to wring the Greek's neck.

Things weren't going well for the Realm troubleshooter. Though he was dressed in a well-cut suit and looked the executive from head to toe, he seemed ill at ease. There seemed to be other things on his mind.

Perhaps the bodies on the beach, Nanos thought. He'd been briefed on the White Brigade's failed attempt on the safehouse. Though Nanos had wanted to be on the operation, Barrabas had ordered him to stay in Paris, and Nanos had to admit Barrabas was right.

Nanos had his own war to fight—with a woman who took no prisoners and a Hitlerian Frenchman who wanted to rule the world. He couldn't afford the risk, now that he and Lee Hatton had gained entry to the outer gates of the Realm. They would have had difficulty explaining away any wounds picked up in battle. It would have seemed more than just coincidental if they'd been injured at exactly the moment the White Brigade went into action.

Nanos knew it was better to play carefully. There would be plenty of time for fighting once he worked his way inside the empire.

And it looked like that would happen soon. The Realm had been counting on taking over the armaments corporation, and not just for supplying weapons to the Realm. The company could be a gold mine, selling unaccountable and untraceable arms on the underground market.

The Realm needed a victory to offset its recent losses in the Netherlands and Belgium. The defection of the Banker had crippled one of its most profitable operations. His financial revelations and Maurice Sordett's military ones had drastically altered the Realm's timetable. Just when Bayard was getting all of the factions in line, these disasters had struck.

Now the Realm was under pressure to show it was more than just a shadow kingdom. Otherwise the grand idea of the movement seemed just a dream—a dream financed by Realmists who were being woken up the hard way.

The Realm needed Manufacture d'Armes de Pontaillier. And so it needed Michael Kioskouras.

The Greek grinned now as he studied Kaspar Ulrich.

"What amuses you?" Ulrich asked.

"The trouble you have taken to appear legitimate in my eyes. The way you try to impress me with your power. So far I have seen none of it, and it seems I never will. So, if there is nothing else you have to say..." The Greek stood and headed toward the door.

"Wait—"

"I am done waiting," he said. "I've been looking for a man of substance, but you have disappointed me with your games. Certainly you can frighten Pontaillier, but not me. Our business is finished."

"But we want the company!" Ulrich protested. He, too, got to his feet and leaned forward over the desk. He gripped the edge tightly. His eyes burned at the Greek. "You and I must come to an arrangement."

Nanos paused at the door. "As I said before, if you really are a messenger of the Realm, you do your outfit a great disservice. So far you've told me little I want to hear."

"I am authorized to negotiate with you," Ulrich said. "You must understand that before we can proceed with our plans."

Nanos stepped away from the door. "Bayard may have authorized you," he said. "If so, his judgment isn't as acute as I prefer. You've made some grand claims about throwing in my lot with the Realm, which I have considered. But after all, any arrangement between businesses is a kind of marriage. I must know my partner."

"Speaking of marriage..." Ulrich began.

"Yes?"

"There is the matter of your wife. And Lili Kavroleira."

"I don't see the connection," Nanos said. He moved back across the room and dropped into the seat facing Kaspar Ulrich.

Ulrich relaxed, back on more familiar territory. "It is just that I noticed a certain closeness between you and Lili. I was concerned for you—wondering if perhaps your wife also noticed it—''

"Leave her out of it!" Nanos thundered.

Ulrich raised his hand, palm outward. "Exactly what I wish to do," he said. "There's no need to be defensive. We are men of the world here. If you and Lili enjoy each other's company, I will do my best to keep it discreet."

Nanos acted stunned for a moment, as if he were really in a trap. "Lili and I..." he said. "We...we just—''

"No need to explain."

The Greek sighed. "Did you attempt a similar trick with Monsieur Pontaillier? Use a woman to get a hold over him? And now Lili is supposed to have a hold over me." He shook his head. "So if I play along, you keep this from my wife?"

"I just have your interests at heart." Ulrich's face was expressionless, his eyes glowing.

Until Nanos smiled. "Lili's beside the point," he said. "Though it's true my wife might not approve of our...attraction, the fact remains that you have no evidence. Yet."

"What do you mean 'yet'?"

"I mean I may see her again," Nanos said. "I may not. Maybe the next time your company spies will catch us in the act. But I doubt it. I am careful in these matters."

Ulrich collapsed in his chair. The Greek had been toying with him again. There was no hold over him. No entrapment. And Michael Kioskouras didn't seem like the kind of man to be intimidated.

Nanos threw him a rope. "The point is, Kaspar, you don't need Lili. You never did. I like what I hear about the Realm. Great profits could be made—enough for me, enough for the Realm. I must admit I would like to make my own fortune, rather than rely on my wife's all the time. I want that kind of power. I'm sure the Realm has ways of making that kind of money. We will all prosper."

Ulrich studied him skeptically, as if this were another of the Greek's gambits. Or was Kioskouras finally leveling with him?

"I mean what I say," Nanos went on. "You don't have to trick me. I'm ready to join in. Lili or no Lili, I want in the Realm."

"Then what is the problem? We can discuss it."

"No," Nanos insisted. "Auguste Bayard and I can discuss it."

Ulrich was about to protest, but Nanos cut him off. "Get me an audience with him or forget all about Pontaillier. You'll never set foot in here again."

"All right," Ulrich said slowly. "I'll see to it."

"See to it now." Nanos nodded at the phone on the corner of the desk.

Ulrich made the call.

"I have no intention of seeing this man," Auguste Bayard said sharply a few moments later.

Kasper Ulrich wiped his brow. There was no sweat there, but he felt feverish just the same. His head was on the chopping block.

So far the conversation had gone badly. It didn't help matters that the Greek was sitting there as if he had first-row seats at a command performance.

Ulrich gripped the phone more tightly. "He insists. It is the only way. Believe me, I have looked into all the alternatives."

"Just as you looked into all the alternatives of your last assignment?"

Ulrich shook his head. He would forever be haunted by the botched mission. He'd handled all the details, planned the hit, brought in Captain Braga's men—and got everyone slaughtered. Coming on the heels of the Amsterdam massacre, it didn't bode well for his future.

Even though Kaspar was working on rebuilding the Netherlands operation, he might have stepped over the line. Perhaps Bayard would send someone along to take care of him the way he'd taken care of Bernhard Vallance. But not until he carried out the assassinations for the Realm.

"Well?" Bayard demanded.

"This is the best way," Ulrich said. "It will be profitable all around. He is most eager to work with us—with you."

"I see," Bayard replied. "Very well. But I want you to know that things are going badly on several fronts. There has been a lot of trouble."

Created by you. The accusation had gone unsaid, but it was there nonetheless, hanging over Ulrich's head. He had risen far by being ruthless. It had taken a long time to reach the top ranks of the Realm. Only now did he realize how quickly he could fall.

"This will have some unexpected advantages," Ulrich said.

"It better."

"It will help us concentrate on some of our new projects," Ulrich said. He spoke slowly, carefully selecting his words. He knew that Bayard would recognize what those projects were.

For one thing, there was the matter of Lili Kavroleira. Her usefulness had passed. She was one of the top candidates on the Realm's hit list. Bayard wanted to cut off the weak links in the chain.

Lili was to be "transported" to another realm—as soon as she finished her job on the Greek. Ulrich was supposed to silence her. Bayard had added another name to the list—Pierre Hubert.

"In that case, bring Kioskouras down here," Bayard replied.

"I'll set it up then," Ulrich said, putting down the phone. Though Auguste Bayard disliked the glad-handing, the wining and dining, it wasn't all that rare to see industrialists in his Paris mansion, men courted by the Realm. The Greek would be made welcome.

As he listened to one side of the conversation, Nanos savored Ulrich's nervousness. Initially the man had seemed like a rock, unafraid of anything. But obviously things had gone wrong for him lately. Dead wrong. He was no longer the golden child of the Realm, but just another gangster.

Nanos knew little about him other than what he could sense of the man and what Pierre Duval's people had put together on him. Kaspar Ulrich hadn't come up through the military. He'd come from the streets of Hamburg, Amsterdam and Paris. He was a bodyguard at first, then an enforcer, one of those types who relished violence regardless of the danger. Violence was the only music he danced to.

Ulrich had graduated into more profitable rackets. He started running girls, drugs, weapons. Naturally that made him noticed by intelligence operatives, who often hung out on the same street corners. Rogue intelligence operatives had brought him into the Realm.

Now it looked as if Ulrich would bring Nanos in.

When Ulrich hung up the phone, he nodded at the Greek. "It will be some time this week. At Monsieur Bayard's convenience. He will notify you when. Is that acceptable?"

"For Monsieur Bayard, yes," Nanos said.

"Good. I'll send a car for you and Mrs. Kioskouras."

"We'll drive ourselves." Nanos pushed off from the chair and headed for the door. "A pleasure doing business with you," he said, looking back at the rattled Ulrich.

ONE HOUR LATER, Alex Nanos met Lee Hatton in a quiet hotel bar on place des Vogues. They sat in a booth by the front window, looking out on the midday crowd.

"Well?" she asked, lifting a glass of white wine. "How did it go?"

"You and I have a date," Nanos said. "With a king."

"When and where?"

"Within the next few days we're going to be guests of Auguste Bayard at his mansion."

"What should I wear?" she asked.

"I'd start with a bulletproof gown."

CHAPTER TWENTY-ONE

Barrabas stood on the slippery rocks, as the waves splashed over his ankles. He spun the black steel grappling hook in an ever-increasing circle. It made a slight whirring sound as it picked up speed. Then, using an underhand throw, he launched it straight up in the air, letting the nylon cord uncoil from his left hand.

The four-pronged hook arced over the lip of the thirty-foot cliff, then caught in one of the jagged crevices.

Barrabas tugged on the line until it grew taut. He tested it a few times, then planted one foot against the sheer cliff wall and began climbing.

Liam O'Toole stood in the surf ten yards down, whirling another grappling hook.

Claude Hayes and Billy Two finished stowing away the SOBs' waterproof bags and lightweight scuba gear in niches gouged out of the cliff. The closed-circuit scuba systems were designed for shallow-depth penetration missions, providing up to three hours of air.

Plenty of time for the SOBs to make it to shore and also back out to their rendezvous a mile down the coast, where the "fishing boat" waited for them in the dark. The boat belonged to Company operatives enlisted from the CIA station in Lisbon.

Barrabas moved silently up the cliff face, walking almost vertically as he moved hand over hand, crevice by crevice. He was the first to scramble over the top, pulling himself up the jagged edge.

Quietly he looked around as O'Toole neared the halfway mark.

Then Barrabas froze. He was standing only a few feet from the edge of the cliff when he detected a slight movement in the grove ahead.

With the sounds of the surf smashing onto the Estoril shore below and O'Toole's harsh breathing as he climbed the steep face of rock, Barrabas could hear nothing in front of him. All he had to go on was that fleeting perception of movement.

Wind raced in from the Atlantic and kicked at his back. But it wasn't a frigid wind. And that meant that the ice-cold sensation on the back of his neck was telling him something was there, watching him.

He sensed rather than saw the guard. It was probably the four-legged kind. Two dogs roamed free on the grounds of Philip Emanuel's sprawling seaside villa, trained to be quiet, and trained to kill. Barrabas had been briefed about them by the CIA station in Portugal.

Barrabas eased the Navy Colt .22 from its rig. The stainless-steel silenced pistol was known as the Hush Puppy because of its most frequent task. But it could take care of more than just dogs.

O'Toole's head rose above the edge of the cliff.

Claude Hayes and Billy Two were standing by below, waiting for the go-ahead signal.

But it didn't come.

Barrabas raised his right hand slowly and signaled O'Toole to halt. Then he stepped forward, keeping his eyes on the woods ahead of him as he tried to goad the creature into showing itself. Leaves rustled. Then finally he saw it.

The Doberman was sitting in the dark shade at the edge of the grove. Its eyes, lit by a curious and hypnotized gaze, were on Barrabas. The canine killer was considering which way it would kill him.

One dog accounted for. Where was the other?

The question vanished as soon as the Doberman moved. It whipped out of the brush like a statue come to life. The sudden transformation was disorienting. One moment it was stock-still, the next it was a blur in the night. It came down once, its nails digging into the dirt, then launched itself straight for Barrabas.

The animal closed the gap faster than anticipated. Barrabas pulled the trigger. The hushed cough of the .22 seemed to have no impact. The dog was still coming.

Then the delayed reaction kicked in. The Doberman's eyes started to fade. A second shot cored through the bridge of its snout and into its brain.

Barrabas tried to step aside, but the dog was already upon him. Like a heat-seeking missile it slammed into him, even after it was dead. Barrabas pivoted with the blow, slashed his arm down around the animal's body, then propelled it over the cliff.

It dropped to the water and rocks below, making a dull splash.

Barrabas looked over the edge. Hayes and Billy Two were approaching the dog, its black form rocking in the water. They lifted the body from the water and put it on a rock.

The second dog appeared just as O'Toole heaved himself over the lip of the cliff. It streaked for him like a bullet, fangs open wide, its hot breath scorching his face with primordial anger.

O'Toole's fangs struck first. He snatched the grappling hook from its perch, yanked it free in one motion and smashed the dog's skull with the curved metal. The blinding strike deflected its attack. But its claws raked the dirt as it went after O'Toole again, still fighting until Barrabas fired the Hush Puppy. The Doberman collapsed in a long bloody sigh.

O'Toole got to his feet and looked down at the slain dog. "And this was supposed to be the easy part," he said.

"Welcome to Portugal," Barrabas said.

They fixed the grappling hook, and helped bring Hayes and Billy Two and their packs up the cliff. Then the SOBs moved into the woods.

Philip Emanuel's villa was perched on the cliffs overlooking the Estoril coastline, some of the most expensive sand in all of Europe.

But the cliff and the woods had seemed like a natural barrier against intruders, with no need for guards beyond the dogs. No one would expect anyone to approach that way. So that was the way the SOBs had come in.

There was another thing in the SOBs' favor. Philip Emanuel was of the old school. He believed in conducting war on foreign territory. He didn't expect it to be brought home.

At the north end of the villa a small walkway had been carved out of the hill. Its wooden steps and two landings led down to the beach and dock and boat house. A guard was usually posted through the night to watch over the yacht.

The yacht had recently come back from a long odyssey—a failed one. Several of the passengers had been left behind in Belgium. Now Emanuel was prepared to lick his wounds and demand reparations from Auguste Bayard before he continued to serve in the Realm.

The SOBs had come to show him that war didn't work that way. It wasn't quite that simple. It had a way of backfiring on you no matter how wealthy and protected you thought you were.

The four-man team moved toward the house where Philip Emanuel slept.

THE KINGS OF PORTUGAL had often lived on the coastline of Estoril, in the mountain palaces of Sintra, in the colder castles of the interior. Long after the monarchies fell the kings still lived in Portugal. After World War II they gathered there from all of the crumbling kingdoms of Europe, bringing whatever treasures they could from their homelands. So many royal exiles lived there that Estoril was called the Coast of Kings. It was also known as the Portuguese Riviera, attracting the royal families of Portugal, who had lived there for decades. Philip Emanuel, the White Brigade leader and would-be king, lived in his seaside villa like a Moorish prince.

The main building was a mixture of whitewashed and sun-washed walls, with stained-glass and rose windows admitting multicolored light into the interior. Hanging gardens decked the walls in a riot of foliage. Brightly tiled fish ponds stood in front of the house, bracketing a mosaic tile path that led toward the wide expanse of coastline—from where the ill-fated attack on the Belgian safehouse had been beached.

It was paradise on earth, a fitting home for a ruler of the Realm.

Nile Barrabas stopped just outside paradise. With dawn a couple of hours away, he and the SOBs looked like black nightmarish creatures about to intrude in the dream.

Barrabas studied one of the stained-glass windows along the side of the house. It was a painting of a knight slaying a dragon, the different panels showing a kingdom basking in light from above. Barrabas covered the painted glass of the lower panel with strips of tape, then punched it hard with black-gloved knuckles. The glass cracked, but remained glued to the tape. Slowly Barrabas removed the shards of glass, unhorsing the now shattered knight as he prepared the way for real-live dragons to enter the ''castle'' of Philip Emanuel.

Billy Two worked quickly and soundlessly on the next panel smashing the glass the same way. After the glass from the two lower panels had been removed, the Osage Indian gripped the black metal window guard that had separated the panels, and hung from it using his full weight. It bent, groaned slightly, then ripped away from the wall.

O'Toole, who'd been standing nearby with a hushed Heckler & Koch MP5 submachine gun, stepped closer as first Barrabas, then Billy Two went inside. Despite his bulk the Irishman moved lightly. He balanced his hands against the window well, swung his feet inward, then lowered himself soundlessly to the floor.

The three SOBs moved toward the inner sanctum of Philip Emanuel.

AN ARMED SENTRY, broad-shouldered and tall, watched over the boathouse. He stood at the end of a dock flanked by powerboats. Now and then he puffed on a cigarette cupped in his hands.

Though he was awake, his eyes had been lulled by the long hours of his watch and by the soothing waves. He was looking out to sea, certain that nothing could come from behind except another sentry. After all, this was neutral territory, guarded by wealth and by the good name of Philip Emanuel.

Claude Hayes took his time moving over the damp and silent slats of the dock. Now and then the anchored boats creaked, covering any sound he might have made.

The guard was sleepy. With three quick steps, Claude Hayes closed out the man's watch by pressing a needle-nosed dart gun to the back of his neck. Hayes pulled the trigger and caught the guard as he fell, instantly knocked out by the powerful drug.

The SOB swung the man around, eased him down the dock and dropped him into one of the powerboats. He propped him behind the steering wheel. "Don't dream too fast now, hear," Hayes said, then backed down the dock.

The guard was hidden and safe, out cold for the duration.

Hayes hadn't come here to murder anyone. Just to silence him for a while.

LIAM O'TOOLE WALKED to the back of the villa, his eyes now adjusted to the darkness.

Two hours before his watch was to begin, a guard slept soundly in a room off the back corridor. The Irishman made sure the man stayed asleep by firing a narcotic dart into his neck. O'Toole backed out of the room, still wielding the gun, then continued to scope out the ground floor.

Like a slightly distorted mirror image—the hair longer, the movements a bit smoother—the Osage duplicated O'Toole's actions on the other side of the house, moving toward the back where another guard was waiting.

This one woke up, saw the looming shape of Billy Two and cried, "No!"

"Yes," Billy Two corrected him, firing a narcotic missile into the man that put him out in seconds. He would wake up hours later, surprised that he was still alive.

The SOBs had come in with enough firepower to blow the guards all away, but they'd also packed the nonlethal weaponry. Tonight's raid was going to be a lesson in applied power. The instructors were the black-clad SOBs.

Barrabas took the stairs.

According to the intelligence provided by the embassy, Emanuel's only houseguest was his mistress, a dark blond habitué of the Estoril coast.

Barrabas paused outside the bedroom door. He held a Heckler & Koch subgun in his right hand, a narco dart gun in his left. If things went down the wrong way, he wasn't going to be the first one to check out the afterlife.

He opened the door upon two soundly sleeping people. The gray-haired commander and his blond companion were stretched out on the bed, barely covered by a sheet crumpled around their legs while sea breezes blew in through the windows.

Barrabas hurried over to the bed and fired a dart into the naked blonde. She squirmed, started to swat at her neck, then dropped her head onto the pillow.

Emanuel stirred. The SOB chieftain walked around the bed. He lowered the sound suppressor on the H&K subgun until the cold metal circle pressed against Emanuel's cheek. He woke with a start.

"Don't move," Barrabas said.

Emanuel nodded, his eyes following the trail of the submachine gun barrel. He was familiar with the damage it could do. More than once he'd been on the other side of one like it.

"I want you to understand something," Barrabas said. "Do what I tell you and you might live long enough to consider this all just a bad dream."

Emanuel nodded again.

"Understand?"

"I understand."

Barrabas stepped back. The Portuguese commander looked at the woman beside him and noticed how still she was. "Veronica," he said. "Is she..."

"She's still," Barrabas assured him. "Isn't that part of the plan? You surround yourself with civilians—like you did on your recent yacht trip—and you figure no one will hurt you."

"The yacht has been here all along."

"That's what I came to talk to you about," Barrabas said. "Get up."

The man stood. He started to reach for his robe at the side of the bed. "Do you mind if I wear this?"

"As long as it's not bulletproof, be my guest."

Barrabas directed him downstairs to a narrow dining room lit by a wall lamp, where O'Toole and Billy Two stood waiting on opposite sides of a long wooden table. The candelabra centered on the table was flanked by bundles of gear the SOBs had brought with them.

From the wall behind the table a regal portrait of Philip Emanuel stared down at them.

Billy Two and O'Toole greeted the Portuguese commander with the silenced barrels of their submachine guns.

"Sit," Barrabas told Emanuel.

He complied quickly, then stared evenly at Barrabas, who sat at the other end of the table, his face streaked with camouflage makeup that gave him a macabre appearance.

"What's this about?" Emanuel asked finally.

Barrabas put down his submachine gun on the clear polished table, pushed it forward, the barrel pointing at the captive, then unzipped one of the packs and took out a packet of photographs. "It's about your pleasure cruise." He pushed the photographs across the table, spilling them in front of the Portuguese commander.

Emanuel gasped.

The photos had been taken from SR-71 Blackbird overflights and KH-11 digitized reconnaissance satellites with resolution so clear one could have counted the polka dots on a bikini. Walker Jessup had arranged the surveillance with just a few words to Teddy Nicholas, the NSA covert tsar. Every bit of the journey had been captured on film. From the moment the yacht left Estoril, through its "pleasure stops" along the coast and its destination in Belgium, where it dropped off its commando cargo, to its return to its home port. The last group of photos showed the White

Brigade commandos who'd fallen on the beach, never to rise again.

"How did you get these?"

Barrabas shrugged. "It's the company we keep," he said. "You could have met some of them personally—if you came ashore in Belgium."

"Who told you I was involved?"

Barrabas paused. One goal of tonight's operation was to alienate Emanuel from the French leader. "Bayard as good as threw you away," he said finally. "It was no great feat to put the puzzle together." Barrabas hoped to turn the man against Bayard. With enough friction, the empire might crumble. Emanuel could provide plenty of damaging information about Bayard.

"The Belgians were fielding a lot of inquiries from intelligence operatives about the whereabouts of Maurice Sordett, a White Brigader in our possession," Barrabas continued. "You may have heard of him."

Emanuel nodded.

"Supposedly these people wanted to question Sordett about cases they were working on. But their requests were transparent. They were obviously working on behalf of the Realm. Fortunately for us, they were very persistent, eager for an answer. That made it easy for us to leak the whereabouts of Sordett. And then, surprise, surprise, your people came looking for him."

Philip Emanuel took a deep breath, let it out and stretched his hands across the table, almost as if he were lifting them in surrender. He'd been in the trade long enough to know that there was only one way out of here, and that that course was determined by the hard-faced man across the table.

The White Brigader didn't bother to deny anything. He knew they had him cold. "It was suggested that I join the operation," he said, "to increase my position in the Realm. I chose to comply." Emanuel glanced up at Billy Two and O'Toole, who looked back at him impassively, as if they were ready to drill him at a nod from their commander. "And so now you came to kill me."

Barrabas shrugged. "The idea has occurred to me."

"But first you want to make me repent."

"Look," Barrabas said, "no one's dead yet. They've only been drugged. Your guards and your girl upstairs will wake up later with varying degrees of nausea and headache. Not bad, considering the alternative."

"And I?"

"That's what we have to settle," Barrabas said. "Where you stand in the Realm. It's harder than you think to build a kingdom on earth. But if you'd like to try for the other kingdom—" he tapped the Heckler & Koch, then flicked the selector to a 3-round burst "—it's as simple as one-two-three."

"What do you want from me?"

"Break with the Realm," Barrabas said. "But not openly. Not until we tell you. Then you come out against Bayard with everything you have."

"That's quite a lot to give up."

"We also want information about Realm activities in the Netherlands. We already have Belgium under control. France is well covered. And Portugal, well, that is finished. Here and now. But we still want to know about the Dutch."

Though the Banker had given the SOBs a look into the financial dealings of the Realm, the military aspect was still unknown.

Emanuel looked up. "What do you want to know?"

"Start with the name of the Dutch White Brigade commander," Barrabas said. "Safehouses. Arms caches. Subordinates. Everything we need to put him out of business."

Philip Emanuel nodded. He had made up his mind even before the demands came. The Realm was a lofty idea that had degenerated into a terrorist network. And now if he stayed with it, he was dead. So at that moment he started unraveling the secrets of the Realm, beginning with the names of the Dutch commander, Albrecht, and aides who worked for him.

Barrabas listened for several minutes, then raised his hand. "Enough for now," he said. "Someone from the Company will contact you tomorrow to make arrangements. You'll be debriefed, defanged, defrocked and dethroned. Do it right and you just might ransom your ass out of this. Just make sure you're as talkative to them as you were to us."

"Why wouldn't I be?"

Barrabas stood up from the table. He picked up the Heckler & Koch. "You might forget how well this little rehearsal went down tonight, once we're gone. You might think if you beef up security we won't be a threat anymore. That we won't come back."

Emanuel stayed rooted in the chair, looking at the submachine gun and wondering if this had all been just part of an act to open him up—and now the hit was coming down.

"Fuck with us once," Barrabas said, "and when we come back it's show time."

He raised the Heckler & Koch, the silenced barrel pointing at Emanuel. Then he shifted his aim and pulled the trigger. The silenced burst thwacked into the shoulder of the portrait of Philip Emanuel. "Get the picture?" Barrabas asked. And then they were gone.

CHAPTER TWENTY-TWO

Auguste Bayard clamped down the phone as if the receiver were a guillotine. For a moment he imagined the head of Philip Emanuel toppling onto his desk, then a hooded executioner picking it up and holding it aloft for the crowd to see.

Emanuel's crime was simple but almost treasonous. He had ignored a royal summons.

For days now the Portuguese commander of the Realm had been incommunicado. Word had reached Bayard of some kind of "incident" at Emanuel's Estoril compound. Bayard's contacts in the Portuguese community knew of a disturbance but had nothing definite to pass on.

The news from Portugal was bad, mainly because there was no news. As the prime mover behind the Realm, Bayard had to know what was happening on its frontiers. But Emanuel was keeping him in the dark.

Bayard had made several attempts to reach Emanuel. The man had not responded. It was as if the Portuguese commander had withdrawn from the Realm. Like a brooding baron, Emanuel seemed to want nothing to do with Bayard. At least for the moment.

Bayard had expected some such problem. Just as in the chivalric kingdoms upon which the Realm had been modeled, there were bound to be feuds now and then. Tests of loyalty and intrigues were inevitable.

Obviously, Emanuel still hadn't recovered from the loss of his men on the Belgium attack. For that matter, neither had Bayard.

Despite his momentary anger, he would take the proper course with Emanuel. He would let him sulk, let him lick his wounds. After a decent interval he would welcome him back into the Realm with open arms. If Emanuel still resisted, then he would welcome him with loaded arms.

In the meantime, he had a kingdom to run. Meetings had been scheduled with industrialists like Michael Kioskouras who wanted to be persuaded firsthand. To allay their suspicions Bayard accommodated them whenever he could. But there was another reason why he saw such men. It added to his cover as an international businessman to have the high and mighty arriving at his Parisian doorstep at all hours. With so many respectable businessmen visiting him, it would be hard for anyone to imagine him as the covert ruler behind the Realm.

While the White Brigade manned the trenches, he brought in the fortunes needed to keep the Realm going. These days the corporate battlefield was his domain. He had no doubt that Michael Kioskouras would take over the armaments company. A preliminary investigation had shown that he was more than capable of completing the maneuver he'd started. When that happened, Bayard would just have to take over the Greek.

Other matters needed attention, too—matters best left in the hands of Kaspar Ulrich.

THE SWEEP BEGAN in the Netherlands.

The Dutch Royal Military Police hit Realm safehouses in Amsterdam and The Hague. At Schiphol

Airport Whiskey Company antiterrorist marines picked up several White Brigade commandos. The Whiskey Company platoon had often trained at Schiphol. Familiar with all the avenues of escape, they sealed them off from the White Brigaders.

The scenario was repeated all across the country in lightning raids conducted by the state, municipal and Royal Military Police.

The overall sweep was headed by Pieter Dietrich, a commander of the Brigade speciaal beveiliginsopdrachten, a police unit activated in emergencies. Since the Realm had almost put the entire nation into a state of emergency, Dietrich threw everything he had into the operation, carefully selecting BSB men who were above suspicion.

The Dutch antiterrorist specialist worked closely with Mitchell Rhodes. The CIA man had provided most of the names and locations acquired from the Realm's Portuguese faction. That began a domino effect, with Philip Emanuel cooperating fully in order to remove the noose from around his neck. In turn, most of the people he named chose to cooperate rather than face the wrath of the covert force. The intense debriefings set in motion a steamroller as one agent after another jumped from the crumbling kingdom, their only parachute a willingness to give up information.

After the first sweep, only one group of White Brigaders remained at large, led by Frederick Albrecht, the commander of the Dutch White Brigade. He and a number of his top aides had managed to escape the net.

But they couldn't evade it much longer. Albrecht was a well-known figure in Holland. Much had been made in the press of his retirement from the Korps commandetroepen a few years back and of his subsequent success in business—a business funded by the Realm. Too many people knew him and his haunts. With his safehouses shut down and his suspected collaborators watched by BSB teams trying to flush him out, there was little chance left for the Dutchman.

Albrecht made his move three days after the sweep began.

He contacted a network unknown to the intelligence men looking for him. It had been selected ahead of time just for an occasion like this. It was a smuggling operation that had for decades been moving arms, cash and—most important—people. It specialized in moving people out of a war zone, which was exactly what the White Brigade leaders found themselves in.

Gunther Dykstra was their only ticket out.

Albrecht was convinced that it was a safe passage. The only White Brigaders who knew of the arrangements he'd made with Dykstra were fleeing with him.

The arrangement was simple. The Dutch smuggler agreed to it after Albrecht made him an extravagant payoff, which Dykstra called a retainer.

At ten o'clock at night Frederick Albrecht strolled through the busy streets of Amsterdam toward a rendezvous with Gunther Dykstra.

Albrecht was a cautious man. When he reached the third floor office above the bookshop on Kalverstraat he looked around as if he expected to find a ghost, or worse, a gunman. Though he was gray-haired and well into middle age, Albrecht had kept himself in fighting shape and was ready to prove it if necessary.

Dykstra's bodyguard stood silently in reserve, guarding the door like a block of cement.

"Relax, Frederick," Dykstra said, walking across the room. "I specialize in making things disappear, not appear. There's no one else coming tonight."

"Good," Albrecht said. "As it is, I'm taking a chance in coming here. But I figured if I couldn't count on you, especially since we were members of the same unit—"

Dykstra laughed. "You figured we were in the same boat."

"Exactly. Old comrades, ready to help each other out in time of need." He dropped into the chair in front of Dykstra's desk.

The rugged blond Dutchman sat on the edge of his desk, looking down at Albrecht. "The only problem is," he said, "we aren't marines anymore. In fact, it's my guess the marines are after us right now. They could be outside my door any moment."

"Not a chance," Albrecht said. "My people have been backing me up every step of the way. They would have picked up any surveillance."

"Where are your people now?" Gunther asked.

Albrecht looked warily at him. "Why?"

"That's a damned silly question. You want my help in moving your people out of here—but you won't tell me where they are?"

Anger flashed across Albrecht's face. "Where do you want them to be?" he snapped. "That's the only question that has to be asked."

Gunther shrugged. "We'll do it your way. But there is one more question."

"What's that?"

"Money," Gunther said. "Fifty thousand guilders a man."

"That's too much," Albrecht protested. "More than we agreed on. I won't pay that."

"Fine." Gunther walked around the desk. "Then take a bus."

"Damn you!" Albrecht shouted. He leaped from his chair and raised his hand to pound on the desk.

Two things happened then. Gunther Dykstra moved forward, his steel grip intercepting Albrecht's fist. And Gunther's bodyguard came to life. Moving quickly, he stood beside the two of them, waiting for a cue from Gunther.

But the blond Dutchman needed no help. He released Albrecht. "That doesn't work with me," he said.

Albrecht was still flustered but he moved away. "You don't know who you're dealing with."

"Yes, I do," Gunther said. "I'm dealing with somebody who has to run for his life. And if you don't have the money for it, then you're out of luck. You'll have a short life."

"I'll pay," Albrecht said.

"Then I'll take you."

"All right, look, forget what just happened," Albrecht said. "People with guns chasing you all the time, makes you a bit crazy."

"Don't worry about it. I've been there."

Albrecht nodded. "Now, where and when do we move?"

"Tonight, two hours from now," Gunther said. "At Damrak Harbor. As part of my import-export business, there's a tramp freighter called the *Zeemeester*. It's leaving in the morning via the North Sea

Canal. We go south and take you to your new home. Then you get off.''

"We'll be there.''

"Bring the money," Gunther said. "But no weapons, in case we are searched. And make sure you dress right in case we have to pass you off as part of the crew.''

"As you say," the Dutch White Brigader said. "In two hours you'll have five new crew members.''

They shook hands.

The following morning the *Zeemeester* passed through the North Sea Canal into the open sea. The five new crew hands stayed below all the while, cramped and hidden away in one of the holds.

The freighter headed south.

Two hours later it slowed, met by a 44-footer that had come to off-load the commando cargo. Four men came aboard the *Zeemeester*. One of them climbed down the ladder into the hold.

Albrecht stood up and massaged his legs to restore the circulation. Then he stepped in front of the newcomer. The four other men, all hardy looking, all tired and cramped, spread out behind him.

They looked at the man with coarse white hair and the dark blue jacket still wet with sea spray. He was armed with a Browning Hi-Power on his hip, but looked as if he didn't have to depend upon the weapon. He looked like the type that could see them through the underground escape route Gunther had mapped out.

"Who are you?" Albrecht asked.

"Nile Barrabas," the man in the jacket said. "The person you've been running from.''

Albrecht froze, suspended between disbelief and fury. "Gunther sold us out!" he shouted. "What is this?"

"You just said it," Barrabas told him. "Gunther had a bad reputation to uphold. With you people anyway. This is the end of the line, Albrecht. The Realm is running out of rulers. We're closing it down."

Albrecht started to go for the newcomer, his hands outstretched. But he stopped halfway, seeing the man's cold unconcerned eyes. There was no fear there, only a knowledge that he could meet whatever came his way.

The Dutch White Brigader saw his death reflected in Barrabas's gaze. It didn't matter to this man if Albrecht lived or died. And he didn't need the Browning to put him down.

The other White Brigaders, equally confused, immobile like their leader, undecided what to do. Billy Two and Claude Hayes made up their minds for them, clambering down into the hold with submachine guns. Liam O'Toole followed them, with a Heckler & Koch MP5.

Albrecht stepped back, collapsing against the wall.

"This is the deal," Barrabas said. "It's cut-and-dried. You want to be free, you can go over the side now and take your chances in the North Sea. You want to stay dry—you start talking about Auguste Bayard."

Frederick Albrecht saw the castle walls falling. He shook his head as if he couldn't believe that he'd been taken by the smuggler.

"What do you want?"

"I want Auguste Bayard dead to rights. And while you're at it," he added, "you can give me the keys to the kingdom."

AUGUSTE BAYARD WAS shell-shocked when he heard the news that Frederick Albrecht had disappeared. The last stronghold in the Netherlands had been smashed.

Bayard was entertaining and he hoped, winning over a quartet of industrialists when Kaspar Ulrich called from Amsterdam. He couldn't dismiss his guests—not then. He had to ride it through. If they saw that his empire was vulnerable, there would be no way of getting them back into the fold.

With Holland out of control, Portugal close to secession and Belgium thrown into chaos, there was little the Realm could do. But it had to be done, and it fell into the hands of the most capable man. Kaspar Ulrich.

It was time to strengthen the Realm by cutting off the weak links. And though Kaspar Ulrich had lost a major battle, in one-on-one situations he was peerless.

Bayard gave Ulrich his marching orders, then went back to the dining table and toasted his guests.

"WE MUST TALK," Kaspar Ulrich said, his eyes hidden behind dark glasses, his weapons hidden beneath his leather jacket.

Pierre Hubert looked out his half-open door at the Realm troubleshooter. Out of habit he looked at Ulrich's car in front of the château to see if he'd brought someone with him. The windows were struck by sunlight, making it hard for him to see.

"It's just me, Pierre," Ulrich said.

"It is more than enough," Hubert said, manufacturing a smile. But the well-fed NATOcrat gripped the side of the door as if he were prepared to close it in his caller's face.

"It concerns the Realm," Ulrich said.

Hubert nodded. The harried diplomat had no choice. Ulrich was the main messenger from Bayard. It wouldn't do at this point to antagonize either of them. But the last thing he needed now was another complication. On Bayard's earlier orders he had had his staff close down the château, then sent them to his Brussels mansion, while he stayed behind to sanitize the place in case there was an investigation.

With the Netherlands under siege and the Dutch White Brigade scattered, they could take no chances. They had to erase the past and shut down the château. There were too many rumors linking the place with the entrapment of the high and the mighty. That part of the operation was going to be furloughed for a while.

Pierre Hubert would busy himself once again in the normal diplomatic intrigues in Brussels. There, he would keep his nose buried in NATO affairs and hope to avoid the heat coming down on the Realm.

"What's it about?" Hubert said.

Sensing that he was nervous, Ulrich smiled and shook his head conspiratorially. "It's a problem that only a man with your skills can solve. It requires finesse. Come outside and talk."

"All right," he said, "but only for a minute. I'm due to leave for Brussels this afternoon."

"It'll be quick."

They walked around the grounds, two country gentlemen discussing the affairs of the state. Ulrich kept talking broadly about the problems that needed to be solved, gradually steering Hubert toward the back of his château. They strolled into the maze of well-clipped hedges.

Halfway through, Hubert assumed his diplomatic persona. "Now, Kaspar," he said, "I insist on an explanation. What requires my...my finesse, as you put it?"

"It involves Lili Kavroleira," Ulrich said. "Some time ago you had a conversation with Monsieur Bayard about the danger she represents to our cause."

Hubert's eyes flickered with anger and sadness. Lili had brought Hubert and countless others into the Realm. She knew too much now. If she was ever apprehended it would be the end of them. "It has to be done," he said. "She's too dangerous now, especially after the fiasco on the coast. But then, I needn't remind you of that. It's obvious we've been penetrated. Damaged. We've got to protect ourselves."

"Yes," Kaspar agreed. "It's time."

Hubert sighed. "There's no choice." The political maven took on the hard-eyed glint of a soldier of the Realm. "But please, just make it quick."

"Yes," Ulrich said. "It will be quick." He leaned forward and looked at Hubert as if about to confide something to him.

Ulrich pushed the Belgian off balance, and as Hubert teetered backward, stabbed him with the dagger that had materialized in his right hand. Up through the ribs, through the chest, into the heart. Hubert gasped. Then he was dead.

As Kaspar had promised, it had been quick. It had taken only three seconds to kill Hubert.

Ulrich used the leverage of the knife to swing the Belgian around. Then he eased him to the ground, sitting upright in a maze from which he would never escape.

CHAPTER TWENTY-THREE

The auburn-haired siren was accustomed to having men breathe down her neck.

But usually she could see them. Today Lili Kavroleira could see no one, hear no one. But she could sense someone.

Perhaps it was only her imagination, but a part of her was certain that her name was being spoken somewhere. That something was in the air.

The Czech actress felt watched and listened to as she prowled around her Brussels mansion on boulevard du Régent. It was only natural. The ocean of paranoia that had flooded through the gates of the Realm was bound to affect her sooner or later. Lili wasn't immune to the problems besieging the Realm. Far from it.

The hardest part was that no one was talking to her. It was as if she were being kept in isolation, cut off from her friends in the Realm. Not that there were many she genuinely could call friends.

Still, it was frustrating. She had been forced to cool her heels for long periods before being sent into action in the past. But Bayard or Ulrich or Hubert had always had a kind word or two for her. Even if the kindness was faked, it had still soothed her.

Of the three only Pierre Hubert seemed to genuinely care for her. She thought of as him the closest thing she had to a friend. Maybe it was just because she spent most of her time at the château south of

Brussels, where the Realm "recruited" so many of their people. She felt at home there. She felt safe. If nothing else, she thought, at least Hubert wasn't a dangerous man. He didn't have the brutal edge that Ulrich did.

Lili picked up the phone and tried again to reach Hubert. There was no answer at the château, or at his Brussels place.

She swore. She felt like a prisoner.

Her most recent word from the Realm had been orders from Kaspar Ulrich to stay put. Ordinarily that would have been simple to do, but as more and more Realmists were rounded up by the authorities, staying here was almost like a death sentence.

The hell with it, she thought. The wrath of the Realm would come down on her if she wasn't here when someone came for her, but she had to get out.

At three in the afternoon she left the house, wearing jeans and a knit top, looking nothing like the Czech actress whose image the public feasted upon in the papers and on television. She looked like a woman with more on her mind than fashion or frolic. She looked like a woman in fear of her life. Her subconsious had warned her—but her conscious mind hadn't yet put it all together.

Almost in a trance she glided past the iron gate and climbed into her white Peugeot. Though she was accustomed to being chauffeured around the city by Kaspar Ulrich, she needed her own transportation from time to time—especially a time like this.

She drove across the city to the Anderlecht district where Hubert maintained his palatial mansion. But it was vacant except for servants. They said he was still at the château.

Maybe he was out walking, she thought, and hadn't heard the phone when she called. He might have gone out to the garden for a final look, or maybe to the nearby woods. Or perhaps he was just returning from a drive.

She took the road south toward Mons.

She needed contact with someone—someone who could share her fear that was emanating from the heart of the Realm.

In front of Hubert's château Lili killed the engine of her Peugeot and rolled to a stop. Two of his cars were parked in the oval drive, but they were no guarantee of his presence.

She slid out of the car and slammed the door, the echo bouncing off the walls and getting lost in the sounds of the forest.

It was quiet here. Too quiet.

Pierre Hubert's château was always alive. Every time she'd been here before, something was going on, whether it was someone demanding her services for the Realm or merely a gathering of the Realm's inner circle. The place had that magical air about it that history was always being made.

Now it was deserted. The once thriving château looked abandoned, just like her.

Lili dug in her purse for the key Hubert had given her months back. Then she unlocked the oval door and pushed it inward.

It was dark inside. Most of the desks, tables and chairs were covered with white cloths, seating only the ghosts of the Realm. But a few pieces of furniture hadn't been covered yet. Hubert was evidently still using part of the château.

Lili called out his name.

Nothing.

She called him again as she moved deeper into the building. Still no answer. He was gone, she thought. But where? Maybe they'd crossed paths along the way, he heading for Brussels while she came down here. Or maybe he was on his way back here to finish closing down the place.

She decided to wait for him.

But not inside. It was too spooky. There were too many rooms where someone could be waiting. Jittery as she was, Lili didn't feel like spending any more time inside this elegant mausoleum.

She went out through the back and stepped into the shade of several ancient oaks. Then she headed for the tall hedges where Hubert was fond of taking her in those few quiet moments they stole together.

Halfway through the maze she saw him. He was sitting propped up against the bushes, looking at a horizon only he could see.

"Pierre!" she shouted. She ran forward, taking in the crimson stain that ran down his shirt like a bloody necktie.

Flies buzzed around him. She brushed them away, then moved back as the scent of death assailed her like a perfume of the Realm.

She felt a cold spear of horror shoot through her chest. Then she started to tremble. Not because he was dead—in that time she knew how much, and how little, he really meant to her. What horrified her was the idea that she was probably due to join him soon.

Someone was closing out accounts for the Realm.

She heard a strange sound coming from her mouth. It was not a scream but a whimper. She didn't want to be heard in case the killer was still around.

She ran through the house. Then she dashed out into the bright afternoon sun, jumped into the Peugeot and screeched away from the château like a woman possessed.

All she could think of was the Greek, the man who had so deftly evaded her trap and had then told her if she ever needed him to come to his hotel in Paris.

Now, as she raced south toward the French border, she remembered the Greek's unflinching eyes. They had seen through her, beyond her. They were eyes that had seen her future—along with the future of everyone else in the Realm.

He had known this was going to happen. In fact, she thought, he probably had a good deal to do with bringing it about.

His offer of help could be a trap, she thought. But the alternative was waiting for the hatchet man to come after her.

THE HOTEL on place des Vogues was busy in the afternoon, its shops, café and bar offering an air-conditioned reprieve from the hot Parisian streets.

Lili Kavroleira was used to that lazy air of elegance—women with stunning figures and stunning clothes, men with stunning bank accounts, all of them scanning the lush surroundings for something to buy or sell, whether it was a bright and shining object or, more likely, an hour or two of affection. They moved around like slow-motion sharks, she thought, as she took the elevator to the third floor.

A few moments later she stepped out into a cream-colored hallway. She walked down a corridor that led toward the front of the hotel, turned right and then stopped in front of room 318.

That was the number the Greek had given her.

Lili started to knock but caught herself at the last moment. Her fist hung suspended in the air. What if it was a trap? What if this was the room where it would come to an end?

She turned around and took several steps down the hall before stopping dead in her tracks.

Where could she go?

To Auguste Bayard? From what she'd learned about him recently, mostly by seeing the dread he inspired, she didn't want to see him face-to-face.

To Kaspar Ulrich? She pictured his cold eyes, his dead smile, like that of an alabaster-skinned ghoul.

Then the image of the Greek came to her. He had told her to come here for help, and he'd meant it. At least that had been her impression. And since she was here, her instincts told her to trust him.

Why not? she thought. He could be no worse than the others, and maybe better. She turned around and headed back toward room 318.

Lili raised her hand to knock on the door. It opened and suddenly she was knocking on air.

Someone grabbed her, yanked her into the room. The door slammed shut behind her.

The room was dim. Even though it was the middle of the afternoon, the curtains were drawn tight.

Lili was about to cry out when she recognized the Greek. He was laughing. He released her hand and said, "Sorry. I just didn't want you to change your mind again."

A soft laugh escaped her lips.

"I was hoping you would come," the Greek said. "In fact, the moment you stepped into the hotel one of my people called me from the lobby. I've been watching for you.''

''It's—I wanted to get away. I had to leave before they came to me—'' she stammered. ''They killed Hubert.''

The Greek raised his eyebrows. ''It's started then,'' he said. ''But we're here to finish it.''

''We?'' she asked.

Just then Lee Hatton stepped into sight. She was carrying an automatic pistol. The silvery barrel was pointed not at the newcomer, but at the doorway behind her.

Soft footsteps sounded from within the suite and two other men came in. The first man had hair that was almost white, but it wasn't from age. It was from the kind of work Lili instinctively knew the Greek was involved in.

''As beautiful as you said, Alex,'' he remarked. ''Let me know as soon as you can if she's in or out.''

The Greek nodded.

''Alex?'' She looked first at the white-haired man, who was obviously in command, then at the Greek. ''I thought your name was Michael.''

''It was,'' the Greek said, ''on the day we met. And as far as the Realm is concerned, I still am Michael Kioskouras, a man about to take over the Pontaillier arms corporation—a man they think *they* are about to take over when I have another meeting with Bayard.''

''What is this all about?'' she asked.

He told her about the state of the Realm and the White Brigade. He told her about the people he and his friends were going after and what they wanted from her.

While he and Lili talked other men came in. A bulky man entered from another room in the suite. From a room across the hall came a tall black man and a red-bearded broad-chested man with laughing eyes. Behind them was a man she'd passed in the lobby. His long black hair was pulled taut in a lock that draped over his collar. He smiled and nodded at her.

They didn't look like businessmen here to advise Michael—Alex—about the finer points of industry. Especially since they were all armed. None of them looked menacing, either. At least, not to her.

She gasped as a man walked into the room whom she'd seen at embassy affairs: Pierre Duval. She also knew him as one of the main enemies of the Realm and of Auguste Bayard.

The hotel suite had the atmosphere of a war room.

They'd been planning a war on the Realm, the Greek explained, and she was one more soldier in the fight. He put her in a corner where she was out of the way. She felt reassured that she'd made the right move. She couldn't imagine anyone getting to her through all these people.

She looked at the woman she believed to be Mrs. Kioskouras. "And your wife?" she asked. "Where does she fit into this?"

Nanos smiled. "She's not my wife. Though she'd like to be."

"I don't understand."

"She played the role of my wife long enough for us to get into the house of Auguste Bayard." He looked at his watch. "Which is where we're going soon. But first, it would help if you told us more about the master of the Realm."

The look of fright returned to her face.

"There's no retribution. Nothing to fear. We know you had no choice. Now we're giving you one."

"What do you want?"

"Make a statement for us about Bayard and the subversive activities of the Realm."

"Bayard will kill me," she said.

"No doubt he would," the Greek said, "if we hadn't come along. But dead men can't kill anyone."

"What do you mean?"

"I mean this is the end of the Realm," he said.

"And Kaspar?"

"He's going down, too. He's been in it all the way."

"But if you know all this," she said, "why do you need me?"

"A chorus is much more important than a solo act. With you on board, we've got the crowning touch."

Lili nodded. She'd already decided to throw in her lot with the Greek. And now that she saw the fire-power behind him—the white-haired man, the high-powered covert operators—she felt even safer. "What do you want me to do?"

Alex smiled broadly. "Now that is a loaded question," he said. "First, let me tell you what I can give you. Your freedom. Your dignity. A chance to wipe the slate clean. After this is over, no one will own you anymore."

"What do you want in return?"

"The truth," he said. "About the entrapment operation. About the people lured into the Realm. We want you to help us spread the news."

"And then what?"

"And then we'll make some news of our own."

CHAPTER TWENTY-FOUR

At seven in the evening an army of guests headed for Auguste Bayard's mansion on avenue René-Coty.

Only two of them were invited. The others trailed a block behind Alex Nanos and Lee Hatton as they walked toward the residence.

Agents in surveillance vans, taxis and sports cars watched the two SOBs carefully. The vans were equipped with cameras, night vision goggles, thermal imagers, automatic weapons with silencers, shotguns, hammers and explosives. Everything needed to crash the private party was there.

Nile Barrabas drove one of the cream-colored surveillance vans. O'Toole sat across from him, while Hayes and Billy Two were in the back, H&K submachine guns slung over their shoulders. They were rolling armories and they were rolling in the direction of the Realm.

Well-dressed men carrying briefcases also moved through the neighborhood. Luxurious and compact, the briefcases contained weapons ranging from a dismantled CETME Ameli machine gun with one hundred rounds, submachine guns, grenade launchers and sniper rifles. A number of "students" carrying similarly loaded knapsacks strolled through the nearby university grounds, ready to move on the house at a moment's notice.

Their business was covert operations; they were select members of GIGN recruited by Pierre Duval, the SDECE head who had returned from retirement for this operation, which was the culmination of his decade-long struggle with Bayard. They were here to contain the war to the manor, seal off the surrounding streets and prevent the bloodbath from spilling into the heart of Paris.

The operation would be spearheaded by the SOBs and a cadre of CIA paras led by Bennett. The members of the paramilitary team were professionals who'd done this kind of work before, serving with Bennett around the globe, most recently in Belgium. Their bodies were nearly as scarred as that of the agency man. They were all outsiders, deniables not attached to the agency.

The assault had been carefully planned. If possible, Nanos was going to take Auguste Bayard alive— although no one gave that much of a chance. Bayard wasn't the surrendering kind. The SOBs were prepared for a room-to-room battle.

If the operation turned sour, the French forces wouldn't be held responsible. If it turned sour, those inside would be dead, with everyone on the outside suddenly forgetting their names.

The cover story would be that a group of terrorist factions had had a shoot-out at the mansion and a GIGN team had arrived on the scene to contain it.

"MONSIEUR KIOSKOURAS," Jacques Rogier said. "Welcome." Almost as if it were an afterthought, he turned to Lee Hatton and said, "And you, of course,

Madame." He spoke very proper French for what he obviously considered improper guests.

She smiled for an instant as she passed.

Nanos nodded slightly at Rogier. There was no love lost between them. Rogier considered anyone not of the Realm to be an outsider. And though the Greek was a prospective member of the Realm, it wasn't as a soldier but as a pigeon.

Rogier was a round-faced man with short hair. His eyes always seemed in motion, as if he were trying to look behind the scenes. Despite his cherubic appearance he had been a decorated sergeant in the Troupe de Marines before he was recruited into the Realm.

With a discreet professionalism, Rogier quickly searched Nanos, patting him down for weapons. He eyed Lee Hatton's figure as impartially as any man could while he studied her for signs of bulging weapons.

"Careful," Nanos warned. "Those curves can be dangerous."

Rogier frowned. "It is a precaution we must take," he said. "A man of Bayard's stature has many enemies. There are too many crazies out there."

"We're not crazies," Nanos said. Just enemies.

Satisfied they were unarmed, Rogier ushered the couple inside. By now they were familiar faces to the White Brigade attendants—millionaire guests who wouldn't go away. But since they still had to be won over, Bayard had proved unusually accommodating to them. He'd agreed to see the Greek on short notice tonight, because the Greek had hinted strongly that he was ready to commit himself once and for all to the Realm.

With all of the misfortunes befalling the Realm, Nanos and the arms company were too great a prize to put aside. Bayard needed a fresh influx of funds—and arms—to maintain his kingdom.

As Rogier led them up the staircase, Nanos and Hatton were watched every step of the way. Bayard had positioned armed guards in the salons, hallways and offices. Most of the guards were stationary, but Nanos knew from previous visits that other guards discreetly followed Bayard. White Brigade gunmen manned posts throughout the mansion.

Possibly the least protected room was the private dining room where Bayard often sat with guests.

"He'll be with you in a moment," Rogier said, leaving Nanos and Hatton alone.

They sat on opposite sides of a long wooden table, where Bayard had previously wined and dined them.

Nanos looked at his watch. It was shortly past seven. In a while the news would break. And then, if all went well, so would the Realm.

After a few moments the Greek stood and casually strolled to the window facing the street below. A slice of sunlight streamed through the glass. Nanos inconspicuously pushed the curtains further apart to let in more light. It was done not to brighten their mood but to brighten their chances of survival.

A GIGN surveillance team had set up a laser bug to monitor the conversation inside Bayard's dining room. The laser beam struck the window, picked up minute vibrations from the voices inside, then bounced back to a telescope receiver, which demodulated the beam and turned it into voices. Pierre Duval was listening in to their conversation, as was Barrabas in the surveillance van. The bug would work so long as the window wasn't masked by curtains or shades.

Nanos looked down at the steady movement of vehicles and pedestrians on the street. No distinct patterns emerged. Good, he thought, no white crows. The term was used for surveillance operatives who stood out from their surroundings and called attention to themselves. But Pierre Duval had selected his operatives with care.

The army was out there, waiting for the signal to strike.

It would be any moment now, Nanos thought.

LILI KAVROLEIRA FIRED the first shot.

It hit the target in the center, right in the heart of the Realm.

The weapon was her voice—loud and clear enough to be heard worldwide. A video of her confession was transmitted by satellite to television and radio networks in France, England, Portugal, The Netherlands, Belgium and throughout Europe. The transmission was simultaneously broadcast in several languages.

"My name is Lili Kavroleira," she began. "Many of you know me as an actress, but my real work has been on behalf of a terrorist organization known as the Realm. For the past several years I have been forced to entrap leading military and political figures across Europe."

She was followed by Philip Emanuel, who somberly told the world that "subversive elements of French intelligence, led by a former leader of the DST, have infiltrated our military and economic system using murder, blackmail and bribery as their means of entry.''

Frederick Albrecht's statement followed. Then came other White Brigade defectors.

The damning testimony pointed relentlessly at the man behind the Realm, Auguste Bayard.

TEN MINUTES PASSED as Alex Nanos waited for Bayard to come in. All hell would break loose any moment now, and he wanted the chief of Hades to be within arm's reach. Otherwise they were dead.

Suddenly there was a slight commotion outside the room. Bayard paraded down the hallway with a retinue of guards trailing in his wake. He dismissed most of them, then stepped into the room with two guards who closed the door behind them. They moved unobtrusively to the corners, sitting down and pointedly not staring at Nanos or Hatton. They were guarding Bayard as much from the outside as from his guests.

Bayard greeted the guests profusely, taking Lee's hand and bestowing on it a regal kiss. Then he shook Nanos's hand and clasped it. It was the grand gesture of a king accepting his lord and lady into the Realm.

Then Bayard sat at the head of the table and motioned for his guests to sit. He chatted with them politely for a few minutes, then one of his men poured wine for them to toast their new agreement.

"Ah, Michael," he said. "There is so much we must discuss. About your place in our—our esteemed Realm."

"We've been giving it a lot of consideration," Alex said. He let the thought hang in the air.

"And?" Bayard said, and his regal gaze assumed a certain hardness.

It was twenty-questions time, Nanos thought. And the wrong answer could mean his life. "And we think we're getting close to a decision."

Bayard frowned. "The Realm is for decisive men," he said. "If you wish to assume your place, you must act now."

"That's why we're here," Nanos said.

The king smiled. "That is good. You see, the situation is now such that a man of your position can fill a void at the highest levels—"

At that moment the door to his inner sanctum flew open, and both guards jumped to their feet.

Bayard stared behind him at the intruder who filled the doorway, looking every bit like a guard dog straining at his leash.

"They've turned on us!" Ulrich shouted. "And they're broadcasting it over every television and radio network in Europe. Philip Emanuel has gone over to the other side. And Albrecht has done the same. Every station is broadcasting the bulletins!"

"What are you talking about?" Bayard shouted.

"We just received an anonymous call about the broadcasts. Most networks are showing the raw unedited footage—"

"Of what?" Bayard demanded, standing.

"Of us, Auguste!" Kaspar snapped. "Philip Emanuel has betrayed us. That's what I'm talking about. He's holding his silence no longer. He's spilling everything he knows. It's all on videotape. Our enemies have penetrated our organization and somehow made them talk. Emanuel and Albrecht have publicly condemned us. And our actress friend has revealed everything. Lili was—"

Suddenly Kaspar looked at Nanos—as if the mention of Lili's name combined with the sight of the Greek suddenly helped him put the pieces of the puzzle together.

The Greek felt a breeze blow into the room. A breeze that came from the River Styx in the underworld.

Ulrich's hand shot forward and he pointed at Nanos and Hatton. "It's them—they're behind it!"

Nanos bolted up for the table and grabbed for the weapon in the holster of the guard to Bayard's left. The man was lost in the chaos and confusion caused by Ulrich's entrance.

The Greek reached him just as the guard cleared his Manurhin .357 Magnum combat revolver from his holster. Nanos grabbed the guard's wrist, then clamped down on it as he threw his left into the man's chin. Alex put all of his weight lifter's strength into the blow, practically raising the man into the air.

The guard's teeth clacked together once, then again as Nanos pushed him against the wall.

He snatched the revolver from the fading guard, then swung it around at Kaspar.

Ulrich had been about to reach for his own weapon—but the sight of the short-barreled pistol looming his way changed his mind. He dropped to the floor just as Nanos pulled the trigger.

The gun's roar drowned out the shouting as the bullet thwacked into the wood down the room. It was like an instant tranquilizer. For a moment everyone in the room froze.

But only for a moment. Angry voices sounded outside the hall as the White Brigaders reacted to the gunshot.

The guard on Bayard's right, a heavyset man with a look of shock on his face, drew his 9 mm automatic and swiveled toward the Greek.

Darting away from the table, Lee Hatton crouched and spun around, landing her right heel smartly into the small of the guard's back.

Jolted off balance, he fired into the floor, then dropped facefirst as Lee's elbow connected sharply with the back of his head. He fell like a chopped tree. He groaned as Auguste Bayard, scrambling to escape from the dining room, stepped on his back.

Tracking him with his weapon, Nanos saw a man fill the doorway, aiming a MAT-49 9 mm submachine gun at him.

Closing in on Bayard, the Greek fired point-blank at the subgun wielder. The .357 slug burst through the gunner's skull. The door was sprayed with gray and red matter.

It was pandemonium then. Dodging a hail of automatic fire from the reinforcements thundering down the hallway, Nanos watched Bayard dash away with Kaspar Ulrich.

Nanos fired two rounds into the gunners, then dived across the table, two steps ahead of a full-auto burst that raked the wood in a splintery fusillade. Several rounds crashed through the window.

Lee Hatton fired a burst from the floor, kicking two of the men off their feet with the MAT-49 she'd inherited from the dead gunman.

Rolling and firing, she kicked the door shut. The move made it harder for the gunmen to zero in on them. Bullet holes appeared in the door and the walls as the White Brigaders fired blindly into the room.

His .357 booming, Nanos returned the favor, splintering body and bone on the other side of the wood.

Suddenly the barrage outside in the hallway stopped. The gunmen had other matters on their minds. Loud explosions ripped through the mansion and automatic fire ripped down into the rooftop.

The angry shout of the White Brigade commando in the sheltered stairwell on the roof was drowned out by the loud whine of the Aérospatiale helicopter. Cradling a submachine gun, he ripped off a burst at the chopper as black nylon ropes dropped from the helicopter.

An answer chattered from the copter, knocking the White Brigader down the stairwell. Five GIGN commandos descended from the aircraft. Since the GIGN routinely practiced rooftop assaults all over Paris, the men made it from rope to rooftop in less than seven seconds per man.

They raked hell out of the rooftop doorway with automatic fire, then descended into the mansion.

THE MANSION'S FRONT ENTRANCE was no more. Shards of glass and wood sliced through the smoke that billowed out of the jagged opening. Two grenades had blown the door off its hinges and shredded the gunman who'd come to investigate.

Liam O'Toole had fired the 40 mm high-explosive grenades from atop the brick wall separating the mansion from the street. He put down the M-203 grenade launcher, then unslung his submachine gun.

Barrabas, Hayes and Billy Two vaulted over the wall from the street side, each hanging on to the ledge with one hand and wielding their H&K submachine guns with the other.

A desperate barrage of wild gunfire drilled into the concrete walls, kicking up chunks of stone and giving flight to the SOBs.

Dropping to the ground, they fired full-auto bursts into the smashed doorway, slapping in fresh magazines as they advanced toward the remnants of the steps.

O'Toole dived as the flash of an automatic weapon lit up the smoky interior. A dotted line of bullet holes perforated the wall behind him.

Barrabas, darting to the right, triggered a burst at the gunman. He heard a scream, then the clatter of a fallen weapon.

"It's a bloody wasp's nest in there," O'Toole shouted.

"Yeah," Barrabas replied. "And Alex and Lee are sitting right in the middle of it. Let's go!" He hurtled forward in a horizontal position across the cindered stoop, triggering another burst as he sailed into the room. Covering him, Hayes sprayed the far wall with a full-auto burst, then followed him inside.

Billy Two also charged through the doorway firing.

O'Toole thumped another grenade into the M-203 launcher, slapped a fresh magazine into his subgun, then joined the war party.

Next came Bennett and his CIA ops, carrying an array of weapons and thermal imagers to help them see through the smoke and darkness.

Behind them trooped a squad of blue-jacketed GIGN men.

"THANK GOD this guy was prepared," Nanos said, rifling the unconscious White Brigader's gun belt and loading another six rounds into the revolver. He took two clips from the other knocked-out guard and slapped one of them into place.

The sounds of war rocked the second floor as bodies ran, bodies fell and bodies bled all over the heart of the Realm. Death screams were punctuated with loud bursts of automatic fire.

"It's a madhouse out there," Nanos said, shaking his head as he neared the door.

"Yeah," Lee said. "But it's our madhouse." She slammed a full magazine into the MAT-49 subgun. "Let's get it done."

They opened the door and came out firing.

At ghosts.

The White Brigaders had fled. Some had gone upstairs to hold off the GIGN team. Others had fled downstairs with Auguste Bayard—following the leader even in panic.

Nanos and Hatton hurtled down the stairs into the smoke and fire.

As he clattered down to the main landing, the Greek shouted and leveled the .357 at a man who stood in a cordite cloud, holding a submachine gun. He held himself in check when the other man shouted, "It's Nile! It's me! Nile!"

Nanos hurried to his side. "Where the hell is Bayard?"

Barrabas gestured toward the back of the house, where a rapid-fire exchange was ripping through the walls. They headed in the direction of the screams and found Bennett lying on the floor, his left arm a ribbon of blood.

The CIA man and his ops had separated from Barrabas, fighting the White Brigade escort that had gathered around Bayard.

"Where is he?" Nile shouted.

A burst of gunfire sounded from an open stairwell that led to the basement. Bennett nodded toward the sound.

The SOBs hurried down the hall, stepping over the bodies. They went down a flight of stairs and headed for a wine cellar. There they found the rest of the CIA ops, lying in a bloody heap on the floor. They'd been chopped down in seconds by someone concealed in the wine cellar.

The SOBs triggered several bursts into the small chamber, raking row upon row of bottles. Bloodred wine streamed from the shattered glass. But the room was empty. Whoever had been there had moved on.

But it was a mystery where they had disappeared. They couldn't have gone outside even if they could have made it upstairs. The GIGN team would have silenced them.

They had to be there somewhere.

The SOBs stepped softly over the dusty gray floor toward the back of the mansion. The basement was huge, a maze of darkened rooms and pipes and old machinery.

The SOBs moved quickly and securely, covering each other as they leapfrogged from point to point.

There was a rumbling sound, as though a heavy door was moving on rollers.

Rounding a corner, Barrabas saw a door-width shadow on the wall. But the shadow was shrinking.

The wall was moving. A stone-colored partition was gliding shut on casters, but it was jammed. A pudgy hand appeared, attempting to push it closed. But the fingers found no purchase on the stony surface. The exertions of the man behind it grew louder.

Barrabas shot a 3-round burst that thwacked into the wall behind the man and sprayed him with chunks of cement. The hand was withdrawn from the wall.

The SOBs spread out behind Barrabas, ready for anything that emerged from behind the sliding door.

"You've got three seconds to come out," Barrabas said.

There was no answer.

Barrabas stepped to the side, and approached the door at an angle. He fired into the wall. "One!" he shouted.

He fired again, the bullets digging in nearer the edge of the open partition. "Two!" he shouted. Then he stepped closer and aimed the submachine gun at a sharper angle. "This is it!" Barrabas said.

"Wait—wait—"

"Guns down and hands up."

A pistol dropped to the floor. Then a round-faced man stepped into the open.

"Rogier!" Nanos said.

"Who is he?" Barrabas asked.

"Bayard's right-hand man."

"Uh-huh." Barrabas leveled the Heckler & Koch at Rogier's middle. "Looks like Bayard just cut off his right hand."

O'Toole leaned against the edge of the stone wall and pushed. It slid back on its rollers, then shuddered into the wall.

Rogier stood perfectly still in the hidden room. It was about six feet deep and twelve feet wide. The inside of the sliding wall had a crossbar in it, with bolt holes, to secure it to the inside walls. If he'd managed to close it, he might have gotten away.

His hands up, his eyes fixed on the weapon in Barrabas's hand, he said, "Please. I had no choice—I had to fight."

"Give up Bayard and you won't have to fight anymore," Barrabas said.

Rogier shook his head. But instinctively he looked to his right. The room was built on an incline with a ramp that led down to another narrow wall.

"Where's Bayard?" Barrabas asked.

"I don't know."

Barrabas thumped the submachine gun into the man's chest, pushing the barrel in so Rogier's head bent forward, his eyes flooding with fear.

"This is the ultimate lie detector test," Barrabas said, pressing on the barrel. "If I don't like your answer, this goes off. Where's Bayard?"

Rogier broke down. "All right," he said. "Down there." He nodded at the blank wall at the end of the incline.

"He walks through walls?"

"That wall opens up."

"To what?"

"A staircase," Rogier said.

"Where does it lead?"

"Down a long corridor," Rogier said. "It takes you into the catacombs."

"I was afraid of that." Barrabas turned to the SOBs. "Unless we get Bayard in the next few minutes, he's gone for good. There's hundreds of miles to get lost in."

His submachine gun was still pointed at Rogier's chest as Barrabas moved toward the wall. "Come with me," he said.

Rogier followed him.

"I press against this wall, it opens up," Barrabas said. "Right?"

Rogier nodded his head urgently. "Yes."

"Where?"

"Right in the corner."

"Here?" Barrabas said, flattening out his free hand and pressing slowly against the stone. He watched Rogier's eyes.

"Yes," Rogier said, remaining calm, as if he had earned his reprieve.

Barrabas pushed the wall. It opened slowly, almost soundlessly. There was just the whisper of stone sliding over stone, followed by a dank musty smell. He saw a flight of stairs leading to a dim corridor.

"So," Barrabas said, "you didn't lie."

The man nodded.

"Will these stairs take us to the catacombs?"

"Yes," Rogier said. "I've given you what you wanted. May I go now?"

"Be my guest," Barrabas said.

Rogier started to ease by the SOBs when Barrabas lashed out. He grabbed Rogier by the collar and spun the surprised man around, catapulting him into the air. Rogier shouted as he sailed toward the stairway, his feet pinwheeling as he tried to avoid contact with the steps.

Barrabas stepped back.

Rogier landed hard on the lower steps, triggering a loud blast as the booby trap went off. The explosion ripped through him, tearing him to pieces. Ribbons of light and rivers of blood shot toward the high ceiling.

While the blast still echoed in the corridor, a blizzard of automatic fire from the far end of the stone hall ripped into the remnants of Rogier's body and the cement behind him. The bullets whined off the rock in an endless murderous barrage.

But the SOBs hadn't fallen for the trap. Rogier had been too eager to help them, too eager to be on his way.

"Now," said Barrabas, leaning forward and triggering a burst down the corridor. He jumped into the corridor, rolled and ripped off another burst.

Splashing a full-auto fusillade toward their ambushers, O'Toole followed suit, then Hayes, Nanos and Billy Two. Each unloaded his clip in full auto in turn, while Barrabas and O'Toole reloaded.

Lee Hatton hung back in reserve, covering them all from the top of the now trashed stairs.

At the end of the corridor Bayard's White Brigade escorts had dropped, cut to pieces by the unexpected volley. As the SOBs advanced toward the bodies, one of them came to life. Regaining his feet, Kaspar Ulrich fired a quick burst from his submachine gun.

Then he darted around the corner through the darkness.

The SOBs moved slowly through the mess of bodies, ready to take on any more spirits who'd come to life. But the rest of them were as stone dead as the skeletons that lined the catacombs.

Barrabas nosed the Heckler & Koch around the corner, then fired a burst to clear the hallway. There was no return fire.

Ulrich had already gone.

Halfway down the corridor the SOBs found a suspicious niche in the wall. Several lanterns and flashlights were lying on the rough-hewn stone shelf. Rubber boots, helmets with built-in lanterns, pickaxes and shovels were hanging on the wall—everything needed to work through the catacombs and make new passages if necessary.

"We've got a phantom of the opera here," Nanos said.

"Just a phantom, if we move fast enough," Barrabas said. "Take what you need and let's move." He grabbed a high-intensity lantern, then led the way into the catacombs in search of the lost king.

Holding the lantern, Barrabas jogged down the narrow corridor. The beam skidded down the sand-colored walls that gradually closed in on him as the tunnel shrank to a height of five feet.

He crouched as he ran, trying to keep his balance as he slogged through brackish water that carried the stench of decomposing earth.

Barrabas heard Kaspar Ulrich running in front of him. He was perhaps three turns ahead. Perhaps not. It was hard to judge the sound.

Barrabas gripped the Heckler & Koch MP-5 in his right hand as he ran. His knuckles repeatedly scraped against the rough limestone.

Here and there the lantern's wide beam illuminated the White Brigader's murky footprints through the subterranean maze.

Finally the tunnel widened again and rose to a height where a man could run upright. The footsteps of the quarry seemed closer now, or perhaps just louder, forming a steady rhythm as Kaspar Ulrich sloshed in and out of the water.

As he drew closer to the sound, Barrabas slowed, half expecting Ulrich to make a stand. The blood pumped through him wildly, beating out a hunting rhythm in his brain.

Behind him came more footfalls. He glanced over his shoulder, seeing Hayes and O'Toole sprinting toward him. More voices were coming from behind, more rapid footsteps, as the GIGN agents filtered through the tunnel, branching out into some of the arteries.

The hunt was on in full force.

Barrabas kept to the right while O'Toole and Hayes fanned out to the left, covering the area ahead.

Suddenly the corridor turned sharply and opened up into a long and wide gallery. The bottom of this chamber was also filled with brackish water.

Barrabas aimed the beam dead-center. It formed a bright yellow moonlike circle on the wall at the far end. He ran forward, slogging through the water.

He was running at full speed on instinct, chasing after the sounds of his quarry whose steps were staggering in an uneven rhythm. Ulrich was an assassin, not a soldier, Barrabas thought. He was probably tiring by now, running wild, running like a maddened creature of the Realm.

Suddenly gunfire reverberated through the chasm.

Barrabas dived to the ground a split second before a river of lead whirred overhead. It was only instinct that saved him. Halfway down the corridor, the footsteps had stopped. Ulrich was making a stand.

Barrabas threw the lantern in front of him and squeezed off an H&K burst, chipping stone from the walls and spraying the corner where Ulrich had fired from.

The White Brigader had ducked out of sight.

Barrabas reached for the lantern, flicked it off. Plunged back into darkness, he dropped the lantern into the water.

Rising to a crouch, Barrabas duck-walked down the dry right side of the corridor, the Heckler & Koch aimed for the corner.

Ulrich stuck the snout of his MAT-49 subgun around the corner and triggered another blind burst.

Barrabas fired at the man's hand and heard a shout. Then he released a shout of his own. The magazine clicked empty.

He heard Ulrich step closer to the corner again, ready for another full-auto burst. Barrabas tossed his weapon ten feet ahead, into the water, and reached for his holstered Browning Hi-Power.

At the sound of the splash, Ulrich popped out from the corner and fired a burst into the water where the empty subgun had fallen. By the time he realized his target wasn't there, Barrabas had managed to bring out the Browning.

It was the last thing the White Brigader would ever realize. Two shots from the Browning blasted through his chest and head, knocking him back against the wall, then down into the water.

Barrabas picked up the lantern.

At the end of the corridor, he flashed the intense beam around the corner, flooding the next corridor with light.

Fifty feet along, several gaps were carved in the wall at waist height. Looking like altar-length niches, the gaps were filled with skulls and bones, some of them thousands of years old, some perhaps only days old. It seemed like a good place to get rid of enemies of the Realm. But how deep were they? Were they large enough to hold a man?

Barrabas shone the light down to the floor. There were footprints on both sides of the muckish canal, smaller than Ulrich's. Bayard's?

He followed the tracks with the light. They ended right at the second gap.

That was why Ulrich had stopped. The king had given out. And that was why Ulrich had had to make his stand.

Barrabas flicked the beam up the wall toward the limestone gap. Then he set the lantern on the floor.

A burst of automatic fire ripped from the niche— the slugs bouncing off the wall to Barrabas's left.

Barrabas triggered two shots toward the gap. Then he moved closer, the lantern illuminating the niche every step of the way. He held the Browning securely in his right hand.

"Give it up, Bayard!" Barrabas shouted. "It's over."

"You don't know what you're doing," Bayard shouted back. His regal voice had changed to that of a crazed man on the run. It was a subterranean shriek, the cry of a rat caught on a sinking ship.

It sounded pitiful, but there was no mercy there. No sorrow.

Barrabas stepped forward.

A skull flew out of the niche, startling him. He tracked it with the Browning for a split second, realizing too late that Bayard was trying to distract him.

By that time the leader of the Realm, pushing the remains of skeletons ahead of him, leaped out of the niche with the MAT-49 submachine gun.

Barrabas fired once at the moving arm, winging him in the shoulder, just enough to ruin his aim. The subgun lowered, emitted a burst into the floor.

Barrabas closed the distance between them and grabbed the man's wrist with his left hand.

"Let it go," Barrabas said. "The gun, the throne, the whole crazy idea. Let it all go! It's over, dammit." He pressed the barrel of the Browning to Bayard's temple. The man grinned. Barrabas didn't want to kill him. He thought the world should learn about such craziness, and learn also from the due process of law.

"I'll die for the kingdom if I have to," Bayard shouted. "Shed my blood for the Realm—" The crazed king was beyond pain, beyond reason. As his empire was falling around him he was intent on destroying the man who toppled it.

Barrabas twisted Bayard's wrist and hand. But still the former DST man held on to the subgun. It was his last card, and he wasn't about to give it up.

Bayard angled the subgun toward him.

The SOB chieftain dropped his Browning, using both hands to work the subgun free.

Bayard screamed then, summoning up all the fury of his madness. His demonic strength was enough to move the barrel a few more degrees toward Barrabas.

"Then die, damn you," Barrabas said. He released Bayard's wrist and like a shot-putter, struck Bayard's chin with the heel of his palm. The blow lifted him off his feet, sent him hurtling back against the wall, breaking his neck.

The submachine gun dropped into the water, and then Bayard dropped into the realm of the dead.

Barrabas picked up the lantern. He moved down the corridor, hearing rushing water. He supposed the corridor ahead led into the sewer system. Bayard and his retinue had probably planned on fleeing up a steel ladder or two to a manhole.

There was movement behind him, and he saw the SOBs heading his way, accompanied by Pierre Duval. The SDECE man had come in for the finish.

Duval hurried over to Barrabas. "The media are swarming all over the street up there," he said. "It's a victory clear and simple. The televised confessions did the trick. Bayard had to fall—and now they want to see the heroes who took him down." Duval jerked his head upward. "You should come up there with me."

Barrabas shook his head. He nodded in the direction of the corridor leading to the manhole. The other SOBs hurried past Duval and continued on through the catacomb maze.

"Thanks, but no," Barrabas said, shaking his hand. He looked after the SOBs, whose footsteps were now fading away. "This is where we get off."

DEATHLANDS.

A different world—a different war

RED EQUINOX $3.95   ☐
Ryan Cawdor and his band of postnuclear survivors enter a
malfunctioning gateway and are transported to Moscow, where
Americans are hated with an almost religious fervor and blamed
for the destruction of the world.

DECTRA CHAIN $3.95   ☐
A gateway that is part of a rambling underwater complex brings
Ryan Cawdor and the group off the coast of what was once
Maine, where they are confronted with mutant creatures and
primitive inhabitants.

ICE & FIRE $3.95   ☐
A startling discovery changes the lives of Ryan Cawdor and his
band of postholocaust survivors when they encounter several
cryogenically preserved bodies.

Total Amount	$ _____
Plus 75¢ Postage	.75
Payment enclosed	$ _____

Please Print

Name: _____

Address: _____

City: _____

State/Prov: _____

Zip/Postal Code: _____

DL-B1

by GAR WILSON

The battle-hardened five-man commando unit known as Phoenix Force continues its onslaught against the hard realities of global terrorism in an endless crusade for freedom, justice and the rights of the individual. Schooled in guerrilla warfare, equipped with the latest in lethal weapons, Phoenix Force's adventures have made them a legend in their own time. Phoenix Force is the free world's foreign legion!

"Gar Wilson is excellent! Raw action attacks the reader on every page."
—Don Pendleton

Phoenix Force titles are available wherever paperbacks are sold.

GOLD EAGLE

PF-1R

More than action adventure . . .
books written by the men who were there

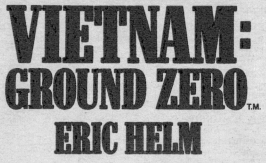

VIETNAM: GROUND ZERO ™

ERIC HELM

Told through the eyes of an American Special Forces squad, an elite jungle fighting group of strike-and-hide specialists fight a dirty war half a world away from home.

These books cut close to the bone, telling it the way it really was.

> "Vietnam at Ground Zero is where this book is written. The author has been there, and he knows. I salute him and I recommend this book to my friends."
> —Don Pendleton
> creator of *The Executioner*

> "Helm writes in an evocative style that gives us Nam as it most likely was, without prettying up or undue bitterness."
> —*Cedar Rapids Gazette*

> "Eric Helm's Vietnam series embodies a literary standard of excellence. These books linger in the mind long after their reading."
> —*Midwest Book Review*

Available wherever paperbacks are sold.

Colonel Nile Barrabas was the last American soldier out of Vietnam and the first man into a new kind of action

THE BARRABAS BLITZ $3.95   ☐
An explosive situation is turned over to a crack commando squad led by Nile Barrabas when a fanatical organization jeopardizes the NATO alliance.

THE BARRABAS STING $3.95   ☐
A former dictator tries to use his political sway in Washington to regain power . . . and only Nile Barrabas and his men can stop him!

THE BARRABAS STRIKE $3.95   ☐
A U.S. defence contractor unable to meet his obligations arranges to have a top-secret weapon disappear. When this supertank shows up in Iran, Nile Barrabas assembles his men to get it back—at any cost.

Total Amount	$ _____
Plus 75¢ Postage	_____.75
Payment enclosed	$ _____

Please send a check or money order payable to Gold Eagle Books.

In the U.S.	In Canada
Gold Eagle Books	Gold Eagle Books
901 Fuhrmann Blvd.	P.O. Box 609
Box 1325	Fort Erie, Ontario
Buffalo, NY 14269-1325	L2A 5X3

Please Print

Name: _____

Address: _____

City: _____

State/Prov: _____

Zip/Postal Code: _____

GOLD EAGLE

SBA-A